Outcast Press

In Filth It

Shall Be Found

Copyright © 2021 Outcast Press

www.Outcast-Press.com

(e-book) 978-1-7353126-6-8

(print) 978-1-7379829-0-6

"Here is to those who write on the edge, who hunt for the fringe, whose stories drive blindfolded down winding mountain roads with no guardrails in the rain. Whose characters are so damaged and flawed they are perfect." —Greg Levin

Dedicated to

Our kind Kickstarter patrons:

BB Prewitt

Poems-For-All.com

Julie Wade Marie

William "Scott" Hannon

LG Thomson

BobbyRoo Smith

Bryce Allen

Marilyn Holt

Richard Gerlach

Rebecca Kullberg

Michael O'Connell

Joanna KW

Don Stoll

Beth Coll

D.M. Clarke

Kristin Peterson

Matthew Tavendale

Mav Skye

Dan Nicholson

Aric Sundquist

Susan Jessen

Seth W. Stauffer

Anne Maguire

Sondra Fielder

Valerie Andrews

Tore Todbjerg Nielson

Thomas Early

Dylan & Sam Doomwarre

Rebecca Walker-Wain

Flipflapje

Chad Kainz

Keith Howell

Amy S Cutler

CBH

Victoria Nations

Sergey Kochergan

Nate Izod

Megan Premo

Jay Bechtol

Shanna Hammerbacher

Aidan Scott

Peter Kell

Table of Contents

About us

"In filth it shall be found" (*in sterquiliniis invenitur*) is a phrase popularized by psychologist Carl Jung, who wrote extensively on "the shadow side" of the psyche. According to Jung, we are less good, less moral, and less virtuous than we appear to others and even ourselves.

He argued that many people operate in a decent manner only because their moral compass hasn't been tested. However, in exploring the shadow side, realizing man's capacity for malevolence, and integrating one's inner monster, people can be actively—rather than passively—moral.

Outcast Press falls in line with this belief that what you need most often lurks in the recesses you least want to tread: taboo topics, disturbing imagery, and the murky gray area within dichotomies.

In this volume, you'll find 20 stories that explore the shadow side of humanity. These stories might disquiet, upset, or even enrage certain readers. Outcast Press doesn't cater to such cries for censorship because we believe that the best art isn't comfortable or comforting. Reading isn't a spectator sport. And since life doesn't come with a trigger warning, neither should literature.

In these stories, we hope each author has explored the shadow side of their mind. Perhaps by working through past trauma or delving into a place that frightens them. For each piece, you won't find easily digestible, stained-glass, or politically correct perspectives. There aren't many commendable characters, and even fewer happy endings.

Here, you'll find the downtrodden and dirty. Because it's in the mud, in the dark—in mainlined misery—that truth reveals herself in all her filth-caked, blood-crusted glory.

Sebastian Vice
Founder

Paige Johnson
Editor-in-Chief

Outcast Press

QP Dollface

By Claudia Santino

My face is caving in on itself. That is what my friend—the bathroom mirror—tells me. It never lies. My skin, once so smooth around the eyes, is now mapped by an invading army of wrinkles. A vast network of them is gaining ground. When did they launch their surprise attack?

And my cheekbones—once sharp like the edge of a cliff—have fallen like a seawall succumbing to climate change. Now, they barely overshadow the sunken apples of flesh that once appeared too ripe for blush.

"C'mon, dinner's almost ready," my husband shouts from the kitchen. He's cooking something special tonight, been telling me for a week.

And, sure, that's nice. But why? He never cooks. Oh, sure, he used to make dinner for me when we started dating, but that was 22 years ago. I guess I never noticed when that changed. But that's different from my face. How could he not notice my face? He, who can spot the slightest typo.

He called me Q, short for Quotations. Then he started calling me QP.

"Like a kewpie doll?" I asked.

"No," he said, "like Quotation and Punctuation."

When we first met, I didn't know what to make of him. He said he'd followed my ankles all the way from the F Train, where he first glimpsed them as I waited for the subway doors to slide open. Said he'd trailed them up the double set of stairs on West Fourth Street Station, into the open air of Sixth Avenue and to the corner of Waverly.

"I'm interested in what you have to say," he said, standing alongside me while I waited for the light to change.

I feigned a New Yorker's deafness, thinking this guy couldn't be talking to me. Then I felt a nudge at my elbow.

"Talk to me," he said.

I took a big step back. He was slightly taller than me, and thin, with doe-shaped, velvet brown eyes that focused like there was no one else in the bustling world around us. No hustling steps in their city shuffle, nobody hopping in and out of yellow taxicabs. He was cute, really cute, but there was something unsettling in that penetrating stare, how it only fixated on me. Maybe because I'd never been looked at that way before.

"Excuse me?" As the words spilled from my mouth, I wanted my feet to start moving. Why was I talking to this guy?

"Your ankles," he said. "I'm intrigued."

It was early summer, but I'd been going sockless since March. The shedding of black tights, sweaters, scarves, hats, and mittens was like a crocus bursting through winter's hard-packed dirt as snow still fell from the sky. I bent my left knee, looked behind my shoulder and at my ankle, as if seeing it for the first time. "Ah," I said and smiled.

Times New Roman black quotation marks were tattooed on each ankle. The left held the open. The right, the closed.

The light changed and I started walking.

He kept stride and I wondered how I'd lose him. "Where are you headed?" he asked.

When we got to the other side of the avenue, I countered, "Are you stalking me?"

He smiled. His big eyes focused on me like a spotlight, unavoidable. "I'm not stalking. I'm just talking. Are you a writer?"

"God, no," I said. "Why would you think that?"

He laughed. "Your tattoos, silly girl."

With those few words, he disarmed me. I nodded in understanding. "I just love to read well-written things."

We met at a Brooklyn Heights bar the next Friday night.

"What's up with you?" I asked. Even though we sat side-by-side in a booth, he never stopped staring.

"Whaddya mean?" he asked, his eyes laser-focused on mine, a goofy grin on his mouth.

I took a good look at him and his clean-cut face. Who was this guy? "I mean, what's up with the staring? I'm sitting right next to you."

His gaze softened into seductive Bambi eyes that settled on me, all bruised. It was impossible to look away. "It's just... You're so beautiful. I can't believe we met."

Who says that?

But he sounded so sincere.

Even though our kissing and petting sessions were marathon, we dated for three weeks before I slept with him. There was something about him that seemed tender, but a voice inside told me to stay away. What it was that I should stay away from, I couldn't pinpoint. There was just something off about him. Like if I let him in, in that way... I don't know, but a little voice inside my head just said not to.

I didn't listen.

As we fumbled in my bedroom, in between kisses and navigating the contours of each other's hip bones, he called me Q.

"Why are you calling me that?" I asked.

"Because of your tattoos," he said. "You'll be my Q and my P. You know, for Punctuation. You're my QP."

More and more, I was reeled by his crazy ways. As Otis Redding sang, "I Been Loving You Too Long to Stop Now," from the mix tape he made, I lined his lips with my tongue, gave him a butterfly kiss, and nodded okay.

"Well then," he said, "like any good punctuation, I want to be inside of you. But first..."

When he went down on me, the world tilted on its axis. For as many guys who'd done that to me before, no one had ever done it like he did. In the background, Tommy James sighed and sang about crimson and clover.

I thought my smile would break my face.

His was a night job. Mine was on the 9 to 5 chain gang. I gave him a set of keys. Every night, he'd let himself in, talk to my dog, and scratch her behind her little ears. Then, he'd kick off his shoes, crawl up through the bottom of my blankets, kiss my tattoos, and wrap my legs around his face to send me spiraling through the solar system.

He read me Abelard and Heloise. I read him Pablo Neruda. I liked doing crossword puzzles, he liked playing Scrabble. He had a Polaroid camera and I loved watching our bodies materialize on the wet film. Naked, he was long and lean with alabaster skin that gleamed in the dawn like the athletic marble forms in Florence's Uffizi Gallery.

One day, he said, "Marry me, QP."

So, I did.

It took me a while to find out about the others. But by then it was too late. I had happily gone under, plumbing the depths of our gratification. The bedroom was my oxygen tank. I swear, he sucked the brains right out of my head. He never, ever let up on the pleasure. And all I wanted was more.

The scent of garlic and roasted ancho chilis twists through the apartment. "QP, it's going to get cold. Stop fussing with yourself. You're beautiful."

What is he playing at? I thought he'd stopped cheating a long time ago. Trust me, I know. All of a sudden, it just stopped. I think he got tired of all the running around; maybe 9/11 made him rethink what he took for granted. But that doesn't stop me from keeping tabs on him. Cracking his phone's passcode was easy because he never hides it. But lately, he's been hiding *something*, acting funny. Is he slipping one past me? Again? Just a month ago, at our local café, he had giggled over something with the new waitress. When I asked him what was so funny, he said nothing, they were just joking.

He's up to something. Maybe not with that waitress, but with somebody. I've seen the photo of that woman on his phone. She stood in semi-profile, resting against him, her perfect ass all snug in a pair of white jeans. His arm wrapped around her waist. In a bar, maybe? I couldn't make out her face but couldn't help but notice her long, brown hair with perfect highlights, her colt-like legs, one arm on top of his hand like she owned him. His face was obscured by her body, but his head poked from the other side of her shoulder, his dirty blond hair tousled like when we'd first met. It was as though he hadn't aged. My own Dorian Gray.

For all the times I've checked his phone, that was the only picture of a woman on it. Why now? Why her? He's turning me into goddamn Sherlock Holmes again. I'm so, so sick of it. How am I supposed to compete with young flesh like that? The beauty he once devoured is as faded as my tattoos. Those quotation marks are as ruined as a newspaper left in the rain.

Last Saturday morning, I overheard him talking on the phone. He thought I was sleeping. When I came into the living room, he quickly ended the call. It must have been her. The woman in the photo. Who else could it have been? He's going to leave me for her. That's why he's fussing with this dinner. Is it an unspoken goodbye?

I shut off the bathroom light and go into the kitchen. His back is to me, inspecting whatever he took out of the oven. The stainless-steel knives on the magnetic strip reflect my distorted image. But all I can see is that damned photo on his phone.

He turns around. "QP," he starts as I slash the knife across his throat.

The meal is good. I have to say, hats off to him. Some kind of shredded, peppered beef. The kitchen is a mess and I've got some cleanup ahead of me, but I'm more concerned about what he's got for dessert. Afterall, it is our anniversary.

It's when I reach for a second piece of Brooklyn blackout cake that I see the present. There it is, on top of the fridge: a shiny box with hot pink wrapping paper, a black-and-white polka dot ribbon. Did he do that? Someone else must have wrapped it.

Either way, it's pretty impressive. I lick the dark chocolate from my fingers. I'm definitely having another piece once I see what's in this box.

Resting in a bed of white tissue paper, a hardcover photobook brings me to tears. I don't know who he got to do it, but it's really something. Photographs from our first year together and every one that followed, all digitally screened into the paper. Photos I'd forgotten existed. Photos I haven't looked at in ages. I rifle back and forth, careful not to sully the pages, until one shot catches my eyes. It's a partial view of me leaning against him, his arm around my waist, my perfect ass all snug in a pair of white jeans.

I think I still have them.

Author Bio

@portsarecalling

Brooklynite Claudia Santino writes fast-paced, George Eliot-inspired stories "with a little bit of romance, a little bit of stalking, and a little bit of paranoia." Such work and other articles can be found in *New York Daily News, Brooklyn Magazine, Catapult, Purple Clover,* and more.

Keep updated on her publications at ClaudiaSantino.com

Sap Tap

By S.M. Fedor

"I fucked your wife last night."

The words hung in the air, tossed about the office on the cold draft that seeped past the single-pane window. Invisible waves of vibrating atoms looking for a target to absorb their tale. They attempted to work their way past copious layers of dust, seep into the cheap plywood sheets I called a desk—with a classy, laminated coating that protected it from spills.

The stains embedded in the faux leather chairs screamed a warning: This was their turf, there was no more room, so kindly fuck off.

In the corner of the room, an end table had been lovingly crafted out of stacks of unread books, pin-up magazines, and paperwork I'd never file. Upon it, sat a potted fern. The fern was dead and not interested in my message.

So, with great resignation and a shrug of the shoulders, the words fluttered over to their target: one Mr. Jonathon Fellows. They whispered to him, with the delicate touch that only a practiced mother could inflect when delivering bad news. *Sorry about the divorce.*

The tiny hairs at the tip of his ear canal twitched, converting the vibrations into an electrical code, then transmitted the signals to the man's cerebral cortex. Despite their best efforts, not much of a spark jolted his brain. Fellows' eyes rolled back in confusion, and he spoke with apprehension. "Pardon?"

"I said, I fucked your wife last night."

This time, the words flew straight and true, delivering their message with pride and gusto.

I'd given it to her good, after all. They should be as loud and proud as any parade.

The sting on my chin and taste of copper upon my lips made it clear he'd understood this time.

I wasn't surprised that he punched me. In fact, I had been looking forward to it. A solid strike was a good motivator, made the rest of the job that much more enjoyable.

Anyone who has ever watched a cat corner a mouse understood: It's fun when the prey struggled, thought it had a chance to escape before the teeth sink in, deep.

I'd won the game the moment he walked through my door.

I had to admit though, I was surprised he managed to draw blood. I expected more so the swat from a mewling child. I may have underestimated his passion for the missus, but I knew that one punch was all he had in him. Jonathon Fellows was of no concern.

That was rule number two for selecting a client: Make sure you can control and handle them.

In case you were wondering, rule number one was to make sure the client had money. I don't come cheap, and I certainly don't do charity.

Fellows was, what we liked to call in the business, a poor-rich man. He operated a couple of small businesses with a partner. He had money coming in, but he needed all that profit to keep his head afloat. That was good enough for me. He could drown after our transaction concluded.

Fellows slumped in the chair, exhausted, and drained of life. Naturally, the client's chair sat six inches below me, designed to look good but sit uncomfortably. Resigned to defeat like the good lad he was, he sustained an angry, beaded glare, but it was all for show. "Wha... Why would you... How? You were supposed to be working for *me*."

I opened my desk drawer, pulled out a half-drunk fifth of Jack, a large manila envelope, and a small plastic baggie.

I unscrewed the cap from the bottle and took a swig. It hit the back of my throat and mixed nicely with the blood. But what didn't whiskey mix good with? With enough shots of Jack and a bleach chaser, I'd soon be singing "YMCA" in a chorus-line.

I offered the bottle to Fellows, who did not budge from his seat. His eyes were open, but his mind was far, far away. I gave him a sad hangdog face, shrugged, and took another long pull.

Satisfied, I put the bottle away. Time to run through my prepared patter and collect the paycheck. "Look, you wanted to know if your wife was having an affair or not, correct?"

"Yes, but—"

"Now, you asked me to find out what she was up to. And I did. I even collected evidence for you." I picked up the manila envelope, wafted imaginary perfume smells from it, and added a dramatic flourish as I sniffed the air around it. Then I placed the package back down, a little bit closer to Fellows. "There're some nice photos and even a video in there, if you want to take a look. Only to confirm my findings, of course."

His eyes darted from me to the envelope, then back again.

I flashed him my most charming smile. Candy, my latest assistant, said it was the Devil's grin, but I think she said that just to encourage the spankings.

I noticed that his mouth was moving. He was trying to talk but had lost the ability to enunciate.

I sighed and leaned in close. "What's that, Jonathon? You need to speak up."

Through hyperventilating gulps of air, he managed to find his words. "I hired you. You were supposed to find out if she was with Rob. Why would you do this to me?"

"Jonathon, you wanted to know if she was having an affair. The *a*-ffair," I said, clicking the A off the roof of my mouth, dancing it like the introduction to *Lolita*, "is the important part, Jonathon. It doesn't matter if she's fucking your partner in the back office while you go run a delivery or if she's sucking off every random guy at the club. Which, if I'm honest—and I hope I can be—seems to be the truth." My fingers rose, counting off the likely number of cocks on the crew.

He interrupted again with his sad stammering, "But y—"

"Listen, my friend, the fact that the little slut is unfaithful to you is what counts. I got here the evidence that she's not honoring your marital vows." I tapped the envelope twice and nudged it closer. "You thought it was your partner. Maybe it is. We all take turns. Listen, I know this is difficult to hear, but I met up with her at a bar, bought her two cheap, fruity cocktails, a bump off the key in the bathroom, and buddy... *amigo*... she was eager to spread those luscious fuckin' legs and teach me all about the Devil's ways." My legs fanned open and closed to cool down. I was unsure if the heat I felt below was imaginary or memory. I nodded towards the envelope on the desk. "Come on, Jonathon. I met her just once and she was ready to do some nasty shit, even make a video of it. You hired me to eat your wife out and give you the details. She's a whore. Now you know."

I was feeling pretty good at that point. Once I started my spiel, I could get myself good and worked up.

Then, the salty metallic taste returned, and my chin throbbed more. I looked at Fellows in disbelief. The poor sap had really loved his wife—and she hadn't even looked that good.

His body shivered with rage and excitement. His hands clenched in tightly curled balls. A man who had never thrown a punch. He was gonna be sore about the broken bones from a poor grip tomorrow.

I flashed him another endearing smile—this time, with a few more tiger teeth. "Listen, Jonathon, you need to try and calm down here. This isn't your fault."

"My fault?" he cried.

I firmly placed my hand on his shoulder and helped him sit back down. The simple action forced him to relax, to submit. A subliminal reminder that I was in control. It's all psychology.

I picked up the plastic baggie from the desk and untied the knot. Inside, was a beautiful off-white powder. The few pieces of paper scattered on the desk were shuffled to the floor to make room for its contents.

I reached into my back pocket and took out my wallet. I pulled out a twenty-dollar bill and grabbed one of my fake IDs. I glanced at the picture and said, "Well, nice to meet you, too, Mr... Saunders."

In ritualistic motion, I tapped the powder with the card over and over, until it felt intrinsically right. With an engineer's precision, I carved two thick lines.

I looked to Fellows, who had fallen back into a stupor and stared at the desk, unseeing. I extended the rolled-up $20. "Here, this will make you feel better. Drift those cares away."

He hesitated for a moment and then, at last, completely surrendered. Game over, kid.

He stood up, took the bill from me, and tried his best to inhale. Snuffleupagus only managed to snort a kiddie-sampler before falling back into the chair, but I gave him an A for effort.

"Not too shabby for a straight fellow, Fellows," I encouraged. I picked up the bill and railed the remaining powder.

Fellows coughed hard, grabbing onto his nose as if it were on fire.

I sat behind my desk again and tilted my head back, waiting to feel the drip. Once the taste hit the back of my throat, I sat upright, and re-opened the drawer. I pulled out the Jack Daniel's and a pack of Marlboro. I swigged another shot to wash down the coke. I tapped out a cigarette, checking over the pack first to see how many I had left. Seven.

Fellows appeared sick. His skin had turned a pale green. Emotional distress and cocaine were not sitting well with him. I calculated the cost-benefit of charging him a clean-up fee if he did vomit versus having to smell the remnants of his breakfast the rest of the year if my girl didn't do a thorough scrub. Money always won out in the end; this place already had plenty of puke stains.

I placed the cigarette to my lips and tried to light it. I amused myself, watching my hands shake from the coke rush as I brought up the flame, before finally taking a nice, deep drag.

The gray smoke drifted out of my mouth and melded into the ceiling tiles. There were a lot of stains on that ceiling. I didn't want to think about what invisible things were probably raining down from their Styrofoam pores. Shaking the image out of my head, I felt my mind was finally in its tip-top state and I was ready to call it a day.

I adjusted myself, sitting with a rigid, authoritative posture and looked squarely at Fellows. "Now, Jonathon, we need to discuss your payment. You had $300 down, so that means you still owe me another $500."

Fellows somehow looked even more sick. "How can you expect me to pay you? You slept with my wife!"

"No, Jonathon, I got you answers. I got you proof."

And that was all that needed to be said. At that point, Jonathon Fellows finally understood. I had fucked his wife and he was going to pay me $800 for that privilege.

Jonathon Fellows began to cry. Snotty-nosed sobs. "I'm such a pathetic loser."

"Ah, you're not a loser. It's just a tough break, kid."

And I answered honestly. He wasn't a loser. He was sap. Which, in my books, was even more pathetic.

You see, a loser had always been a loser. Would always be a loser. Since the day they were born. A loser was a li'l bastard child of a loser and would grow to be a loser of an adult. But—and this was key—they knew their lot in life. They knew what they were. They understood their place and role in society. Knew they'd get knocked down and take kicks to the head. They accepted it. A loser always knew there was nothing else for them in this world but to be beat.

But a sap... Well, that poor, deluded fool thought they had a chance. Thought they might be one of the few who could rise above the muck that us normal, everyday lowlifes swim in. A sap would get knocked down, but—unlike the loser—would try to get up again, not realizing there's no hope. They'd get beaten down more. And again, they'd get up—clinging to the ropes for life—only to receive a brutal uppercut once that glass jaw was revealed.

A sap did not just lose. A sap would be broken.

Jonathon Fellows was not a loser. He was a poor, poor Sap with a capital 'S.'

I watched him shake with tears for another minute, then decided enough was enough. I stood and took a nice, long stretch. Reached my hands out to the Styrofoam sky, letting my vertebrates get some air. I picked up the baggie, tied it tight once more, then tucked it into my pocket. I collected the manila envelope filled with my pictures and intimate recordings.

Fellows noticed and looked at me through watery eyes.

"Listen, Jonathon, I'm going to get out of here. I have some dinner plans I need to get ready for, so I'll leave you to yourself. When you're ready, you come out here and you can give Candice the check. OK? I'll hold onto this evidence if you don't mind. It has some... sentimental value."

I reached the office door and opened it. Through it, was the small reception area, where Candy's short skirt smiled from beneath the equivalent of a foldout card-table.

I took one last look at the empty shell of Jonathon Fellows. "Oh, and Dolores will probably come home late tonight, so don't wait up for her, kid." I shut the door behind me. I was already calculating the expense report to file him for another round.

Author Bio

@S_M_Fedor SMFedor.com

S.M. Fedor has appeared in *Punk Noir Magazine*, *Burning Love & Bleeding Hearts*, and will be in the anthology, *Mickey Finn, Vol. 2* (Down & Out Books, 2022). He splits his time between writing neo-noir and creating award-winning VFX for film and TV.

He currently resides in Montreal, beneath a mountain of cat fur.

Fixer Upper

By Greg Levin

I spent three full days deciding on the perfect drawer pulls for the kitchen, and this clown isn't even competent enough to center them. Like there isn't enough shit off-kilter in my life.

Best in town, my ass. I ought to sue Mr. Fix-It and his fancy website for false advertising. But then what's the point of taking legal action against someone with a knack for getting out of trouble? Serious trouble.

Jesus Christ, I can't bear to look at this flooring anymore. The nerve of this guy, insisting I told him five-inch white oak planks when he knows good and goddamn well that I said eight-inch. Even have it circled in the catalog.

Had a feeling this would happen. Sort of assumed this guy would be like most contractors. He's obviously thinking, *Meh, it's just a cabin in the woods. It's not her HOME home. How great a job would I really need to do?*

The answer: a helluva lot better than this, sir.

Plenty of people buy and renovate cabins like this out in the woods because we've had it up to *here* with HOME homes. With everyone. With everything. I'm not someone with whom you want to skimp on materials or rush the work or pad your prices. Just ask Mr. Fix-It.

The incessant pinging coming from what was *supposed* to be the wine cellar is driving me nuts. I've brought it to Mr. Fix-It's attention a few times and yet it continues. Next time, I'm not going to be so nice about it.

The more I think about what he's done and what he hasn't done, the more I want to wring his neck. And I'm not a violent person. This asshole brings out the worst in me. Still, it's nothing compared to what he's brought out of my cabin.

I start walking toward the bathroom, over the three-inch too-thin floorboards, and stop to swear at the open floor plan that isn't. I glare at the dividing wall—the one I was originally told wasn't a supporting one, the one I was told could be completely

knocked out, the one keeping the entire goddamn cabin standing...
and from coming to life.

There's that goddamn pinging again. More like clanging,
now. And lasting longer than the pinging did. It's enough to take
my mind off the dividing wall.

I continue toward the bathroom. It's the nearest room
with a mirror and seeing myself this upset sometimes helps calm
me down, reminds me to think things through. Gives Mr. Fix-It a
fighting chance.

Not this time. Looking at my reflection—the clenched
jaw, the flaring nostrils, the eyes squinted thin as razor blades—
merely reminds me of the smirk on Mr. Fix-It's face the first time
he told me to "relax, lady." There hasn't been a next time. It's
unlikely there will ever be. But who knows? Perhaps he'll try to
be brave. Part of me wants him to be.

I bring the fleshy underbelly of my fist down upon the
sink like a sledgehammer. Luckily, Mr. Fix-It hasn't touched this
bathroom; otherwise, my punch might have broken the whole
damn vanity.

My snorts propel me back into the hallway. I pass the
bedroom, where the walls aren't even close to the color I
requested. Mr. Fix-It tried to quiet me with, "Paint never looks
exactly like it does on the swatch. Changes color once it dries."

Yeah, so does blood.

I sigh, bow my head, and keep walking. Pacing, really.
The wrong flooring only exacerbates my mood, so I avert my
eyes, fix my gaze on the far wall—the wall where three spackled
holes still haven't been sanded or painted over, despite my
reminders to Mr. Fix-It over the past month. Everywhere I look,
there's the promise of manslaughter.

Below me, the pinging and clanging picks back up, and I
stomp like I'm trying to open a portal to Hell. Like I'm not
already halfway there.

The door to the cellar stares at me, coaxes me toward it,
whispers it's time to fix the problem myself.

I twist the knob and quietly warn all the spiders and
earwigs to keep their appendages to themselves. I let them know I
have size-10 flats and I'm not afraid to use them. I tell them that
it's nothing personal, ask them to imagine how they'd feel if two

months ago they were told they'd have a beautiful wine cellar in three weeks only to now be reduced to bargaining with arachnids. I tell them there's no offense intended.

The only good thing about all the pinging and clanging is how it masks the squeaking of the staircase—the staircase I was promised would be repaired "today" 40 or 50 yesterdays ago. The clanging and pinging pauses. The flashlight feature on my phone solves the issue of no electricity down here. I stop at the base of the stairs and illuminate all my problems.

"Good morning," I say to the source. "You keep banging your head against that support beam, you'll split your skull open."

Mr. Fix-It blocks the blinding glare with his eyelids and curls up as much as the restraints allow. I tell him to remain calm, then rip the electrical tape off his face. He cries out for half his mustache. I take several steps back in case his bound ankles manage to sweep my legs. "Please," he says, eyes still shut, head turned toward the wall where my wine should be. "Let me go and I'll do everything you've asked, fix everything that needs fixing."

I hop off the last step and angle my phone so Mr. Fix-It can look me in the eyes. "Feels like you're still just saying what you think I want to hear. I'm not sensing any conviction, any real integrity."

Mr. Fix-It's chin drops to his chest. If he had the use of his hands, his face would be buried in them.

I tell him to buck up, to not give up so easily. I tell him there's still hope. "I just need to know beyond the shadow of a doubt that if I cut you loose, you won't try anything stupid or vengeful. Won't try to escape and go to the cops."

Mr. Fix-It frantically nods, flashes me those you-have-my-word eyes. Unfortunately, they're the same eyes he flashed when I hired him. And several times since.

I take a few more steps back, away from the stench of piss and onions. Not really his fault—I gave him plenty of water and some bread last night, but no deodorant or bathroom breaks.

I point my phone straight at him, put him back in the spotlight. "You don't understand," I say. "I really had my heart set on this cabin turning out like the plans I gave you, the plans you signed off on. It's one of the only things I care about."

"I understand and am so sorry I didn't give you my best effort," says Mr. Fix-It, fighting back tears. "So sorry I took advantage of you, your trust, your patience. You deserve much better, ma'am."

I take a step closer and flip the phone to my left hand. Then I reach around my back with my right, resting two fingers on the wire-cutters sticking out of my jeans. "What else are you sorry about?"

Mr. Fix-It remains still, as if any motion might shatter the thin ice that he's on. He just stares at me like he has no idea what to say. "I, uh... What do you mean?"

"Well, aside from the shoddy work and questionable ethics you've displayed throughout the renovation of this place," I say, shuffling closer, wire cutters out, "what ELSE are you sorry about?"

Mr. Fix-It eyes the wire cutters as if they asked the question. His Adam's apple is an elevator in his throat.

"Oh," I say, tracing his terror to the sharp metal in my hand, "don't worry about these. They're just for snipping you free—assuming you cooperate."

Mr. Fix-It lightly closes his eyes, exhales.

I take a step closer and go, "Please, answer the question."

He searches my face for the correct response, glancing a couple times at the wire cutters. A bead of sweat forms on his forehead, splits his eyes, ski-jumps off his nose. "So, you mean something besides the work I've done on your cabin?"

I shrug and flash him what-do-you-think eyes.

He closes his to search what I imagine is a warehouse full of regrettable transgressions. "Uh," he says, eyes still shut, "I guess, maybe, um..."

"Let me help you," I say while reaching my free hand into my front pocket and pulling out the photo I've been carrying since hiring Mr. Fix-It.

He opens his eyes and watches as I unfold the photo and hold it in front of his face.

"Have a good look," I say. "Tell me if this makes answering my question any easier."

Mr. Fix-It squints, blinks several times to bring my sister into focus. The elevator in his throat hits every floor, twice.

I smile at the fear I've been waiting years to see. "Remember her?" I ask.

Mr. Fix-It looks from the photo to me, then back to the photo, his eyes a couple panicked fireflies. His mouth drops open, but nothing comes out.

This is almost worth all the incompetence I've had to endure since concocting my plan. All the restraint I've had to exhibit. I point again at the last ever photo of Ella alive. "Did you really think the story ended the day you walked out of that courtroom an 'innocent' man?"

Mr. Fix-It looks down at his feet. "I didn't do anything," he says. Like he's mistaking me for someone with patience to waste. Like he's forgotten the wire cutters. "What's it got to do with you, anyway?" he asks.

I squat, pull my hair back off my face, and shine the phone at my profile. "She was always much prettier than me and a lot more petite, but surely you see some resemblance."

Even with the light off him, Mr. Fix-It looks fucked. "So," he says, his face a defeated silhouette, "she's your..."

We jinx each other on "sister."

"No," I say. "She WAS my sister." I turn the light back around to catch Mr. Fix-It totally in the dark.

"You mean she's... She's..."

I jinx him again, this time on "dead."

The size of his eyeballs says he really had no idea. Not that it makes Ella any more alive. "When? How? What happened?"

I glare at him and his overdue concern, hard enough to leave a scar. "Four months ago. It was ruled an accidental overdose." I move the phone in like I'm fitting him for contacts. "But you and I both know she died three years ago."

Mr. Fix-It's eyebrows and forehead scream pity, remorse, compassion. When none of it lands, he shakes his head, jerks the restraints. "I swear, I never hurt her." He says it almost like he believes it.

Lie to yourself and everyone else long enough, and your face will stay that way.

"Please," I say. "Show some respect." I rise from my squat and lower my phone to erase Mr. Fix-It's face, mute his panic, black out his desperation. I can be a real softy and don't want now to be one of those times.

"Look, I'm real sorry 'bout your sister and all the aggravation of that court case, but I'm telling you, I didn't do—"

"Not another word." I brandish the wire cutters, holding them like a buck knife inches from his mouth. He doesn't need good lighting to see that one slip of the tongue means he risks losing it. "Before that night," I say, "Ella was a strong, confident, witty, independent woman. Then, suddenly, she wasn't. You stripped her of everything, turned her into a shell of herself."

Mr. Fix-It starts to shake his head.

I grab hold of his left earlobe with the wire cutters and squeeze just shy of a bisection. A shriek loud enough for nobody else to hear assaults my eardrums. I release.

"You're crazy," shouts Mr. Fix-It, tilting his head to massage his ear with his shoulder. "Please, I have kids."

"No, you don't," I say. "I did my research."

Mr. Fix-It buries his chin in his chest and goes, "So, what, you're going to kill me out here? If so, get it over with."

"It took my sister a year to die after her run-in with you," I say. "Why should I do you any favors?"

Mr. Fix-It looks up, a glint comes off a tear. "Please, I'll do anything you say."

"I know. So, let's get started."

I walk over to a tall box I stowed here yesterday, just before slipping Mr. Fix-It his sleep aid. 200 milligrams of GHB— a popular date-rape drug, but I want him awake for this part.

"I don't get it," says Mr. Fix-It. "Why would you hire me, pay me, let me do work on your cabin for months if you were just out for revenge?"

I stop dragging the box across the floor to tell him, "Credibility." Seeing how little clarity that provides, I go, "It'll all make sense later. Maybe."

I finish pulling the box to him, then set my phone on the floor—flashlight-up, so he can see. I reach into the box and pull out a floor mirror, an aluminum baseball bat, and a tube of lube.

I wish I had a good camera. With a flash.

"What the hell?" says Mr. Fix-It, shrinking.

I take the floor mirror and set it just behind him, then retrieve the wire cutters. "I'm going to cut your hands loose from this beam but keep them bound," I say. "Then you're going to turn around and face the mirror, propping yourself up on your knees and elbows."

Mr. Fix-It shudders. "What? No. Please."

I shoot him a scowl and go, "That's what SHE said."

"It wasn't like that. I'm telling you. It was consent—"

"If you finish that sentence, you can forget about the lube. Your call."

Mr. Fix-It starts whimpering.

I put in my earbuds, play "Here I Come" by The Roots, and turn it up so loud that it drowns out any remnants of pity rattling inside me. "Get into position now."

Mr. Fix-It says something that doesn't stand a chance against the music. Judging from his eyes and all the muscles in his face, he isn't chatting about the weather. I pick up the bat, point to the mirror, repeat my command. Mr. Fix-It hesitates while begging me with his entire body.

"Don't force me to use this bat the way bats are intended," I say. "You wouldn't survive that. What I have planned is merely extremely uncomfortable and humiliating. Now, on your knees and elbows."

Mr. Fix-It shakes his head. I cock the bat back and eye his melon like a hanging curveball. "Wait! Okay! Okay!" breaks through the music as he braces for impact.

I freeze my swing, a sense of relief washing over me. The last thing I want is a mess to clean up.

Mr. Fix-It reluctantly gets into position, crying so fiercely that I can almost hear it. On his knees and facing the mirror, he turns his head back for one more plea.

My fingers tap the thick of the bat barrel, marking off the seconds of patience I have left. "Drop down and balance on your forearms." My words are inaudible even to myself. "If you've ever done yoga, think of dolphin pose."

In the mirror, Mr. Fix-It's face is a ball of panic.

I smile at it, then crouch to cut the music. "Here I Come" turns into here we go. I remove my headphones and grab the lube. Pretty sure Mr. Fix-It can't see what I'm doing in the mirror, what with the bad angle and sole light on him, so I give the tube of lube a loud, sloppy-fart squeeze to help orient him. The reflection of his jaw slackens. He contorts his neck in hopes of getting a better view of his punishment. "Eyes forward," I say, despite enjoying his dread-clad curiosity.

"I'm begging you," he says, voice quaking. "What do you want from me? Name it."

"What I want is for you to have never set eyes or hands on my sister. But since it's too late for that, I want this. Exactly this."

Mr. Fix-It turns to the mirror again. His head drops like an anchor. From where I'm standing, he looks decapitated.

He wishes.

I pick up the bat and accidentally on-purpose drop it. The metal knocks and pings off the concrete, loud and forever. I pick it back up. "Try to relax," I say. "Otherwise, this will be way worse than it needs to be."

Mr. Fix-It answers with a sob.

"Okay, now listen up. I need to reach around to undo your jeans. If you make any sudden movements, this will end more painfully than you can imagine. Got it?"

Mr. Fix-It says something I can't make out through the crying, though I'm pretty sure it isn't the simple affirmative I'm looking for.

"You mind repeating that?"

Mr. Fix-It calms himself enough to be intelligible. "Please, please. I'm sorry. So very sorry."

"Sorry for what? You keep saying you didn't do anything." I take a step forward. "Now, we need to drop those pants."

Mr. Fix-It writhes and bucks, falls over on his side, curled into fetal position.

"See," I say, "that's one of those sudden, stupid moves I specifically told you not to make."

Mr. Fix-It goes into a fit on the floor that would make an epileptic attack look like gentle stretching.

I wait for him to still, then go, "Now that you've got that out of your system, are you ready to resume?"

Mr. Fix-It heaves and hacks and pants like there's only enough oxygen down here for one of us. His conniption kicked up the stench of fear and urine.

I cover my nose and mouth with one hand, use the other to prod his foot with the bat. "Okay, back on your knees and—"

"Kill me. Just fucking kill me."

"Uh-uh. You're not getting out of this that easy."

"I'm just trying to make it easier for you," he says. "Cause I'm telling you, if you try to stick that bat in me, no way I'm not gonna kick and jab and fight back with everything I've got. You could get hurt—and that ain't a threat, just me trying to save you a lot of effort and trouble, probably even some teeth." His tone is much calmer than before.

I don't like it. It's the same tone he used every time he assured me that he was going to finish or fix something I'd reminded him to. Very triggering. "Relax," I say. "Did you really think I was going to rape you with a bat? What kind of sicko do you take me for?"

Mr. Fix-It's face twitches, then slackens. Like he thinks the worst is behind him. Like he thinks all of that was just to put the fear of God into him.

What he doesn't realize is that Ella deserves more than his humiliation.

And there is no God.

I set the bat down and wipe the excess lube off my hand, then reach back into the box to pull out my .38.

"No! Wait!" Mr. Fix-It's fetal position tightens. He squints through the scraped and bleeding knuckles of his bound hands. "Don't shoot!"

I shrug, roll my eyes. "Didn't you just tell me to kill you? For Chrissakes, make up your mind."

"I'll do anything, give you anything!"

I scratch my chin with the muzzle of the .38, pretend to contemplate. "Give me my sister back. Do that and we're square."

Mr. Fix-It squeezes his eyes shut and grits his teeth, as if trying to generate enough heat to melt the zip ties.

"Okay, okay, that wasn't really fair of me," I say. "How about this: Can you tell me the truth?"

Any more vigorous a nod, he'd be risking paralysis.

"Good," I say. "Then tell me, did you rape my sister?"

Mr. Fix-It looks at me, then away. He purses his lips, swallows hard. Tears or sweat or both drip off the tip of his nose. "I never meant to," he mutters.

The gun and I stare him down as he breaks into sobs that test the cabin's foundation. But they don't put even a dent in me. After all, this motherfucker's acting skills are good enough to fool a jury. "Thank you for confessing, for finally taking accountability," I say, lowering the revolver. "I already knew you were guilty, but it helps to hear it from you."

Mr. Fix-It nods through the cry.

"Still," I say, "I can't help but think you're coming clean simply because I'm holding a gun."

Mr. Fix-It shakes his head, says, "I'm telling the truth. Wish I weren't."

I tell him I know he's not lying. I tell him that I never would have gone through all this if there were a single doubt in my mind that he did what Ella swore he did, did what she failed to convince 12 court-appointed strangers he did, did what she ended her life over. "But it shouldn't have come to this," I say. "Shouldn't have required me breaking all sorts of laws for you to utter the words you should have when my sister was breathing."

"You're right," says Mr. Fix-It.

"Yeah, of course I'm right. Lot of good being right gets me. Gets Ella." I raise the .38 again and point it at his three-years-too-late repentance. His pleading and flinching bounce right off me. "So, guess what happens now."

He cries something incoherent.

I lower the gun and say, "I call the police."

Mr. Fix-It makes a face like I've switched languages, started speaking Mandarin. He watches me walk toward the box and place the gun back inside. "You... You're going to call the police?"

"Yup," I say. "Well, in a minute, anyway."

Mr. Fix-It pinches his eyes closed, then opens them and searches the ceiling for an explanation. "Why?"

"To report you," I say.

Mr. Fix-It stares at me, his face a knot of confusion. "Okay, but... you do know a person can't be tried or nothing for a crime they've already been cleared of, don't you? Not even if they confess."

I smile and nod, then shake my head. "Oh, I'm not reporting you for what you did to Ella."

The knot of confusion tightens.

Without waiting for any more questions, I reach into the box and pull out an 18-inch plank—one left over from or waiting to be used on the deck out front. I hold it up, lock eyes with him. "This is going to hurt," I say, then hold up my free hand, rear back with the other, and crack the side of my forearm with the board. Hard enough to leave a nice defensive wound.

Mr. Fix-It and I jinx each other on "Fuck!" His, out of shock. Mine, of pain.

I switch the 2" x 4" to my other hand and—fighting off the fire running down my radius—thwack my other forearm. I growl and curse through the sting.

Mr. Fix-It just lies there, mouth slightly agape. Shouldn't take much longer for him to figure things out.

I drop the weapon and simultaneously massage my injuries, looking like a genie granting an agonizing wish. Then it's back to the box, where I pull out a bungee cord Mr. Fix-It used to strap down an outdoor tarp covering his tools. I grip the cord taut at both ends and rest the middle against my throat, pausing to take a couple deep breaths.

"Please stop," says my witness-slash-attacker.

"Too late. I've already suffered a couple possible hairline fractures. Can't stop now." I wrap the cord around my neck.

Mr. Fix-It grimaces, tries to look away. "Jesus, stop. Come on, I would never strangle a woman."

I shrug my elbows, keeping the cord in position. "You sure about that? Forensics will say otherwise." Another deep breath, and my near-death experience begins. I can smell the lack of blood getting to my brain. I even scream and beg for mercy, for good measure. I develop tremendous pity for anyone who has died that way. Almost as much as I have for a failed rapist in a prison shower.

The pulse in my ears is a midnight rave. Part of me doesn't want to let go. Hard to tell if the voice shouting to stop is the other part of me, or if it's Mr. Fix-It.

I release the cord and double over, gasping for air, hoping I've broken enough blood vessels to convince investigators.

"Enough, enough," cries Mr. Fix-It. "For God's sake, lady, you're crazy!"

He's just upset he doesn't have control this time.

I've never appreciated the metal hooks at the ends of bungee cords as much as now. They can really leave a mark, especially when you untuck your blouse to expose your belly and scrape it across your skin. And those hooks can tear through the waistband of women's underwear like nobody's business, leaving yet another painful scratch on the hip.

Mr. Fix-It doesn't get to see any of the hook-work I'm doing on his behalf, seeing as I turn away from him. What can I say, I'm a modest lady.

After fighting off his imaginary hands before he's able to do more harm, it's time to make sure the physical evidence of self-defense lines up. I take a few steps toward Mr. Fix-It, stopping just shy of any kick he might try. A girl's gotta be careful when staging her own sexual assault.

"Need to borrow you for a sec," I say. "Same rules as before: You try anything stupid, you're going to pay way worse than what's coming."

"What are you going to—"

I swoop down and claw at his face, taking off a bit more skin than intended. He shrieks like a man half his size, then burrows in his hands. I bite down on one before bouncing back to my feet and backpedaling. He pulls his hands away, revealing puma-like scratches from ear to chin. He brings his bite wound to his mouth and sucks the broken knuckle, keeping a frightened eye on me as I catch my breath from a narrow, heroic escape.

I pick up my phone and tap selfie mode to make sure I've done enough damage. Despite the poor lighting, it seems my cuts and bruises are coming along nicely.

There's just one problem: None of Mr. Fix-It's injuries seem severe enough to have incapacitated him to the point I could've shackled him. I weigh my options, then walk over to him.

"Please, no more," he says, his gaze fixed on the wood I'm gripping.

"Sorry," I say. "Really am, but I've come too far to half-ass this. Hope you understand."

He shakes his head. "I don't think I'll ever under—"

My foot meets his crotch with World Cup precision, and out of his mouth comes a sound best described as a dying oak tree moaning in a hurricane. To help take his mind off his smashed testicles, I bring the 2" x 4" down the side of his head, careful not to catch too much temple. That would be dangerous.

I'm no doctor, but the pain Mr. Fix-It's exhibiting seems to scream moderate concussion more than lethal hematoma. Good thing, too. After all this planning, if he were to die and miss out on all the misery that's awaiting him in some maximum security facility, I'd never forgive myself.

I retrieve my phone, click the call icon, then the keypad. I close my eyes and think about Ella and that night and her absence everywhere I look. My fury and sadness choke me just the way they need to right now.

And I tap 9, then 1, then 1 again.

@Greg_Levin GregLevin.com

Greg Levin writes subversive thrillers and crime fiction. His novels include *The Exit Man, Sick to Death* and *In Wolves' Clothing*. With work optioned by HBO and Showtime, he's won two Independent Publisher Book Awards and been a finalist for a National Indie Excellence Book Award twice. *Publishers Weekly* wrote, "This author deserves a wide audience." His agent and mother agree.

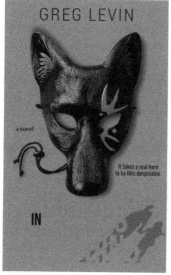

Levin lived in Austin, Texas, until authorities were after him for refusing to say "y'all." He currently resides with his wife, dog, and cat in Sydney, Australia, where he's already in trouble for refusing to say "g'day."

Bricked Up

By Stephen J. Golds

In the daytime the place had looked like one of those chateaus you see on postcards. Classic. All white. Ivy of the deepest green crawling up half the place. The grounds more like a luxury golf course than the gardens of an estate. At night, with the moon asphyxiated by the clouds, it looked haunted. A ghost house from a book you'd read as a kid. A crypt for the resentful and unrestful dead. Either way, the millionaire owner and his family were away in the Caribbean for two weeks.

The skeleton crew: a guard with a panting Alsatian patrolling the perimeter, and another holding a newspaper up to his face in a small hut under a smaller bulb.

I put two bullets through the front-page headlines. Some bullshit about another conflict in some far-flung Middle Eastern country. Confetti rained over the dead man as though celebrating his demise. A faded, curling photograph of his family was taped to the desk.

My backup, Number One, came strolling across the lawn under the glare of a security light. He put the guard and Alsatian out of commission with the silenced pistol in his gloved fist. Then he disappeared behind a brick and glass gazebo while I reached over the bloody photograph to punch the main gate's button.

Number Three slowly pulled into the driveway, grit popping underneath the tires of the Jeep he'd stolen yesterday. He might have been grinning underneath the silk, skin-tone stocking pulled over his face, but I couldn't tell. Since 0 introduced us, ran down the details of the job and our working numbers, Number Three hadn't stopped grinning. I didn't like it. It made me uneasy.

When I turned around, Number One was looming behind me. Too close. As though he had a point to prove to himself and to me. I adjusted the stocking on my face to disguise my surprise, cleared my throat. "What?" I said.

"I counted two out of the three maids. In the kitchen, yammering," he said.

"How do you know?"

He shrugged. "Big windows. A lot to see."

I straightened my stance. Switched the pistol from my left hand to my right.

He shrugged again. "I'll take care of those two. You go in the front and find the third before she sets off any alarms."

I opened my mouth to say something, but he was already halfway across the lawn, the dark navy overalls fading him out in the shadows. I yanked off the stocking, stood squinting into the moonlight. He reappeared like magic, hacking into an access panel next to a side door. The light on the small box flashed green as he slid into the mansion. Disappearing again.

I stepped around the guard hut and gave Number Three the O.K. to drive up. He came to a stop just before the huge porch underneath a willow tree and fountain. Put it in park and turned his head to watch me walk up to the driver's door. I tapped the window with the muzzle of my silencer.

He rolled it down and pulled his stocking up, exposing a thick-stumbled jaw and that grin of his. He hissed, "What's up? Why you ain't in the place already? Why ain't you wearing your mask? There a problem?"

"Nah, nothing like that, I need you to hold onto something for me."

"Sure thing, man." He grinned.

I saw the flash of a gold tooth I hadn't seen before, snaked the silencer through the window gap. "Here, hold onto these." I shot him twice in the chest, until he slumped over the steering wheel, an exhausted man.

I pulled open the door, undid his safety belt and let him fall onto the hard, damp ground. I took the keys out of the ignition and shoved them in the pocket of my jet-black military pants. Quickly dragging the skinny, little bastard into a flower garden, I left him there for the cops, the crows or the flies. Whatever found him first.

I followed Number One through the side door. Came into some kind of terrarium: tropical plants and trees draping branches like emerald crucifixions. The heavy stench of ozone vice-gripped my throat. Trippy as hell. I followed a tunnel of light into a small kitchen, stepping over one of the maids. A jagged rip in her throat. So deep, I could glimpse the pale purple of a ruptured windpipe. She was young. Wearing the same black and white uniform a girl had worn for me on a few occasions. Couldn't remember her name now, but the recollection made me smile.

Moving away from the body, I realized I was tracking blood across the checkerboard floor and cursed under my breath. The whole job was another fucking cold case for the books.

The other maid was slumped against the counter. Bullet holes creating a crimson pyramid. Left breast. Right breast. Forehead. It was becoming more difficult to find robbery crews who didn't have at least one sick fuck within their numbers. 0 should have known better. He was getting desperate and greedy. A bad combination for any fixer and fence. Teaming professionals with thrill-seekers, maniacs, and addicts? Clearly, the recessions affected every market. Even the black market.

I popped a mint to take away the stink of blood, made my way down a hall. Paintings of dead people framed the walls. A large Iranian rug spread across the floor like a stain. I followed growled words and treaded softly, heel first. Pistol pointed from the hip, I slid around a doorway into something that looked like a library: leatherbound books on shelves collecting dust and a globe I was sure housed a minibar.

Number One was standing over a naked woman cowering on a chesterfield couch. Her uniform was torn to shreds and tossed near a dead fireplace. "Where's the fucking safe?" he said, pressing his pistol against the top of her head.

It was my turn to surprise him. "What the fuck do you think you're doing?"

He startled. His voice went soprano. "What's it look like?" he said over his shoulder. "I'm getting information."

"Are you a fucking moron? We already know where the safe is." I was in control now.

"I'm getting confirmation. Where's your face cover?"

"Look," I said, limply waving my pistol at the woman, "I don't care how you get your sick little thrills, but you're on someone else's clock. We don't have time for this shit."

Number One exaggerated his sigh. Apologized to the woman.

She wailed. Blood splashed the rear wall like a psychotherapist's flashcard. *What do you see in this pattern?*

We both stood, giving the woman a glance. She looked as though she could've been sleeping.

"Let's hurry this up already," I said, waving One back to the hall with the rug that concealed the walk-in safe. "You got the code?"

He tapped his temple as though trying to blow out his brains. "All in here, my man."

We stood, gazing down at the rug the same way we had the departed maid. A large target on the off-white marble. Pay day. The big one. I already had my flight booked somewhere hot and was contemplating what to order at the airport bar. I imagined 0's face when none of us made it to the drop-off point. Sweating and wiping that fat fucking face of his. Looking at his watch, wondering if it paid to be a cheap, careless bastard all these years.

Number One gripped the right corner of the rug, and I snatched the left, rolling it up like a huge Twinkie bar and exposing the thick, blast-proof trapdoor underneath. Number One got down on his hands and knees, starting to punch numbers into a keypad like the one he hacked earlier. A soft *beep, beep, beep* emitted into the silence of the mansion.

Something clanked, sprung. Then we could feel the mechanisms shifting, vibrating up through our boots. The trapdoor pushed up, out, and began sliding away on a track. A lifeless backdraft hit us in the face. Number One coughed and hacked. There was a brightly lit hole in the foundation. A ladder. It made me remember reading *Alice in Wonderland* to my children a lifetime ago. I rubbed a latex hand over my face. The sweat of anticipation never dried up. I remembered the pistol still pointed at my hip. I bucked it back twice, sharp.

Number One continued stepping toward the hole before his heart knew it was dead. He collapsed face-first onto the floor, his nose bursting like an overripe tomato. I kicked him aside, slipped the pistol back into my belt. Lowered myself into the hole. Down the ladder. *Whiskey on the rocks. Whiskey chaser. Fuck it, champagne. Cristal.* I was sure one of the bars would have a bottle. Looking at the contents of the basement vault, I knew I could afford five-thousand bottles of the stuff. Things down there, I had only seen from behind Plexiglass in museums: Egyptian relics. Fabrics. Some kind of deformed skeleton on display. A baseball autographed by Babe Ruth. The videotape we were sent to retrieve.

I picked it up. No idea what was on it, but someone wanted it bad enough to give the job to 0 in the first place. A lot of the shit down there I had no idea about, but one thing I knew for sure were the piles of money. Stacks and stacks. I found a brown leather hold-all tossed in a corner and started stuffing the green inside. Crisp, never used. Beautiful bricks of emerald.

I was trying to zip the overflowing bag when I heard it. Wasn't sure at first. An alarm? I froze. Listened. A soft *beep, beep, beep* emanated through the vault. Something clanked, sprung. Then the mechanisms shifted. Fuck!

The door was closing. I struggled to lift the hold-all. Too heavy. I dragged the damned thing like a corpse. The heavy door clang shut. The lights cut out. I stood in the pitch-black, attempting to gather my bearings. A fucking timer lock! And the man with the code was as dead as my chances of getting out.

Sure, I could hear Number One moving around on the first floor. Or was it the cops? I screamed until my throat burned. I gagged. I vomited. Thinking about that Edgar Allen Poe story. I was bricked up. A skeleton in a wall. Fuck Cristal. I just wanted water. Ice-cold water. Tap water.

The vault stank, rancid. Shit, piss, and sick. I kicked the hold-all until I heard it split and the bundles scatter. My breath became shorter or was that my imagination? Felt someone's eyes on me or was that my imagination, too?

Author Bio

@SteveGone58

Stephen J. Golds was born in North London but has lived in Japan most of his adult life. As co-editor of *Punk Noir Magazine*, he writes noir and dirty realism.

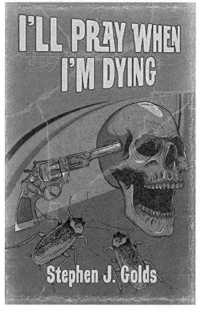

Golds' novels include *Say Goodbye When I'm Gone, I'll Pray When I'm Dying, Always the Dead, Poems for Ghosts in Empty Tenement Windows I Thought I Saw Once, Cut-throat & Tongue-tied, Bullet Riddled & Gun Shy,* and the story-slash-poetry collection, *Love Like Bleeding Out With an Empty Gun in Your Hand.*

The Harpy

By Lauren Sapala

The screaming began the day they moved in.

"Oh, god. What *is* that? Is that coming from next door?" James said as he chucked another box on the floor.

Katie stopped scooting furniture into place and cocked her head. It was definitely coming from next door, and it was definitely a woman screaming. She sighed and shrugged and looked back at him. They thought they'd been lucky to find a San Francisco apartment at this price. "I guess now we know why rent is so cheap," she said.

James only grimaced, then went downstairs to retrieve more boxes.

In the weeks that followed, they heard the same woman screaming every day. It wasn't the kind of screaming where it sounded like she was being murdered. It was more like she was screaming at someone else, and they could only assume that "someone else" was Don, the old guy they'd seen come and go from the apartment. James found out his name when he ran into him at the mailbox.

"He's 65, can you believe it?" he told Katie. "I mean, he does look older, but he sure doesn't look 65. And you'd think he'd be hella stressed from that crazy bitch screeching at him all day long."

Katie massaged her temples. Everything was quiet now, but she was sure it would start back up soon.

"She used to be his wife," James went on. "A long time ago, he said, and then they split up for some reason. He said he left SF for a while and traveled, and, when he came back, they decided to live together again to save on rent." He paused and glanced at the wall they shared with them. "I gotta say, no matter how much he's saving, it can't be worth it."

As if on cue, the screaming started again.

James gave Katie a look. "I don't know how he stands it."

Katie slumped on the couch and buried her head beneath a pillow.

They heard other noises through the wall, too. It sounded like a couple of parakeets, or maybe finches. Sometimes they chirped and sometimes they cheeped, so Katie thought maybe there was a mix of both. She also assumed the neighbors didn't cover the cages at night, because—even when getting up to use the bathroom at 3AM—she could hear the birds. Like the woman next door, it seemed they never shut the fuck up.

But the strangest thing about the situation was that, even though the woman constantly screamed, James and Katie never heard Don yell back. In fact, they never heard his voice at all. They felt beyond pity for the poor guy; it was almost impossible not to picture her as a witch or a demon, her face all screwed up and red and evil-looking, her teeth long and yellow, her eyes blazing with fury as she screamed, and screamed, and screamed.

When Katie thought about the face behind those screams, she shuddered.

Don had met Lena in San Francisco in the late '70s. He'd walked into a bar in North Beach and instantly noticed her flashing an innocent smile as she adjusted her emerald dress over her hips. From the first moment he'd set eyes on her, he'd been entranced by her glossy red mane and pin-up figure.

When Don found a cheap apartment three days later, they moved in together and were married not long after. The marriage lasted a few years before Don called it quits. He never cheated on her, and the sex was always great. Fantastic, in fact. But with every day that passed, Don felt the walls closing in. Like time was running out, and escape would soon be impossible. He couldn't explain the feeling, even to himself, and he knew it wasn't Lena's fault, but still, he had to go. Oddly enough, she didn't take it personally when he left. She watched him pack with a smile, as if she knew a delicious secret that she wasn't ready to tell him.

After he left San Francisco, he headed north. He thought about Lena a lot in those first few months. He remembered how warm and full of life she was when they met. Once there was some distance between them, he could see it more clearly: She wasn't the person he married. She still wore tight skirts and sexy stilettos, that *come-fuck-me* vibe, but underneath all that, she'd turned cold. He thought back to how her eyes gleamed before he left, as if she were calculating something, how she smiled.

It gave him a cold, sick feeling.

Don spent the following decades moving between Oregon and Washington, then Alaska, where the itch to go back to San Francisco crept upon him. Lena popped into his mind, then consumed him: her face, her eyes, her laughter, and the way he'd felt while holding her. The thoughts circled and swooped through his mind like a flock of birds flying in formation against a cold, gray sky. They dipped this way and that, effortlessly gliding in graceful spirals of obsession that soon filled his every waking moment. He wanted her again. In fact, it seemed he *needed* her again, more than he ever needed anything in his life. He had to find her, even though more than 30 years had passed.

A week later, he took off for San Francisco.

That had been three years ago, and, when he tried to think about those years spent up north... Well, it was like he couldn't, not really. What he did there and where he worked, the people he had known, it was all hazy. He couldn't remember anything clearly, not one concrete item—except Lena. She was the only memory that remained sharp, the only one that felt real. But when you got right down to it, Don supposed, that was the only thing that mattered.

When he got back to the city, he looked up their old apartment and discovered Lena was still there. It was so easy; it was almost unbelievable. She opened the door and greeted him as if he'd never left. A few days later, he moved in again, permanently. He knew after seeing her that he would never want to be anywhere else. He was home.

It was only a few weeks after their happy reunion that he noticed Lena had begun growing feathers.

At night, Don went out.

As soon as the sun was down, he was in the car, headed to the Tenderloin. He drove fast to get there but took his time once he arrived. He cruised the vicinity.

He drove down Eddy Street, then turned around and drove back up Golden Gate. He passed by all the bars, eyeing the clusters of people outside the doors and the dark pockets that showed the openings of alleyways. He inspected them for stragglers, anyone alone, anyone who wouldn't be missed—at least for a day or so. He slowed down when he saw an opportunity but sped up when he saw the cops, trying to look like a normal driver passing through the neighborhood.

He usually found what he needed without having to get out of the car, and, over time, it only got easier. He didn't need to cruise for as long, but he stretched the time anyway. A heady anticipation flooded his body as he drove up and down the streets, searching for his mark, and he wanted to savor it. Everything that came after was for her, but in those few moments before the kill, there was something given only to him.

Sometimes, as he stalked his next victim, Don wondered if he had changed as much as Lena. At these times, he felt almost like waking up, as if he'd been asleep at the wheel for an indeterminate time. He had the feeling of floating outside his body, watching himself as a witness of the soul trapped within.

He saw that what was inside him now was dark and predatory, murderous, and that it was linked to something that had taken up residence inside Lena, too, something evil. Another part of his mind—a deeper, unknown, and unacknowledged part— whispered that it was a demon that sat and waited, always waited, for Don to feed it, and knew Don always would.

But then, Don would spot his next kill and forget all this. The distraction of the next victim—the *relief* of being pulled away from that horrible floating sensation and the unbearable consciousness of watching himself—was so great that Don's arms and legs trembled, and he felt as though he might cry. Because many times, right before he was pulled away by the task at hand, he'd seen something he couldn't deny. There was no escape. Don had been empty when the demon found him, just as Lena had been. Neither of them even questioned it when the demon told them they were ready to be filled.

Shortly after Don moved back in with Lena, he bought her two parrakeets as a gift. Lena had loved them and fussed over them so much that he ended up buying her two more birds—finches, this time. The birds twittered and cheeped at each other in their cages over by the window, on the side of the apartment that looked down on busy Noriega Street. The parrakeets were the brilliant green and blue of a tropical sea, and the finches were white with red eyes that seemed to glow whenever Don looked at them. Albino, they call that, Don thought, they must be albino if they have red eyes. Although he didn't think about it too long, those little, white birds with red eyes gave him the creeps. He tried to stay away from those windows as much as possible.

Lena sat in her rocking chair, not too far from the birds or window, where she couldn't be seen by any passersby. When she'd started sprouting feathers, Don stopped letting her leave the apartment. Soon after, she changed so rapidly that he thought he could see overnight transformations, as if whatever force were at work tripled in strength while he'd slept.

The few natural wrinkles she'd had as a 62-year-old had multiplied, ruthlessly cutting into her skin until every inch of her face was spiderwebbed with lines—some so deep, it looked as if she'd been gashed with a knife. Her eyes had gone from green to dark brown, then finally to black. The eyeballs themselves seemed to have sunken deeper into her sockets, giving her the appearance of a talking skull. They reminded Don of hot coals, malevolently winking at him from the back of two dark caves.

Another day he awoke to discover her hair had turned white, most of it fallen out, leaving just a few wisps clinging to a scalp that shed hunks of old skin like a burn victim. She stooped, her back bending into a permanent bow. The only place that could comfortably house her was the rocking chair, which was fortunate, because the chair had begun to meld to her body, and she probably couldn't get out of it if she tried. In this newly deformed shape, it seemed she was now part of the chair, and it was part of her. There was no separation. Alarmed, Don considered trying to pry her out, but then decided against it. He didn't want to hurt her.

As the days went on, Lena's nose grew into a hooked shape to jut over her mouth like a beak. It turned red, then a deep purple, and finally grew a hard, shell-like covering. The bones in her arms grew too, lengthening and stretching, and her elbows formed into new angles, until Don couldn't deny what he saw anymore: Lena had wings.

But possibly the worst change was her voice, the screaming.

Not that Don ever considered her old voice beautiful. She could never carry a tune, but it had been nothing to complain about. It had been normal. Human. But now it scraped over the ears. It cut down into the psyche and dragged nails over the chalkboard it found there, until Don felt like his brain had been put through a meat tenderizer.

After this grotesque rebirth (and Don could think of nothing else to call it), Lena needed things, a lot of things. Since she couldn't leave the chair, she was helpless. She depended on Don for everything. Because she couldn't move, she ended up shitting right where she sat. It was gooey and white when it oozed out of her, and then quickly dried into a pasty gray clay that formed layers of crust beneath her. Don used a screwdriver or an icepick, whatever was handy, to chip at the mound whenever he could, but it was hard to stay on top of it. Lena ate a lot, so it seemed like she was constantly shitting.

As for her eating habits—specifically, what she ate— well, that was hard to stay on top of, too. If Lena didn't get enough food, she seemed to shrink. Her skin shriveled and her cawing became raspier, as if she were drying out like an old chicken bone right before his eyes.

Once Don realized the extent of what and how much Lena needed to consume, he had to make some adjustments to the apartment bathroom. He'd gutted the 1970s tub-shower combo and replaced it with a bigger, metal tub that sat flush against the wall and fit over the drain. Then he installed steel doors over the tub that could be opened whenever he needed access. It gave him just enough room to maneuver as he cut up the bodies and prevented any blood from leaking onto the floor.

The main thing Don was concerned about was the smell. By keeping as much liquid and tissue contained as possible, he hoped to prevent any stench of rotting flesh from wafting down the hall. He remembered the sensational accounts of how Jeffrey Dahmer had been caught in the early '90s because his neighbors smelled something foul coming from his apartment. He figured he could take a lesson from Dahmer and not fuck up so stupidly.

He'd bought the rest of what he needed at the hardware store down the street, adding to his tool kit here and there as he got better at dismemberment and more adept at clean-up. He found, too, that actual killing did nothing for him. It was a job and not much more, like catching a fish and clubbing it over the head. Don had done a lot of fishing work up in Alaska and it was never something he enjoyed. But what came after—*that* was when Don hit his stride.

A calm, contemplative sort of state fell over him as he cut and sawed. He lost all track of time, all awareness of himself, and floated blissfully on a warm sea of effortless, flowing energy that seemed like it could fill him, and go on filling him, forever. Flashes of memories from his life came to him from time to time as he worked, but they never stuck in his mind. They grew stagnant and soured, as so many other memories had before. These images floated in, then floated out again, and there was no worry in them, no fear. Don could see them as they formed and let them go as they passed. He didn't need them to stay. In this state, he was finding that he didn't *need* anything at all.

All he needed was to go on cutting and sawing through skin and muscle and bone, and everything would be all right.

It seemed like it had been a long time since Don knew what day it was or how much time had passed, or how many bodies he'd cut up and brought to Lena. He never saw the sun rise or set because he never opened the blinds anymore. It also seemed he didn't hear Lena's birds chirping anymore, but he couldn't really be sure of that either. Every time he tried to think about it— every time his mind tried to settle definitively on something—it seemed to fly away again, as if it were a bird itself.

And going out at night, well, that was different too. He didn't use the car anymore. He didn't need it. In fact, he wasn't sure he was going out at all. He couldn't be certain he was even leaving the apartment. Although, he had memories of hunting and killing, and there was always another body waiting for him in the bathroom. There was always more work to do to fill his time, and to fill himself up. But possibly, he was only dreaming these things... even though the crunch of bone and the wet, ripping of skin sounded so incredibly real, the blood on his fingers so slippery it had to be happening... but no, he just couldn't be certain. There was really no way to know for sure.

Whether he was dreaming or not, the one thing that *was* clear was that now Don could fly. It was painful every time it happened, but he found he was getting used to the pain. First, his shoulders seemed to rearrange themselves on his torso, until his arms were almost turned around backward. When he looked down at himself, he saw he was covered in shiny black feathers. He felt the gap between his eyes stretch farther apart on his skull, until it felt like his eyes were on the sides of his head. His teeth shrank and shifted and then his voice disappeared.

He beat his wings behind him, then opened and closed his beak, letting out an ugly squawking sound. It was then that he would look toward the apartment windows and see that they were wide open, as if someone wanted to let in the cool fog from the San Francisco night, although who that might have been, he couldn't say—and besides, it didn't matter now. They were open and that meant he was free.

As Don flew over the city and away, out over the water, and then back inland, over fields and forests below, he saw everything. His vision had sharpened until he could see rodents running on the ground, even in total darkness. He could feel the wind rushing over his wings and he rode on it, as if it were a wave carrying him back and forth over the swells of the ocean. He had never felt so at peace.

When he returned to the apartment and shifted back into his normal form, he oftentimes discovered he had brought a victim back with him. As a human again, he found himself ripping away long strips of skin from the bodies with his teeth, the faces already erased, pecked into a bloody, mangled mess by a

bird of prey with a merciless jackhammer of a beak. That was
okay though, because Don didn't need the details of their faces;
he only needed the raw materials he could harvest from their
corpses. Skin and hair, muscle and tendon, globs of fatty tissue.
This was the stuff out of which he made miracles. He had
transformed (a few weeks or months ago, he could never be sure)
from a meticulous clean-up man into a true artist.

Don began to paint.

Canvases had appeared out of nowhere. Or at least, he
didn't remember buying them. But here they were, fresh ones set
up and waiting for him every night. They stood and smiled
blankly at him, begging to be filled, just as Lena had begged him
so many years ago, when they were young and couldn't get
enough of each other. Just as Don himself was filled these days
by something he could not name, but which terrified him,
nonetheless. It was okay though, too, when he had thoughts like
that. Because now he had the painting, and whenever those
thoughts surfaced, it was easy to push them away and just
concentrate on the empty canvas in front of him.

He didn't need brushes. It was enough to use his hands.
In fact, he preferred it. With every picture he created, he felt like
he was getting younger. He felt astonishingly strong, like he was
18 again and ready to take on the world. He wanted direct contact
with the materials because he needed to feel this new vital energy
coursing through him. He rubbed and smeared and pressed
different shapes together, using the lightest touch in some places
and clawing at the canvas in others. He scraped and spread
various forms of matter as he hummed under his breath, then
paused and stepped back before he returned for more. When he
finished, each picture was an explosion of color, an orgy of
textures, everything smashed together and simultaneously
splintered to pieces.

He thought he'd never been this happy in his entire life.

But then, one night, after he'd returned through the
window and torn apart the latest body, he passed by the mirror in
the bathroom, and for no reason at all, he looked over. He saw a
man there. An old man, with clots of blood in his teeth and a
piece of spongy flesh stuck to his cheek. The man looked as if he
were being chased, and hunted. His eyes rolled frantically in his

head like a spooked horse, and when he saw the man's eyes move, he found that he too was looking all around the small room, seemingly without being able to control his gaze.

He tore his vision away from the mirror. He didn't know who that man was. He'd never seen him before. And yet... He was sure it wasn't important now.

Later that night, James and Katie heard a gunshot from next door and called the police. They'd been noticing a weird— and *gross*, Katie had added to the police report—smell coming from Don's apartment for a few days, but they chalked it up to garbage that needed to be taken out. They knew Don and Lena were older and had trouble getting around. They never even saw Lena, in fact, they explained to the cops. They only heard her. "Although that was something weird too," Katie said. In the past week or so they hadn't heard a peep out of her, either. Her, or those damn birds she kept.

When the cops broke into the apartment next door, they found Don slumped on the floor in front of the bathroom sink, dead of a self-inflicted headshot. Pieces from the back of his skull were sprayed all over the mirror.

Lena had been dead a few days. She'd been propped up in a rocking chair out in the living room, her body so bloated that it seemed the chair could barely contain her. Two black rivers of fluid ran out of her nose. The detectives called to the scene found the remains of the parakeets and finches she'd loved so much— stuffed into her mouth, rectum, and vagina.

The walls were covered in what looked like primitive paintings. Floor-to-ceiling was emblazoned with wild splashes of blood and long ribbons of skin glued into place, interrupted periodically by gobs of decomposing tissue that were nailed to the wall so they hung like pieces of expensive jewelry, meant to draw the viewer's eyes to their beauty. All of it had obviously come from the pile of bodies in the recently remodeled shower stall. They were wedged in there so tightly, one of the detectives wondered out loud how they would even begin to get them out.

"I can't believe someone would defile a sweet old lady like that," said one detective, nodding to Lena, where she sat rotting in the chair.

The other detective shook his head, then glanced around the walls. "The really sad thing," he said, "is that if this guy hadn't been a serial killer, he probably could have been a fucking Picasso."

Author Bio

@LoSapala LaurenSapala.com

Writing coach Lauren Sapala has authored transgressive novels about overcoming alcoholism, including *Between the Shadow and Lo* and *West is San Francisco*. She has also produced several highly acclaimed non-fiction books on creatives with highly sensitive personality types, such as *The INFJ Writer* and its sequel, *The INFJ Revolution*.

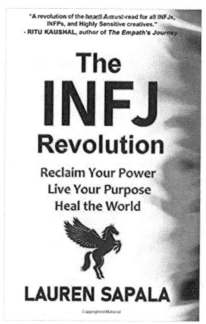

When Sapala is not wrangling her six-year-old son, she can be found hosting online workshops and seminars.

Sugar Baby

By CT Marie

The drugs are better in my neighborhood. At Boyfriend's request, I score a bag of H.

Discreetly, I hand my dealer five $20s. "*Gracias, Señor Wizz.*"

He says, "Take care of yourself," and palms me the plump, little baggie of China white.

It's not my first choice. I prefer Vicodin, Percocet, Oxycodone, or, on occasion, a tranquilizer like Valium or Xanax. I used to buy from some old lady down the street with a whole pharmacy in her lilac bathroom. Every time I'd visit, she'd offer me a cup of Darjeeling, real hospitable. I'd sip it and watch her count each white pill.

She'd go, "One, two... You don't have a problem with this stuff, do you? Three, four..."

"Just for fun," I assured her.

"Mine is marijuana," she said before handing me a pouch of pills.

I haven't seen her in two months. She won't return my phone calls. Hopefully she didn't get caught. That would be a major bummer.

I walk to the subway. From across the street, my neighbor calls out and waves hello. I wave back. New York City is not a small town, but, when you grow up here, it feels like one.

Boyfriend told me he was sick of his neighbors, sick of his parents. He moved down here from Cape Cod to redefine himself. By chance two years ago, we met at a seedy bar in the East Village. He reminded me of Robert Mapplethorpe: lanky, pale, with a head of brown curls. He bought me a beer and we sipped our cool drinks with Velvet Underground's "Venus in Furs" playing in the background.

Friend does not like Boyfriend. She says his relationship with opiates is highly contagious. So critical. Her boyfriend turned her into a vegan, and I don't judge that.

Boyfriend lives in Brooklyn, so I descend the stairs of the 181 Street Station to catch the downtown A Train.

I'm wearing a new outfit, picked specifically for this mission. I'm hoping we can go out tonight. I'm hoping he will see me as someone to keep. I figure this outfit gives off an air of confidence, a chicness not to be outdone by the '90s. I washed my hair, shaved my legs, painted my nails a cool blue and my lips a deep red.

On the platform, I pace back and forth. The buzz from the wine I drank earlier is wearing off. I'm shaking in my too-tight purple skirt. Why am I trying so hard? It doesn't matter what I wear, Boyfriend won't care. Women are too thoughtful and men not at all.

I stare into the mouth of the tunnel, willing the train to come pick me up. I lightly squeeze the H in my purse to reassure myself. I'm not a junkie. It's just a hobby, an occasional activity. People binge drink every weekend, smoke pot every morning, and do bumps of cocaine at every party. Bartenders like to shout, "Pick your poison!"

Well, I have! Why do I deserve such a bad rap? Friend talks a lot of shit.

Finally, the eyes of the train light up the station. It's the weekend, but, damn, with delays like this, the subway should be half off or free.

I sit next to the window, facing forward. The overhead fluorescent lights flicker. Goosebumps snake up my arms. The air conditioning is on full blast, snuffing out my sense of smell. Pity, I prefer the stink of strangers: the pheromones, the sweat, the perfume. When did everyone become so cold and tasteless?

"Next stop, 175 Street," the tired voiceover says.

Fuck, not only is this train slow, but running local, and all that I poured down my throat has evaporated.

I have an ugly urge to pick at my face, redo my lipstick, and play with myself. Sober thoughts bore and scare me. I should have bought a bottle of beer to suck on.

I glance at the people in the train car. I don't recognize anyone. I feel like a tourist.

I reach into my bag and close my fist around the bag of H. I got this for Boyfriend, but I think I need it now. I did just spend my entire unemployment check, and it's only Tuesday.

Over the years, Friend has told me she'd do anything for me, that I could ask anything of her. Yesterday, I asked for money, and she declined. And she calls me a liar?

People think they know what users look like, but I change my appearance daily. It's not like Boyfriend and I sleep on dark corners of side streets. We aren't the dirty type. My parents aren't suspicious. Boyfriend even has a job.

I don't shoot up in fitting rooms and Boyfriend doesn't use toilet water to clean our needles. I don't go dumpster diving for Kmart receipts to "return" the item I just stole. I have morals. I'm responsible. I don't think I'll ever have children.

Boyfriend attempted to get clean before he moved here. How he got into painkillers is still a mystery: no accident, no poor upbringing, no reason. I wish it were tragic. Then maybe things would seem more romantic.

Boyfriend never goes out in short sleeves anymore. He did when we first met, but that was when he was only taking pills: Before. That was when he said I got him high just by touching him. I miss the Before, but I don't know how to turn back time. We used to go to the midnight screenings of cult classics at IFC Center, we used to get lost in Central Park, we used to talk to friends. Now, we rarely visit places or see anyone. Too expensive. Too exhausting. Too stressful. I'm still recovering from the last time we had coffee.

We were sitting across from each other, and he stood up to use the restroom—with a spoon in his pocket. I prefer to snort the stuff.

"Don't be too long," I told him. "Or everyone's gonna think you're blowing up the bathroom."

"Good." Boyfriend walked off.

Twenty minutes later, I knocked on the door. Boyfriend had fallen asleep on the toilet. He's ruined Starbucks for me.

"135th Street," Train Conductor announces.

The doors open. A large homeless man in a winter coat shuffles on. People look up from their phones and newspapers to throw dirty looks in his direction. He sits perpendicular to me and opens his coat to take out a plastic bottle of whiskey. He gulps down the amber liquid in bliss. Who would notice if I indulged, too? The bum spreads out, shielding me from everyone's view, and shuts his eyes.

I carefully pour a bump of powder on my hand, between thumb and forefinger. I quickly snort it up my left nostril. I need to make a living! The thought explodes in my mind, as I feel the dope drip down my throat, tasting like something you shouldn't eat, like poison, like bitter chalk.

"125th Street." The train stops.

I jerk my head up just as the doors open, and someone beautiful walks on. My eyes snake up Dream Guy's body. His hair slicked back and blonde. His blue eyes meet mine. Too quick! So easy...

Dream Guy sits next to me. Up close, I hold my breath. He looks like a rockabilly boy from the 1950s. He looks like a healthier version of Jim Carroll from *The Basketball Diaries*. I can't decide which fantasy I want to go with. I am really high. Cue the music.

"Hey," Dream Guy says.

"Hi." I lick my lips.

"Come here often?"

The line is stupid, but I giggle anyway.

He touches his hair, looks at my crossed feet. "I like your legs."

"Me too." I uncross them. Somewhat of an invitation. "Where you coming from?" I ask.

"The Bronx."

"Is that where you live?"

"Born and bred," he confirms.

"Good."

"Good?" He raises an eyebrow.

"We're a dying breed!" I look right into his eyes. A boy this cute would usually make me nervous, but I'm feeling brave.

"What part of the Bronx are you from?" he asks.

"I'm Washington Heights, baby!"

"I'm no baby," he says. "You can call me daddy."

"What kind of daddy?"

"The sweet kind." Dream Guy winks at me.

Recently, I made a profile on a sugar daddy dating site in hopes of meeting someone like Richard Gere in *Pretty Woman*. But all I attract are sleazy icks with small dicks and big egos. Maybe my luck has changed.

"What do you do?" Dream Guy asks.

"I'm jobless, but thanks for asking."

"Baby, if you're with me, you wouldn't have to work."

"Oh, yeah?"

"Yeah," he assures. "I'd treat you real nice."

"Is that a promise?"

"What would I get in return?"

"Unwavering devotion," I say. Boyfriend *who*?

"Pretty girl like you..." Dream Guy whispers more compliments into my ear. He sounds like he knows me. Finally, someone who appreciates all I've put into my appearance.

Maybe I should keep him around instead. "You want?" I ask, revealing my party favor.

He offers his right nostril and I'm flattered by the instant camaraderie.

My eyes dart around as he does a bump. The unconscious bum keeps us hidden. I do one more bump. The people on the train go out of focus and the tired voice of Train Conductor fades away.

I look down at Dream Guy's warm hands. I imagine them around my waist, holding me with purpose as I lean in, weighing my existence on someone else. "Don't let me go," I sing under my breath.

"Huh?"

"Where you headed?" I ask, smoothing down my checkered skirt.

"I was supposed to get off several stops ago." He smiles. "Where you going?"

"It doesn't matter." I touch his face.

Dream Guy's hand makes his way up my skirt and, just as he brushes that private part of me, the homeless drunk belches awake. People turn. Dream Guy jerks away.

"14th Street."

My stop.

"Can I come with you?" Dream Guy asks.

Boyfriend and I haven't fucked in weeks, maybe a month. I've lost track. My body hums with excitement. I stand and hold out my hand. His palm is soft. I press on it like a doorbell. "To Bushwick, we go." I lead him out.

The L Train is packed, and we are up smushed up against the doors. With our bodies pushed together, we start to kiss. My body craves adventure. Perhaps this self-proclaimed sugar daddy is my ticket. He rubs his thumb on the inside of my wrist.

He follows me up the stairs of Jefferson Street Station, and I feel like a leader.

"Where we going now?" Dream Guy asks.

Boyfriend will have to wait. Fuck him. I'm suddenly angry that I told him I was coming over. Boyfriend isn't worried. Boyfriend hasn't even called.

"I want to take care of you," Dream Guy says, as if reading my mind.

I think of a destination, look at the sky for answers. Whatever is happening here, it doesn't feel wrong. I light a cigarette and contemplate.

We come across a house of worship. We walk through the gate and into the open grass. Not a person in sight. I take out the bag of H and we each do a bump.

Soon, we are all over each other: our saliva, his hard-on, my wanting. Dream Guy turns me around and pulls down my underwear. I look up and am face-to-face with a statue of Virgin Mary. He undoes his jeans.

"Oh, Jesus," I mutter.

"Oh, Jesus!" he screams a few moments later.

We didn't use a condom. No biggie, I will get tested later. I pull up my underwear.

I turn and stare hard at Dream Guy. He no longer looks so dreamy. He has too many teeth, smashed together, and going every which way. I fight the urge to punch him in the mouth. My mistake. "I should go." I walk past him. He follows. The gate is now closed.

"Shit!" I look around for another exit.

"I think we have to climb it," Mistake says.

I watch him hoist himself over the spiky top and make his way down. There's no choice, I'm going to have to do the same.

It's not so bad. I'm more careful than I look. From below, Mistake offers his head to balance my foot on, which makes me think he doesn't use it very often. I'll let him learn the hard way. He groans under the weight of me.

"Give me your shoulder!" I call down to him.

My feet finally hit ground and I sigh in relief. The dope has worn off and I take a quick hit to boost myself back up. Mistake doesn't ask for more.

"I don't feel good," he mutters. "I feel sick." He grabs his stomach.

"Go ahead and puke. I won't judge" I say, walking away.

"Where to?" he calls after me.

I snap, "I'm going to my boyfriend's!"

He follows.

30 minutes ago, I wished this guy would pin me to the ground so I wouldn't float out of existence. Now, I wish I could pin him to a pole or something. I swivel around, "Will you fuck off?"

"Look, I don't feel so good. Whatever you gave me... I don't feel so good."

"Go home," I say.

"Yeah, the thing is..."

"What?!"

"I actually got mugged before I got on the train, and I don't have anything. They got my wallet."

What a lying, little weasel! His talk of riches, his claim of wanting to take care of me... BULLSHIT!

"I think I'd feel better if I ate something," he says.

He follows me into a convenience store. I go into the bathroom to fix my makeup and check my nose.

I didn't see the signs until Boyfriend and I got serious: He absentmindedly scratched a track mark.

I was eating chips. "What are you scratching at?"

"Mosquito bite," Boyfriend said, ashamed. He pulled his sleeve down.

"It's okay," I said. I rolled it back up and licked salt into his open wound. "I love you."

I blow my nose, reapply my lipstick, and wet a paper towel to rub between my legs. Now I miss Boyfriend. I think about curling up on the couch with him, watching Scottish horror films while eating something cold and sweet.

Out of the bathroom, I approach the freezer section. I grab a pint of chocolate ice cream.

"Maybe we could do mint chip?" Mistake says, sneaking up behind me.

"I'm getting this for me and my boyfriend!"

"What about me?" he whines. "Can't you get me something? I came all the way to Brooklyn for you."

"I thought you were made of money. Weren't you going to spoil me with presents?"

The sad sap looks away.

I roll my eyes and tell him to pick out a candy bar. He picks up a Snickers. "Fine," I say.

He picks up a soda.

"Just the chocolate bar!" I feel like I'm talking to a child.

I pay and walk in the direction of Boyfriend's house.

"Hey, wait a minute," he calls.

"Go away!"

"Yeah, the thing is... I used the last of my Metro Card to get here."

I stop walking. "I thought your wallet got stolen."

"Yeah, in the subway, right before I met you."

"Okay, whatever."

I lead him back to the station.

He chews on the candy bar. "Well, I guess that's it," he says, looking down the stairs. So immature.

"Hey, how old are you?" Why didn't I ask before?

"17," he confesses. "But I love older women! You're like 34, right?"

"I'm 25!"

"Oh, I thought you were older."

I swipe him into the train station and immediately block him out of my mind.

When I make it to Boyfriend's house, he jumps up from the couch. "Where were you?"

"I was... I got ice cream!" I hold up the plastic bag.

"I was worried!"

"About me or the stuff I brought?" I throw the bag of H on the coffee table in front of him.

"Hey..." Boyfriend puts his arms around me. "Are you okay? Why were you so late?"

Shrugging him off, I put the ice cream in the freezer and tell him. "...Then I got high and fiddled with myself in the grass, and kinda fell asleep... And then I was locked in and had to climb over the gate." I leave Dream Guy/Mistake out of it. He might as well have been imaginary.

If Boyfriend doesn't believe me, he doesn't let on. He returns to the couch.

"I'm gonna take a shower," I say.

In the bathroom, I pull off my soiled underwear and throw them in the trash.

I step into the hot spray of water, feeling grateful. I love Boyfriend. Really, I do, and there is nothing wrong with that.

We're charming. We're special. We're edgy. We are a team. We are like the characters in *Trainspotting*. We know our limits and, if we overdo it, someone will come around and bring us back with a hit of Narcan, and if no one comes, well...

The world is overpopulated anyway.

Author Bio

@CTMarie92 /CTMarie

Writer, producer, and performer, CT Marie is a New Yorker most notable for creating the web series, *Rent Control*, an official selection at the 2020 T.O. WebFest and 2021 London Web Fest, as well as winner of the 2020 NYC Web Fest. Her essay, "Ugly Couple," is published in the anthology *Dating and Sex: The Theory of Mutual Self-Destruction*, edited by Amir Said.

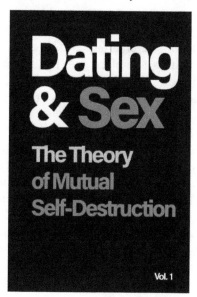

Other publications include "Sexual Assault by a Bunch of Nobodies" (*4W Publication*) and "Being Single Is Underrated" (*Sylvia Magazine*).

Still

By Sue Petty

Heart pumps, blood cruises through blue canals on a journey to nowhere. She can choose not to breathe. She holds it, slipping deeper into the void. Quiet in the clouds. Gulping, like a fish out of water, she gasps stale air. Lungs expand. Eyes open.
Darkness.

What time is it? She feels for the alarm clock on the bedside table, then presses cold plastic against her ear. Nothing. She had gone for a Costa Coffee, rather than long-life batteries.

"You get what you pay for," old Mam always says. True as with time as money.

She listens hard. Nothing. She tumbles out of bed, stubs her foot on a dead weight, winces and rubs her toe. Dropping to her knees, she feels for scattered fag-ends, in case one's smoldering. In case the whole place goes up like that Grenfell Tower block on the news. Just because they used cheap cladding to cut costs. People jumping out of windows to their death. A real-life horror.

Go to the light. Go to the light.

She makes her way to the shaft in the curtains and grabs the frayed edge. No one can see inside her cell in the sky, but she keeps them drawn day and night because she watched a movie where a stalker spied on a young woman through binoculars. She ended up raped and slashed to death. The body laid undiscovered for months, until someone complained about the stink to the housing authority. They found her rotting corpse—all liquid and bone—melded to the limp carpet.

She's not sleeping, and with the electric bill due, she daren't switch on the light.

In the daytime, the view makes her light-headed. Microscopic men mend dirty roads while angry cars jostle on narrow streets. Skipping kids in schoolyards run willy-nilly, throwing balls, kicking balls, and climbing walls. Self-absorbed lovers in dewy parks and dank alleys hold hands, kissing and caressing. All aboard for the sliding, slippery slope of love. Women lug bulging bags, backs bent, heading home, dwarfed by gigantic billboards on rush-hour pavements: Lynx Africa body spray, saying, "Find your magic," while Britney Spears hawks Hidden Fantasy fragrance mist.

She shivers, breathes on the glass, and sketches her name. A skywriter, far out.

At night, she belongs in the starlit sky. Otherworldly. An unknown entity, eons away. Part of a special constellation, exiled from Earth for heinous deeds and sent to dwell in outer space. An astral body. She's an alien on a special mission, observing earthlings from a most strategic position. A stranded ET, deteriorating in a hostile environment: translucent skin blemished with redness and pustulous sores, a hacking cough, sleepless nights and days, and pounding headaches. She awaits the mothership. Phone home.

Nothing.

"One, two... One, two... One, two, three," she whispers, seeing if she remembers how to speak when the time comes for communication. Mam was the last person she'd spoken to. But Mam has her own problems: her asthma, her knees, her stepdad.

The week before last, the man at the Department of Social Security spoke. She must get a job, whether she likes it or not. They won't keep her in idleness much longer, that's for sure. Plenty of work for those who want it. The kid can go to nursery.

She listens hard. Nothing. Dead to the world.

She'd hoped for something better. She wanted better for her own child. But it's hard. Real hard. She looks out of the window, and a shadowy reflection of her mother stares back.

The spiteful cactus on the sill pricks her hand. Mam bought it for her eighteenth. She came wheezing up ten flights of stairs on the 20th of June, like a derailed locomotive all out of steam. Forty fags a day and a cleaning job that plays havoc with her knees, catching up.

"Stairway to Heaven," Mam called it. "All that glitters ain't gold," she croaked, trying to make her feel better. A mournful dirge. A throwback to Mam's misspent youth. "Ah, them were the days.'"

The lift's not worked for weeks. She started counting the steps to give her focus and take her mind off things. But she lost her place, so she made landmarks.

Step 50 – cobwebby turd and a dry patch of stale piss. Someone didn't make the grade. The smell makes her gag, and she pinches her nose for the next ten steps.

Step 60 – pebble dash stucco and kebab up the wall. Brown streaks and meaty red lumps. An aesthetic contrast with the housing authority's standard orange, like a modern art-piece.

Step 70 – Swastikas, a cock, and balls mingle with the legends, "Paki go home" and "Boris is a cunt," drawn by some politically minded artistic type.

"Same old shit," Mam reminisced.

A long, claustrophobic corridor. Gray plastic floor tiles exude dead horses and sweaty council employees. Then her front door. Regulation dark blue, a square of opaque glass with thin, crisscrossing black lines and a tiny spy-hole she appreciates all the more since watching the horror channel. Same as the rest, except for a glittering 110 marking her place. She rattles the security chain and catches her breath, exhausted from the climb.

She eyes the cactus. It used to be lime green with a flower spilling out like molten lava on a sunny day, but the blossom dropped off in no time, leaving a shriveled finger ready to stab her with last-chance, sagging spikes.

The kid's goldfish didn't last long, either. Found floating on the surface of green liquid, like a grated, moldy carrot. Haunted by distant memories of clear, cool water, flowing streams and glistening horizons, it surely dreamt of escape like that pixelated fish, Nemo. But this one lacked comrades. Overcome with sadness, it knew things weren't working out and gave up on a frosty midwinter morning.

"It's not suited to the altitude," Mam said. "Because fish like depth, not height, don't they?" But she'd go the same way, swimming around that bowl all day.

Nothing grows here.

She stifles a yawn and goes back to bed. No idea of the time, but it doesn't matter. Maybe later, she'll finish counting the steps.

Author Bio

@TheRealSuePetty

Hailing from Leicestershire, UK, Sue Petty is working on her 2022 debut short story collection, entitled *Women of the Working Class*. It reimagines the lives of sixteen females from the Industrial Revolution to the present.

Still
by
Sue Petty

"Still," one of the contemporary narratives from this collection, is a stark reminder that—despite political advances—some women still suffer the modern constraints of gender and class.

The Blue Hour

By Paige Johnson

Strip club selfies: the last I'll ever take. Tomorrow, I'm setting up my webcam so I can hang up my fishnets, trade them in for cat ears and knee-highs to become the ultimate eWhore. Gamer girl by day, cam doll by night. Twitch THOT. Chatterbait titty-streamer. Simp princess of YouTube. Whichever flavor of prostitution pays the best without contact.

No more club fees, catfights, scheduling conflicts, or creepy customers. Color me content.

"I'm so jelly," Sissy says, waving out our Polaroid from her kawaii pink Fujifilm. She must've borrowed it from her daughter since she was hoarding tips for her quinceañera last month. "You're gonna reel in a million followers, a million bucks, and I'm stuck in this small pond." She glances around the dusky club, grimacing at a ham planet eating sushi with his bare hands. "Wish I didn't care about anonymity."

"Wish you could collab sometime. I'll miss your pretty face." I kiss her cheek, careful not to smear the blush, bronzer, or highlight. "Plus, I hear girl-girl scenes pull the most views."

"No way, girlie. Don't need my identity plastered all over the internet. Those sites are crawling with kids, gaming or otherwise. I'd be outed in a second by one of Olivia's schoolmates. 'Sides, the only game I play is solitaire."

I nod, taking hold of our picture. Two smiling faces beneath the scarlet lights, two tiny brunettes who go too heavy on the eyeliner. No need for bunny ears. We're wearing our own plus detachable cuffs and collars for tonight's *Playboy* theme.

Sissy laughs at the photo, tapping at people in the background. The bartender yawns next to a lonely guido. The latter leans into one hand, stretching his eye into a pointy, little slit. He wears his hair in a pompadour fade, button-down loose, black at the shoulders and fading to white at the bottom like a spent cigarette. Amongst our shlubby clientele, he stands out like an oversaturated image.

"Pauly D from *Jersey Shore*'s fallen on tough times, eh?" Sissy jokes, nudging me towards the bar.

"Looks more like a mob boss nursing a breakup. Easy money. You can take the loud assholes on the left." I throw my eyes to the hooting bachelor party sitting centerstage, tossing crumpled bills at the new girl. She stops and starts grinding on the pole, unsure if she should take the money now or wait until Doja Cat stops playing. "Uh, maybe help a sis out. Newbie might not know how to say no when the wolves ask for 'extras.'"

"Gotcha, chickie. On it. Good luck working Mr. Mafia."

"Have fun taming the pack. Maybe you can pickpocket something good. One time I got fresh AirPods." I stuff our photograph in my bustier and head towards my mark. Along the way, I steal a spritz of vanilla perfume off the DJ booth. The corner bar drowns in cyan light, its tiered shelf the focal point, liquor bottles seemingly glowing from within. At $15 a martini, they should illuminate the room, eliminate a bad mood. Must admit that's my job, too. At least for another half hour.

Slinking behind the slumped Italiano, I say, "You sure are a pretty boy, but are you really bored by a bunch of half-naked girls?"

He turns around, all smirk and shrug. "Pretty boy? I see why you wear glasses."

I adjust the oversize frames. "They're an aesthetic choice, actually. So, the compliment's genuine."

He glances about to ask if anything can be authentic in a place like this. "Guess standards are set pretty low with tourists sporting Donald Duck tees, but thanks... Not to brag, but I'm usually surrounded by naked women." There's a vibrance to his pool-blue eyes. Must not be sauced to the gills like most of our clients. A squat glass fizzes in his hand, a silver can to his side. Diet cola, like my mom drinks.

I bite my lip so I can't laugh, thinking about Mom sipping Slim Fast on a soap opera bender. "Oh, so you're a regular, a club connoisseur? Back in New York, I'm guessing from your accent." It's calm and nasally like a noir broadcast. "I hear the law doesn't require pasties and panties up there. No wonder you're yawning down here in the Sunshine State."

"Ah, that's not it. Left Brooklyn years ago. My hometown buddies," he nods toward the rowdy group spellbound by Sissy's gyrating, "they flew down to party 'cause one's getting married. So, they're all boozing, Disney cruising, and gambling at the Hard Rock. I'm just third-wheeling... Well, more like I'm the spare tire that fell off the back and nobody's noticed yet." His gaze shifts between me and the bubbles. "Thankfully."

I sit next to him, motion for the barkeep to bring me a gin and tonic. "So, let me get this straight. You're not into bare-naked ladies, theme parks, or frat charades. Got it." I wink as a barback drops a slice of lime into my drink.

"Don't get me wrong on the first count. I'm just burnt out from photographing them all day."

"With their consent, I hope." My tongue peeks out from behind my lips as my drink arrives. I taste like Vaseline and Belvedere.

His first time laughing. It's squealy and infectious like a cartoon character. I see why he keeps it under wraps but enjoy its warmth. "I'm no peeping tom," he says, "but there's a gray area."

I slow the stirring of my cocktail. "Oh? Have I been your secret muse all night? You been taking snaps of me taking Snaps?"

He smiles at his soda. "Trust me, you don't want me taking your photo... I'm a morgue photographer."

"*Sexy*," I laugh. Glad I haven't taken a shot to come out my nose. "I didn't know morgues needed photographers. I mean, photo-ops for the dead? Seems a little gratuitous." I shake my head, banishing my flattening curls from sheeny shoulders. "Who wants the pictures? Fetishists? Doctors in training? Newspapers?"

"Nah, nobody that exciting. More like lawyers, insurance companies, and toxicologists. You see, you have to document every step of an autopsy to look for signs of foul play or malpractice. Then you edit the copies to look more presentable for the family who has to identify the body. Then comes the *fun* part. Like Photoshopping bullet holes into moles."

"Damn, and people think *I* have a gruesome job."

"Eh. Both of us deal with stiffs every day." He slips the bartender a $20 for my drink. "Is what it is, pays the bills."

"You like it any?" I watch him shift like there's a mouse scampering under his shirt. "You can be candid; I can still find you hot if you're into the science of it. Like, I thought dissecting frogs in middle school was cool." Especially when I hid the guts around the classroom to get back at the teacher who flunked me for attendance. Who knew each organ would be a different candy color? "Don't worry. You can't scare me, I'm a true millennial."

"What's that supposed to mean? Something about recessions or 9/11?"

"I mean, that doesn't help. But I was talking 'bout being raised by the internet. My brothers used to show me LiveLeak videos. Ya know, like a modern form of teasing. 'You cry at this car crash and you're a baby.' But after a while, the brutality turns boring. That's life, get over it. Like with the shootings streamed on Facebook that the news shows or squid porn schoolgirls swap to giggle over. Not like I was looking for any of it, but that shit circulates, you know?" This makes me wonder if I'll ever get as many hits camming as an ISIS beheading on Twitter. Maybe if I wear something as meme-worthy as a Pepe the Frog mask.

He rolls his eyes, tittering. "Jeez, I wonder what desensitized us before social media and the 24-hour news cycle."

"I'm sure every generation has their specialty." I shrug. The draft wasn't real cool. Or dying of dysentery.

"Hell, I remember watching cops beat the shit out of Rodney King in the '90s. Seen a carjacker blow his brains out live on Fox News, too. Me and all my buddies would sing along to 'Hey Man, Nice Shot,' not knowing it was about a politician's public suicide." He shakes his head. "Madness."

I take a swig off my drink. Smells like pine, tastes perfectly bitter. "If it bleeds, it leads." At least, that's what I heard the lead singer of Twisted Sister say. "Way of the world. But don't deflect. Do you dig it? Getting to immortalize corpses in photos. Course it's messy and depressing, but what are the good parts?" Health benefits, great pay, discounted coffins?

He shrugs. "I suppose the job feels like getting in on a secret. It's sort of a privilege to know what happens after you die. How they milk you and stitch you up. Drain you of fluids, send them off for testing. Hose you down, dress your wounds, then doll you up for the 'big party' that is your funeral. All in all, I guess it's kind of comforting to know so many people have a vested interest—*care*—to find out your story. As gory as it is to get there."

"That's a neat way to look at it. Optimistic even. You're helping people, too. Finding out the truth, giving families closure." I caress his arm, trying to peep his watch brand. Valentino? Diesel? I wonder if Patrick Bateman would approve.

"I'm not the one with the scalpel." He finishes his Pepsi. "All I do is *click, click, click.* Sunday will put my camera to better use. Gino's paying me to film his wedding ceremony. It's my side hustle to keep sane."

"Corpses Monday through Friday, weddings on the weekend. What a difference a few days make."

"Right? Peace and quiet all week, followed by free cake and champagne."

"You got it made." My drink's starting to fizz my brain. I can't remember if it's my second or sixth. "A li'l blood and odor? No big deal. You got dancing with loose bridesmaids to look forward to."

"Ah, you're right. Enough about my doom and gloom. What's your deal? Let's start with a name. Mine's Matteo."

"I'm Peaches."

"Oh?" he patronizes. "Like the princess from *Mario.*"

"Uh, I think she only had one peach, so I'm better." My wink lasts longer than my drink. The bartender carts it away. "Princess Peach's modesty would never cut it in the Playboy Mansion." I wiggle my butt on the seat, making my puffball of a tail twitch. I'm surprised it doesn't fall off.

"Reminds me of my rabbit growing up," Matteo laughs. "A brown floppy-ear. Called him Patches 'cause he had hair missing by the nose."

"Other buns musta kissed him too hard. What happened to him?"

A frown forms. "Neighbors didn't appreciate him eating from their turnip patch. So, uh... it didn't end well."

So much for making an I'd-pull-on-your-carrot joke. "Sorry to keep turning things sour. I meant what happened that made his hair go missing, not him entirely, but whatever. I get why you got a lot on your mind. Listen, if you wanna lighten things up, get to know me better, you should join me in Paradise." My head tips back toward the aptly labeled door. "You'll be my last hurrah for the night. Ever at this place, in fact."

"Ever? What do you mean, you're quitting? Damn, I tried warning you I'm a killjoy."

"Got nothing to do with you, big guy. This funny bunny is moving on to greener pastures." Bright lights, smaller cameras. I stand up and grab his wrist. This time, I can make out the watch name. An unfamiliar make, but a beautiful one. Roman numerals, unbusy design. Silver bezel, black inlay, stainless and gleaming. "I'm in the mood to celebrate. Only the most deserving get my time tonight. I'm even willing to break my no-touch policy." Another wink and tug at his arm. My fingers slide up his chest, tickle the hairs popping out of his open collar. "Consider it a prize for holding decent conversation."

He follows me like a leash-bound Maltese.

In the VIP room, a see-through pole stands in the middle of a sleek stage. Cream and chrome tuffets, marshmallows of seats, border it. The walls are diamond-plated while the ceiling houses magenta LEDs.

I step onto the stage, waiting for Matteo to pay the DJ while I admire the girly modern décor. It's something I'll have to replicate in my streaming room. Turn tedious memories into entertaining ones, twice as many dollar signs. Excited to pick out more furniture and paint swatches once I get home, I grin as he approaches. He sits at one of the ottomans, unsure where to look at such close range. "Relax," I say. "A little sin never hurt no one."

Electronica pumps through the speakers. One hand grabs the pole. I hang from it as I circle with a ballerina's gait. We share a smirk, his lips looking so soft and full in this Valentine light. With eyes as piercing as quartz, he makes me feel exposed but in an exhilarating way. The bass drops and I spring. As effortless a hop as my bunny costume suggests. One knee keeps me glued to the pole as I swing, dipping into dramatic shapes that show off my cottontail or cleavage. I kick my heels as I twist, narrowly dodging his face, dropping a few more dollars out of him. Pointed toes, arched back, vertical splits. Hypnotizing a man is a game of flexibility and flourish, lighting and angles.

I climb to spin in a flying X, then slip back into *Titanic* pose. This corset is too small for jumps. My cups overflow, revealing daisy pasties. Whoops! My fingers cover a shy smile as my toes touch the ground. "What a terrible *accident*."

I suppose another fifty is a good bandage. Good bondage, enough to make Matteo appear extra sweet under the fluorescent strobes. I sashay my way into a lap dance, swaying to the beat. His dress pants are easy to slide over, much better than the concrete jeans construction workers come in with. It's easier to feel and see what I'm doing to him. My fingertips run over the top, kneading the little, plastic button. "We can have even more fun at your place," I whisper into his ear. My cheek presses against his. Lava hot. "You grow any more roses there, huh?" I'm not one for extras, one of those Craigslist escorts asking for 100 "roses" a lay, but Matteo seems the perfect client to end a career built on teasing: unimposing, gorge as fuck, and generous enough to earn me a better ring light for my recording room.

I grind until he gets my meaning, until I squeeze a yes out of him.

As the song sizzles out, I kiss him. One of those real suctiony, before-the-plane-departs type smooches. "Good choice. Let me grab my coat."

In a matter of minutes, I promise to text Sissy the deets of my conquest, pay the staffs' cut, and tell the bouncer not to worry about me. "Won't rough the boy up too bad," I tell him as he walks us to my car.

Bouncer kind of rolls his eyes, but it's not like he hasn't seen "private shows" or "field trips" arranged before. Plus, I'm not his problem anymore. "*Sayonara, sour-pussies!*" I wave to him and the rest of the club, who ignore or laugh me off.

"You okay to drive?" Matteo asks once I'm behind the wheel. His apartment is within walking distance but I'm not leaving my Mazda to get defaced by ex-coworkers.

"If my balance looked funky, it had to do with my stilettos. Nothing I slung back." When I pull out, my whip-it dispenser rolls out from under the seat. It shouldn't instill any confidence in my cognitive abilities but leaves my passenger giggly. "You do nitrous shots?"

Ordinally, I'd blush at the discovery of my middle school hobby/high, but my cheeks are already burning from Sailor Jerry kisses. And Matteo doesn't seem judgmental.

He kicks the device up to his hand, admiring its peeling Pusheen stickers. "Mind if I take a crack?"

"You find any juice left in it, it's your lucky day."

He shakes it and finds a couple unused bulbs under the floormat. "Must be. This'll pair great with what I have at home."

"What's at home?" We gonna use the canister for its intended purpose, lick whip cream off each other? Smoke while dissociated? Do I tell him now or later that I'm not into weed's goldfish memory or cat piss stench?

"You'll see."

Matteo's apartment isn't boyish or barren. Half-drunk Diet Coke cans spot each surface. Everything's wooden and wiped down with lemon-scented bleach, by the smell of it. There are a few blown-up Georgia O'Keefe vignettes on the walls: cattle skulls and black-stemmed flowers, making for an interesting contrast, clash of the sexes. Yet the most striking art pieces are handmade. Stuffed and mounted animal heads. On the side table stands a crow with a feathered fedora who seems to be winking. On the back wall, there's a mounted lamb's head donning a crown of knotted honeysuckle. At the coffee table where we kneel, there's...

"Is this...?" I tilt its tiny sunhat, staring into beady eyes.

"Yep, that's Patches." Looking away, Matteo chuckles without sincerity. "Sorry. If I was expecting company, I woulda stowed them away." He taps out the contents of a couple baggies onto a plastic tray. The kind for developing pictures and hopefully not for draining the blood of a bludgeoned pet. "Taxidermy's super weird, I get it, but I try to have fun with them, you know? Remember them as happily as I can."

"Sure. Of course." My Ss stick and I haven't even bumped any of the coke yet. I'm still trying to figure out if he's hot enough to justify a plush cemetery. Either way, my purse's taser gun is within reach. "I guess the accessories are cute." And the thought of Patches getting banished to a closet or cardboard box makes me sadder than knowing he gets to spend most of his days channel-surfing with his dad.

"Thanks. You're a pretty cool, macabre chick, so I'd hoped you wouldn't mind so much."

"Hey, man, as far as Florida drug dens go, this is top-notch. The most Orlando Disney version I could ask for."

He laughs like one of the mascots might. Not a villain, but maybe one of Cinderella's rats or Stich from *Lilo*. "I mean, we're celebrating your last day at Midnight Blue, right? Gotta class it up." As I nod, he asks, "So, what're you gonna do now?"

You, stupid. "Uh, ya know, freelance work. Online jobs."

He raises an eyebrow, catching my drift. "Hopefully, that's safer and more rewarding."

"For sure. I've been streaming video games a while now. It puts a dent in my rent, but I'm ready to take it to the next level. Those platforms are all about a consistent upload schedule to make the real scratch."

He nods slowly. "I'm familiar. Suggestive gameplay and clickbait commentary rule the web. Got a cousin who bought a Porsche from screaming his head off, playing *Grand Theft Auto*."

I smile. "Makes you wonder if masturbating for money is really the more shameful thing."

He takes his ID from his wallet—a hefty one, might I add—and crunches up the mold-white substances. "When you've logged as many hours into dating sims or staging drama as him, then yeah. Definitely."

We laugh, scraping and mushing powder like play sand. I tell him I've already got a little audience from my YouTube channel. "I'm sure you'd help draw views with cadaver talk. The beauty gurus on there are all about murder mysteries. You've probably photographed a serial killer or two, huh?"

He nods gravely. "At least one."

I fantasize about all the necrophile jokes and games we can play on camera: bullet hole bingo, shots for stab wounds, tier-listing the hottest dead celebrities. "We can dress as Gomez and Morticia," I squeal before knocking back one of his old sodas.

"And I'll get you a real-deal digital camera once your channel really kicks off." He winks.

I agree, "Don't wanna be one of those Playmates of yesteryear doing perms to make ends meet."

We work until one of our piles is reduced to powder, the other shards. They're lopsided, uneven, like Sissy's boobs.

"So," Matteo says, clacking his card clean, "what I have here is called Calvin Klein. I figure a designer drug suits such a luxurious lady." Our laughter is as hollow as our friend Patches. "Two parts ketamine, one part cocaine. 'The safer speedball.'"

"Safer?"

"Rather do heroin?" he deadpans.

"That smile could make me." I pick up a straw. It's like I've always said: Strippers and coke go together like rum and Coke. Every businesswoman needs a little pick-me-up before sitting down to her desk.

"And if we suck in a little nitrous as soon as the ket kicks in, the effects will last way longer."

"Wow. You're like a mad scientist."

"More like a sad artist, wasting all my time on these dumb concoctions." He shakes his head and I stare at Patches to make sure he doesn't do the same. "Whatever. Is what it is." He shovels out four lines like a crop farmer, giving me the healthier yields. "Ladies first."

"Appreciated, but I should probably freshen up first. I have more creative ideas for a play surface." Technically, railing snow off a hooker's ass is cliché, but maybe snorting ketamine out of a stripper's navel counts as novel.

Those big, blue eyes don't say no. My tongue senses no objection.

Whatever we do, I just don't wanna come off smelling like beef stew topped with sugar cookies. So, I head for the shower.

In the bathroom, no roaches or shampoo spills: good sign.

I wash off a day's worth of sweat, glitter, and body spray. I'm not worried about a *Psycho* situation because a clothing rack kind of blocks the door anyway. Goodbye strip club stink, hello a deliciously strange man's bodywash. Peachy cream and lemon musk.

Shimmering in the last of the shower's dew, I smile in the mirror. Check my teeth for lime residue and my crotch for razor burn. None. Picture-perfect.

Shimmying back into my perfumed leotard, my so-long selfie from Sissy falls out. *The story I'm gonna have for you tomorrow, girl! Might even make good YouTube content.* Hell, maybe I should've pretended to quit every night of my life. Something about a girl on the edge seems to draw out the sexiest men, the most money. Maybe Matteo thinks I'm a charity case, but whatever. Free drugs. Fine dick.

It doesn't take me long to revitalize and reappear in the threshold of the living room, dripping like the fruit I'm named after. "Alright, Mr. Photographer, ready for my close-up!"

He is not.

He's facedown next to Patches.

I walk forward, shivering from the draft. "Hey, save some for me." I crouch next to him.

Freeze.

Framed by red rivulets that start from his nose, Matteo sticks to the coffee table. Complexion ashen, posture coiled like celluloid.

As I wait for his breath to return, unsure if it ever will, all I wonder is:

Who'll take his picture?

What grim portfolio will he become part of?

Who's gonna stitch him up for a shoot?

Then I remember the last photo of him alive. It rests between my breasts, and now probably will forever.

Author Bio

f /ThePoliticiansDaughter **y** @KettyKat8

Paige Johnson is the editor-in-chief at Outcast Press (including this very anthology). She writes about pharmaceuticals, pedophiles, and prostitutes just to keep her Florida residency. The taboo romance and navel-gazing cost extra, like her Amazon novella, *Imperative Fate*.

Influenced by *American Psycho* as much as *Lolita*, she's up for anything that reads like a degenerate's diary. Submit likewise novels, poems, and short stories to her at Outcast-Press.com

When Your Parents Are Junkies

By T.W. Garland

When your parents are junkies, you don't have to stress about Mother's Day or Father's Day. If Walmart clears out the card section before you stumble upon it, it's not a problem. Dad isn't going to shame you about how bad Mom feels that you forgot to buy the cheap box of chocolates she likes. Mom isn't going to guilt trip you with messages about when her flowers are going to arrive. And you're not going to miss the family dinner on her special day. None of that will happen.

You don't have to set your week by regular phone calls or voicemails full of blame. Your parents aren't going to drop in for a surprise visit and you don't have to invite them to help at your kid's birthday. You don't have to bother with any of that. It's not a surprise. You know what to expect.

Growing up, you weren't surprised to find Mom giving a blow job to a guy who left her a small baggy or hear Dad unloading a house full of electrical goods at midnight. When you came home to watch *Power Rangers* only to find that the TV had disappeared, you spent the afternoon depressed—not shocked. You didn't sit at the empty kitchen table, wondering when dinner was going to arrive. You didn't open your wardrobe and feel confused when there were no clean clothes.

You knew the TV was a temporary fixture, dinner wouldn't be made, and laundry wouldn't be done. You also knew no one would show up when you played point guard in the divisionals, no matter how many reminders you wrote. Yet it didn't stop you from looking into the stands and missing that extra point.

You weren't surprised when the ten bucks you earned washing cars disappeared, even when you hid it in that super-secret place under your bed, beneath the carpet. Toys disappeared. There were no books. Family treasures never existed. There was nothing new or worth any money in the house.

The milk was rotten, and the bread was moldy. You ate whenever you got the chance. You ate anything because you weren't sure when you'd eat again. It certainly wouldn't be a packed meal in a novelty lunchbox. You were lucky to have a paper bag with receipts from the liquor store.

Lying wasn't a problem for you. Claiming your parents were ill was easy when Mrs. Parker's phone call was answered by a coughing, retching parent. Telling the cafeteria lady that the big kids stole your money got you lunch. Telling a neighbor that Mom was working late got you dinner. When kids at school called you a mooch, you pushed down the embarrassment and called it surviving.

At some point in early adolescence, as you held onto the last fragments of childhood, you decided to fix everything. You kept your parents away from cigarettes, drink, drugs. You knew the hiding places. You knew what Class A drugs looked like and how to get them, but it was a full-time job without holidays or benefits, yet your parents never gave in or up.

In better times, your parents were half-asleep on the couch, watching daytime TV, then the next day they were gone. They didn't have a cell phone. You couldn't call them. They wouldn't call you. They just disappeared.

You expected to find them passed out on the lawn each morning like a newspaper no one wanted to touch, because it's full of nothing but bad news you've already read.

If you had the kind of luck that delivers normal people winning lottery tickets, you'd never see them again. Either way, you keep going and do what you think normal people do: You get a job, go to work, earn money, spend money, rent an apartment. Then you meet someone. She asks you about your day and wants to spend time with you. She hugs you when you're sad and you feel better. She looks at you and smiles.

You know you should smile back.

She says you should move in together. You smile back, rent a bigger apartment, have a kid, then another, and keep going. In the house she decorates, there are no pictures of your parents. They don't come to visit. You rarely give money to the homeless just in case your eyes lock on a familiar pair. If your kids ask about grandparents, you say they passed away. It's the same lie you tell anyone who asks, except your wife.

She looks at you with sympathy but doesn't understand. She makes fun of the wall of tinned food you build in the cupboard and calls you insensitive when you don't cry at sad films. She rolls her eyes when you check the locks a third time. She wants you to turn off the TV before falling asleep, but you like seeing the *Power Rangers* reruns in the morning.

At her parent's anniversary party, you smile politely and avoid eye-contact. She bounces around the room, giving out hugs like Halloween candies. As the party moves into the fourth hour and the kids whine, she hovers around a guy who has put in more gym time this week than you've managed all year. You get to your feet and don't remember much else until she's calling you an embarrassing drunk.

When the kids don't have anything to give her on Mother's Day, she looks at you. You tell her she isn't your mother, and she doesn't speak to you until the youngest has a dinner-time tantrum. She wants to have a long talk on the cause of the tantrum and dons a red veil of anger when you don't have any suggestions.

On the phone to her mom, she retells the Mother's Day incident. She brings it up at a dinner party. You protest, telling everyone the kids aren't old enough to dress themselves, let alone buy a card or present. She tells you she knows; it was *your* job.

You have another drink.

As date night looms, she asks if you've finally picked the right tie for your shirt and insists you pick the restaurant. When you can't, she tells you to grow a pair.

You get home late after a business meal, and she shouts at you because you didn't phone. You start getting undressed and climb into bed. She's still talking about the kids, about taking out the bins, mowing the lawn, servicing the car, organizing the family vacation, inviting the neighbors over for dinner.

As the bile rises, you dash to the bathroom like a patient running down the halls of an asylum.

She follows you, waving a credit card bill and telling you to stop buying things you don't need. She yells at you for keeping a stash of money. She asks what else you've been hiding.

You can't answer. You can't think about anything but having another drink.

Author Bio

 TWgarland.wordpress.com @TWGarland

T.W. Garland looks out from an inner city of books more numerous than the minutes he has to read. He hopes to throw insight on the complexity of human emotion or at least avoid unnecessary trips to the psychiatrist. His stories have been accepted by *Shotgun Honey, Punk Noir Magazine, Dwelling Literary, Dash Literary Journal, The Daily Drunk, Dark Dossier,* and *Schlock!*

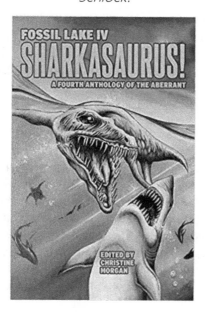

His short story, "The Lost Island of the Sharkasaurus," appears in this Sabledrake anthology on Amazon.

Ten

By Gregory J. Wolos

 Part 1

The man who finds her stands with the moon over his shoulder, his slim silhouette a hole in the desert night-sky. He's darker than the greater darkness surrounding them because he blocks the stars.

"Why are you in my yard?" he asks. "Can I help you?" He crouches as he speaks, still two-dimensional.

Her head is cold, her throat dry. "Sick," she says, which is a kind of truth. "Cancer," she lies to explain her baldness. "Attacked," she says of the dried blood streaked from her thighs to her bare feet.

Hands emerge from his silhouette and slide under her. Only after she's hoisted like a husk, does she feel the shape of the rocks she's been lying on. She's swung away from the moon, wants to see it, but hasn't the strength to turn her head.

She wakes swathed in cool sheets in a lit room. Poster-sized artwork covers stucco walls. Her abdomen aches. She touches herself, peers under the sheets that are so white, they seem fluorescent. Crust edges her wounds, but the blood has been washed off. Red spots startle her—just the polish on her toenails; she's not hemorrhaging. But when she hears a male voice, pain wracks her. The speaker stands in the door-less threshold of the room. He is tan, with hair like straw. The voice and thin body match those of her rescuer. He won't allow his gaze to shift from her eyes. His are blue.

"I cleaned your wounds," he says. I haven't called an ambulance or notified the authorities. Do you want me to?"

She remembers—before she'd become too dizzy with
exhaustion to think straight, that she'd created the beginning of a
story—cancer; she'd been on her way to Mexico City for
alternative treatment when her car broke down and a gang of
young men in a beat-up car stopped to help; though she was
suspicious, the day was so hot and the road so empty that she had
to accept. What rescuer, seeing the blood, wouldn't believe she'd
been assaulted? Who wouldn't marvel at the will to survive
demonstrated by her escape? And she had run—that much was
true—but she'd lost consciousness before coming up with a
reason why the police shouldn't be summoned.

The man in the doorway purses his lips. He isn't young—
age spots mark his hairline, and his leathery face is deeply
creased. His beard is so white, it makes his teeth appear stained.
"You've been on television," he says. "We're less than a hundred
miles over the border, and I get American TV. They know who
you are. The child you gave birth to is healthy. A boy. Did you
know that? Did you see? Before you ran? If you're hungry, I've
got soup, Jenna. Your name is Jenna something, right?"

"Water, please," Jenna whispers.

"Beside you." The man nods to the glass on a nightstand.

When Jenna reaches for it, her ribs ache, and her thighs
cramp. What's the right play here? Should she hide her pain or
exaggerate it? But when she tries to lift the water, her palm stings,
and she sets the cup back down with a short cry. She looks at the
heel of her hand, the heels of both hands—tiny puncture wounds.
Had her nails done that when she clenched her fists? She picks up
the glass with her fingertips and drinks. The water sears her throat
like cool fire. Screaming has left her hoarse.

"'Cancer,'" the man quotes. His voice echoes—the floor
is tiled, the ceiling high with track lights to illuminate its pictures.

Jenna reaches for her bald head. How much does this man
know? Does he know there's no chemo, that she's hairless
because of alopecia? Does he know that she's not perfectly
smooth? Patches surface: one on her thigh, another under her
arm, and an inch-wide strip on her head like an off-center bird's
crest. Almost perfect. Being absolutely hairless would be divine,
but her patches are an insult. Shaving herself smooth has been a

lifelong chore. Her fingers ease over her scalp until... bristles. When she groans, her uterus spasms.

"The reporter on the news said, 'Look for a young woman in a yellow raincoat. It might be blood-stained. She could be wearing a wig because she doesn't grow hair.' Did you lose the wig?" The man shakes his head and lowers his voice. "Cancer is something you shouldn't fake," he says, as if that's the worst of her crimes.

Jenna's nostrils flare. Instinct tells her to flee, but she knows her body wouldn't obey. Where would she go? Her eyes glide around the room, over the pictures, then the large windows: three on the wall to her left, one in front of her, set above the pictures, too high to reach and black because it's night. To her right is a small bathroom. She sees a shower stall, a sink, and toilet—no window or door. The only way into or out of the room is through the doorway that frames her host.

"Don't call anyone," she says. "I just need rest. Where am I?"

"You're where you fled to. No one expected you to run. You confused the border patrol. They underestimated your strength. But they found your bag and ID, Jenna—and your gun. They're looking for the man whose vehicle got you to the border. They know he was your doctor. They assume he was your accomplice. He must not be a very brave man to leave you alone."

He's dead, Jenna remembers. She kidnapped him back home—to drive and in case she went into labor early—and she shot him in an arroyo when they got close to the border. No one will ever find him, she told herself. But she'd miscalculated her needs—her first contraction came just moments after she pulled the trigger—the gunshot had been so loud that she had nothing to compare it to. She thought she could still make it over the border to her Mexican connections. And they did find her, too late, recognizing her yellow raincoat as she dodged traffic. When they swept her into their black-windowed car, she was empty-armed and exhausted.

"Where is the baby?" they'd demanded as she gasped and bled over a creamy leather seat. The man in back with her offered his handkerchief. She thought they'd shoot her, but instead they drove and drove on shrinking, rutted roads, until the red sun dropped behind scorched hills, and they pushed her out of the car.

"Call us when you got something, *puta*," she heard before the car spun off, spitting pebbles.

"Hungry," she says now. When her host—captor?—first found and cleaned her, he must have wiped away her drawn-on eyebrows. What did he think as he erased her rakish expression? What else had he noticed? Certainly, the drops of mother's milk tattooed beneath her nipple that some of her lovers mistook for tears. And the whole world now knows, she's smooth. Did her bristly patches confuse him? She would rather shave than eat, but she won't ask for a razor—he might think she's desperate and dangerous. Where are the mirrors? None even over the bathroom sink. Just pictures, everywhere.

"Soup," the man says, "but—" Before he can finish, something bursts between his legs, streaks across the floor, and leaps onto Jenna's bed: a speckled, piglet-sized dog with radar-dish ears and blazing eyes. Its sudden weight rocks her and wakes her pain.

"*Mee*-go!" Jenna hears as she covers her face and lifts her knees, her last sight a lolling tongue between grinning jaws. The snorting creature digs at the sheet between her legs and tries to tug it away, and Jenna screams as if she's giving birth again.

 Part 2

"I find that I'm a different person in different rooms of my house," Claude says without looking up from the wooden tablet he cuts into with one of his knives. Every morning he brings a tablet, a portable worktable, a folding chair, and a leather case of carving tools into Jenna's sunlit bedroom. While he works, Jenna often gazes up at the windows, waiting for a bird, an airplane, or even a cloud to pass. When something does float by—or when it rains, and the glass seems to melt—Jenna's heart beats faster, as if she's about to learn a secret. Then the windows return to rectangles of skim-milk blue, white, or gray. At night, they're always black. Beneath the windows, the pictures—prints made from woodblocks, she's been informed—are bright with colors, but Jenna focuses on their figures only when Claude points them out.

This morning, she's staring at the carving tool in Claude's hand. When he lifts it, her eyes trace its path as if it's a magic wand. The blade reminds her that she hasn't shaved in over thirty days—since she woke up in this room. She's marked the passing of time by notching the bedpost with her thumbnail. Claude pares her nails, but not too short. Migo curls against Jenna's thighs, his snout against his hindquarters, as if he's one of those snakes that swallow themselves.

"I only have this room, so that's all I am," Jenna says. She has no idea how many rooms are in this house.

"But you had a life back in The States. You lived somewhere. Who were you then? Always the same, no matter which room?" Claude peers up from his work, his forehead grooved like his tablet.

"Each woodblock I cut is for a different color of a print," he's told her before. "After all of them are inked and printed onto the paper, the picture is complete." She imagines that Claude is cutting her face and figure into his tablets, and when he inks the print, she'll be able to see herself. But what he's actually fashioning are poster-sized versions of small works produced by Yoshitoshi, a 19th century Japanese master of woodblock prints. Claude's "expansions" hang on Jenna's walls. "You'd be surprised what they sell for," Claude has said. "Only the most foolish tourists mistake them for originals. But they are original, in a sense. It's like making a movie out of a book: a different version of the same thing, just bigger. I contribute size."

Rooms? Who was she in the tiny customs booth where she disgorged someone else's child? There was space only for herself and the sweating official between her legs. A roll of unfurling paper towels flew over her and struck one of the windows filled with faces and white and blue uniforms. Pain—a Milky Way of exploding stars—then a wail, and then the blinding sunlight, confused shouts, and car horns.

History: the night before the customs booth, a room at the Blue Daisy Motel with fat Doctor Morrison—Doc Mo. He spent the night chained to the drainpipe under the sink. He'd have never guessed that the bathroom would be his final sight. Who was

Jenna as she dry-shaved her head-strip—for the last time—on the
Blue Daisy's sagging mattress? She'd been someone who
thought that the $75,000 awaiting her in Mexico was three times
better than the fee she'd been contracted for in The States.

 Part 3

"Migo is blind and deaf," Claude says, and Jenna would
have never guessed. "He knows you by your scent."
Jenna runs her hand along the dog's rash of spots. His
eyes glow white. Sometimes, she strains to see herself in them.
"His name is Amigo without the 'A,'" she says as she watches
Claude cut into a fresh woodblock with a thin blade. Purple ink
stains his fingers. "Does that mean he is or isn't a friend?"
Claude's glance lasts a blink. It's morning, and Jenna
spoons oatmeal sweetened with brown sugar from her breakfast
tray. Claude prints a few hundred copies of each enlargement.
The prints he hangs in Jenna's room are first runs, their colors
especially vibrant. "Friend," Claude mutters, as if it's an idea he
hasn't considered. Jenna still doesn't know if she's a guest or a
prisoner. Since Claude has established no restrictions, if she asks
for nothing, then nothing is denied.
This is freedom. She's brought three meals a day, and the
bathroom is stocked with shampoo, soap, toothpaste, fresh towels,
and the terrycloth robes that are her only clothing. Before Jenna
settled in, she wondered if anyone else lived in the house, that
maybe it's honey-combed with dozens of chambers just like hers,
like a hive. But Claude couldn't care for so many guests and still
spends most of his day in her room, working. She's free to
explore, as far as she knows, and free to inquire, but the curiosity
that might prove her freedom false has shriveled. She's quit
counting days. There's no more room for fresh grooves on her
bedposts and headboard, and no point in deepening the old ones.

 Part 4

Jenna recognizes two universes: her room and her body.
Bored with the windows, she leaves her bed to study the prints

that surround her. Claude has told her that the men and women in the prints represent figures from Chinese and Japanese history, literature, and legend. Today, while Claude works, she lingers before a new print, hoping that Claude will explain it.

"That's Wu Gang," he says, putting down his knife. "Because he abused the practice of Taoist magic, he's doomed to chop down the golden-blossomed cassia trees that give the moon its brightness. Every time he cuts down a tree, a new one grows in its place. The print shows Wu Gang resting over his ax. The moon hangs over him, his perpetual burden."

"That's like the myth of what's-his-name," Jenna says. "The guy who pushed the rock up the hill, and it kept rolling down."

"Sisyphus," Claude says. "Same idea."

Later, alone, Jenna returns to the print of Wu Gang and the moon made of gilded flowers. It's the magician's ax—not the blossoms—that attracts her. With a blade like his, she could shave off the lengthening hair on her head, thigh, and underarm. And if she polished the ax, it could serve as a mirror. She runs her hand over her scalp until her fingertips bump against her lop-sided crest. Jenna remembers seeing horses with braided manes, then winds a finger around a lock of crest-hair, thinking of ribbons. It's a wonder that Claude never mentions her unusual feature, or the other two fuzzy places that mar her smoothness. His only involvement with her appearance is the trimming of her nails.

When Claude slices off her nails with one of his cutting tools, he works quickly but delicately with the same intense concentration he gives his woodblocks. Jenna holds out each hand like the brides she's seen on TV shows: palm down, fingers spread, in anticipation of a ring. When he's finished, he shifts back to his worktable while Jenna eats, examines the prints on her wall, or showers.

Jenna often sings while she showers. She runs a bar of soap over her flesh and kinked patches as if she's shaving and hears in her own voice the sing-song rhythm her mother used when she scraped away her little girl's unsightly bristles: *sooo-smooth, sooo-smooth.* Or Jenna mimics hip-hop performers and sways her hips and slaps her wet ass—mothah-fuckah this and mothah-fucka that—memories and tunes that are rootless and carry only sound. Jenna's crest-hair has grown long enough to shampoo, so massaging it to a soapy froth delights her. *Mine*, she thinks as she squeezes her fists through the foam, *all mine*.

Often after showering, when she returns to her bed in a clean, white terrycloth robe, Jenna discovers that Claude has hung new prints. This morning, as she lies back on her pillow, water leaking from her crest and down her neck, she notices two.

"Prostitutes," Claude says with a swipe of his tool in the direction of the prints. "Yoshitoshi called the first 'Moon of the Pleasure Garden' and the second 'Streetwalker at Night.'"

Jenna tugs her robe to cover her cleavage. Migo, already comfortable against her hip, lifts his head and stares toward her like a blind sphinx. Her first day in this room, the dog had crawled onto her legs, stretched himself along her sore abdomen, and tucked his muzzle under her ripe breasts. He wants my milk, she remembers thinking. Then, as now, she'd thought of her tattooed droplets and clamped her arms over her chest. "Migo is ugly," she says.

"Migo is a beautiful and perfectly bred truth," Claude says, returning a blade to the tool case and selecting another.

"His head comes to a point, like a sharpened pencil. And his spots look like some kind of filthy disease."

"Both result from generations of street-breeding. The pointy head so he can stick it in tight spaces to eat, and the spots for camouflage in trash heaps."

"He has fishy breath. How did he get here?" It's the new prints that vex her—not the dog—Jenna knows.

"I found him in my yard with a broken leg. Probably hit by a car. A dog like him isn't likely to wander this far away from a populated area, so he's something of a mystery."

"Was he blind when you found him?"

"No, but his vision was probably failing, which may be why he got hit. And drivers here often aim for small animals."

"They hit things on purpose?"

"Dogs, armadillos, tortoises, anything that isn't likely to damage their vehicle. Not much regard for life."

Claude finishes for the afternoon, leaving Jenna alone until dinnertime. The sky in the high windows is the washed-out blue of the streetwalker's scarf in one of the new prints. The depiction of this prostitute includes a verse in Japanese, which Claude translates for Jenna, "Like reflections in the rice paddies, the faces of streetwalkers in the darkness are exposed by the autumn moonlight." The woman in the print is of the lowest class of prostitutes, and she carries her rolled straw mat along a riverbank. For what purpose will she next roll out the mat, Jenna wonders—to sleep or to ply her trade? Jenna turns from the white-faced streetwalker to the elaborately robed courtesan lucky enough to reside in "pleasure quarters." This woman's face is hidden as she watches cherry blossoms sift from tall trees like moonlit snow. An attending child watches the falling blossoms with the mistress.

What's to become of this little girl? She's sure to follow the mistress's trade, but will she inherit the "pleasure quarters" or will she be dismissed to the streets with a rolled mat? Jenna presses her hand against her stomach, anticipating a pain that doesn't come.

 Part 5

"Can you bring me ribbon?" Jenna asks Claude. It's the first request she's made since occupying the room. If she pulls the hair from her crest over her ear, it reaches her jaw. The hair is honey-colored, much lighter than the patches in her armpit or on her thigh. At night, she lies on her back and tickles her nose with strands of it. She hopes Claude will bring a pair of polished sheers along with the ribbon. She imagines admiring herself in the blades after she's decorated her crest. A fragment of a nursery rhyme floats to Jenna like a moth: about Johnny who went to a fair, and, in trade for a kiss, "He promised to buy me a bunch of blue ribbons, to tie up my bonny brown hair."

Jenna blushes at the idea that Claude might think of kissing her. She peeks at his crimped face as he works. He's so old. Is he frowning because he's mulling over her request for ribbon? In what ways does she inhabit his thoughts? The eyes of many men have run over her like thirsty fingers after they've learned of her smoothness. To kiss Claude—Jenna watches him bite his lower lip with stained teeth as he works, and her mouth clogs as if she's stuffed it with hardboiled yolks.

"What color ribbon?" Claude asks, flashing his eyes.

"Blue." Jenna clears her mouth with her tongue and blinks from Claude's face to the sky in her windows. She gasps—bisecting the view from the middle window to the left of her bed is a thinly branched tree. "There's a tree!" she exclaims, shrugging herself up on her elbows, turning back and forth from the tree and Claude. Her flesh goosebumps. Her underarm and thigh tingle under their growths.

"That's Migo's tree. I planted it last night. It's a Mexican sycamore."

"Migo's?" Jenna's excitement contracts into a knot deep in her chest. It's been days since she's seen the dog. "Where's Migo?" she whispers.

"Migo's dead," Claude says. Does his gaze slip from her eyes to her crest? "He didn't wake up the other morning. I mixed his ashes in with the roots when I planted the tree last night." He arches an eyebrow. "You had feelings for him?"

Jenna sinks back into her pillow and stares at the tree. Its trunk and branches remind her of a fish skeleton hanging from the lip of a trashcan. She remembers the feel of Migo's mottled coat under her hand, his weight against her side. Claude had said Migo was "beautiful."

"I got used to him," Jenna murmurs. "He was familiar."

A groove deepens between Claude's eyes. "He was a killer. Did you know that? Before I took him in, my house was full of life. I had a parrot and a cat. And another dog: an old husky. The parrot talked. '*Buenos noches*,' he could say and 'hermosa luna' like 'goodnight' and 'beautiful moon.' One day Migo brought me the parrot's body. He jumped on the couch next to me, with it in his jaws like he was carrying a rolled newspaper—and dropped it in my lap. The perch was too high for Migo to reach. I don't know how he lured Rodrigo down. The cat—which I admit I never liked much—I found murdered in the yard. And Migo tortured my old friend, the husky, for months, biting him on his back and belly and ears when I wasn't around. I'd find Mukluk bleeding. I tried to separate them, but the husky whined to be with his tormenter—Mukluk understood that murdering was part of Migo's nature, part of his perfect breeding, and he longed for the company, even if it was killing him.

Eventually, his big heart burst. So, for a long time—until you came—it was just Migo and me."

Jenna shivers and pulls the sheet up to her neck. She runs a palm over her bare scalp, finds her crest, and pets it.

Claude nods toward the window with the tree, the creases on his face lengthening with his smile. "Keep your eyes on those leaves," he says. "See if they don't grow bloody teeth."

 Part 6

For the first time since she gave birth, Jenna dreams: She is behind the wheel of Doc Mo's SUV. She's moved from the passenger seat after forcing him out of the vehicle. She winces against a blistering sun and at the fat doctor, who lumbers past cacti, stones, and tumbleweeds toward a parched gully. "Look for the wounded animal I saw," she's insisted. "It's your job to take care of the injured." Her swollen belly presses against the wheel. She knows driving will be difficult, but the border isn't far. The baby inside her kicks through her flesh, sounding the horn, and the doctor looks back over his shoulder. He can't see the pistol— it feels like a toy in Jenna's palm. "Further." She waves with her free hand. "The animal I saw was limping further away. Do your duty." She's never shot at anything but a target. Should she aim at his head or his body? Jenna's dream-perspective shifts: Now, she sees herself from outside the SUV. Is that really her in the curly, black wig and yellow raincoat? And that belly! It seems so long ago. The doctor turns his back to her and throws back his shoulders—a puny act of defiance—or maybe resignation. Jenna watches herself calculate. Is she sure she won't need him? The phone on the passenger seat buzzes like a snake's rattle, and she's looking at a close-up of the gun's muzzle. She feels her finger jerk the trigger—and a silent explosion engulfs her in black.

Jenna's eyes spring open. She's safe in her room. It's morning. Migo's tree—its branches thick with leaves—blots out most of the ashy sky in the middle window. Lately, Claude has been replacing the prints on her walls as she sleeps instead of when she showers, so she glances about for any changes. She expects to see the Yoshitoshi print he described the previous afternoon, though he'd told her its lack of color would make it unprofitable to reproduce: "In the print, the ghost of a maid rises from the well she's haunting. She committed suicide because she broke a dish, part of an extremely valuable table setting. The ghost counts to nine, over and over again."

"She killed herself because of a broken dish?"

"Why not? It was her duty to maintain a complete set. But people needed the well she haunted. How do you think her ghost was exorcised?"

Jenna had tried to picture the obsessively counting ghost but saw her mother instead: emerging from a fog, waving the pink Lady Schick razor she'd used to shave Jenna clean. "Oh," Jenna sobbed. Claude's head had snapped up from his work, and she found herself staring at him. "A broken dish," she repeated. "Oh, your hand—"

"Ah—" Claude lowered his gaze. He'd sliced open his index finger. Blood ran along it and dripped onto his woodblock. He'd wryly grinned before wrapping his finger in a white handkerchief until a red stain bloomed. He gathered his things awkwardly and left without a word.

 Part 7

Jenna's dream and memory of Claude's blood spreading on the handkerchief left her restless. Now, he's late with her breakfast. Should she take a shower before eating? She reaches for her crest. It's festooned with blue ribbons that dangle past her shoulders. Each shower soaks the ribbons, which stiffen after drying and rustle like wind-blown branches when Jenna tosses her crest-hair. She looks at Migo's tree, as she does a hundred times a day, and remembers the feel of the dog's body against hers. She shakes her head a second time, glimpsing fluttering bits of blue. Claude had brought her the roll of blue ribbon, but not the shears with mirroring blades she'd hoped for—he'd sliced the ribbon into pieces with one of his knives. As Jenna cranes her neck, enjoying the weight of her hair, she discovers two new prints side-by-side over the headboard. Hung while she dreamed. Turning, she looks up at them from her knees.

The first print depicts a nobleman squatting on a mat. In a nearby water dish, he sees the reflection of a female demon about to attack him from behind, so his hand tightens around the hilt of his sword. Jenna sucks in a breath. The puddles on the floor of her shower, had she ever tried to see herself in them? She hops off her bed, sheds her robe, and hurries into her bathroom. But when she steps into the shower and turns the faucets, nothing happens. She twists until her palms hurt, but no water. She tries the sink. Again, nothing. And the toilet, which might have provided the most reflective surface of all, is dry. Jenna licks her lips. Her mouth and tongue are pasty. Where is Claude? Disappointed, thirsty, and hungry, she returns to her bed. Glancing again at the "demon in the water dish," she heaves a sigh, slumps onto her side, and frowns at the second print. It's of a lovely young woman.

This woman contemplates a broken wooden bucket lying at her feet. Like many of the prints on Jenna's walls, this one features a Japanese inscription. Examining the calligraphy, Jenna feels her lips move, as if she's uttering a prayer, and a translation emerges: "The bottom of the bucket has fallen out—the moon has no home in the water." But I don't understand Japanese, she thinks, bewildered. What can this mean? She hears herself whisper an answer: "No reflections."

Jenna's face drops onto her pillow. Lying on her stomach, she scratches the itchy patch on her thigh, then picks at the hair under her arm and sniffs her fingers. She worries that her crest is really nothing more than a lop-sided Mohawk. Its dry ribbons irritate her neck. She imagines quenching her thirst from the nobleman's water dish, despite the demon in it.

 Part 8

She waits. Darkness comes, then light, then darkness again. Maybe it's the same day with rare dark clouds, maybe many days pass. When it's light, the leaves on Migo's tree glisten, sharp and dangerous. From her bed, she calls, or thinks she might call Claude, but she doesn't hear her voice or feel it in her throat. "I'm hungry," she whimpers with closed eyes, as if she's a baby. It's hard to fill her lungs. When she lifts her lids, the pictures on the walls spin around her like a color wheel. The wheel slows and stops. Directly across from her, right where it's always been, is the print of Daruma, the founder of Zen Buddhism. Daruma sits in his red robe, his legs folded under him. "It took Daruma nine years of meditation to reach enlightenment," Claude had told her. "So much time that he lost the use of his legs. But you can buy little round figures of him. Dharma dolls, they're called. You can get them anywhere, even in the shops that sell my prints. The little, red dolls are self-righting: Tip one over, it pops back up. They symbolize optimism."

Jenna tries to hold the image of the meditating holy man. Red spheres swirl like tiny planets around her head—no, not planets—Dharma dolls. Jenna hugs herself and draws her knees to her breasts, curling around an emptiness that's the size and shape of one of those dolls.

An acrid odor burns her sinuses. Is that her? Her eyes would tear if they weren't so dry. No water to drink or wash with or see herself in. She reaches for her crest, her arm as weightless as paper mâché. The ribbons, stuck in clumps of waxy hair, crumble at her touch. Has Claude been allowing her ugliness to ferment? She thought he was protecting and nurturing her, but maybe he's been trying to protect the rest of the world. From her. Had he been saving the world from Migo, too? At the expense of his other pets?

Jenna pictures Doc Mo collapsing in the arroyo, feels the volume of the gunshot that started her labor. How long would it have taken the doctor's fat body to decompose in the desert heat? Bacteria first, insects next, crawling inside his clothes, then winged and four-footed carrion eaters—like the Mad Hatter's tea party, Jenna imagines. But now she sees herself perched on the dinner table, and the guests surrounding her are the legendary figures of Claude's Yoshitoshi prints: warriors and poets, buddhas and courtesans, demons and ghosts. Circling the table is the mad young woman from a print Jenna had forgotten: The woman wanders the streets at midnight, her letter to a dead lover unspooling all the way to a silver moon.

Who would be looking for Jenna? Authorities couldn't be bothered. The parents of the baby she failed to steal are $25,000 better off. Her Mexican associates have surely found another willing thief. Would she recognize the child she bore? He's no kin to her, though her blood fed him. She winces at meditating Dharma. How long until her legs become useless? She lifts herself to her hands and knees in the center of the mattress. Her robe hangs open, and her breasts dangle like forgotten fruit, the tattooed drops of milk crawling like ants from her nipple. The strip of stucco between her headboard and the prints is daubed with red—Claude's blood? She looks at the doorway and it seems as impenetrable as the prints covering her walls.

 Part 9

The doorway—Jenna's hand is a lily on its dark frame. The wall outside it is close enough to touch. She feels the weight of the stone tile beneath her feet. She closes her eyes and tries to remember the exhilaration of her rush to freedom after giving birth: being too numb for pain, the blinding sun thrown at her from the metal and glass of a thousand cars, and the baby she'd hoped to barter but left behind.

To her left, the hallway ends abruptly. To the right, she blinks, startled: a print stands on an easel, more colorful than any in her room: yellow, green, blue, red, purple, orange. A print like this would have required a dozen woodblocks. She leans on the doorframe, one foot hovering over the threshold. The print is less than ten feet away, its colors swirl, and Jenna understands: It isn't a print at all, it's a mirror. The mirror is angled so it reflects not her, but something incredibly beautiful—a garden?—at the end of a connecting corridor. A few paces and she'll see herself, then run to paradise. But she hesitates. At the base of the easel, there's a little, red globe—a Dharma doll. Stuck in its head like a pick in a 'fro is a gleaming blade. An invitation to shave? Jenna grabs her crest, and ribbon-dust falls into her eyes. There's a mark on the Dharma doll's belly.

"X," Jenna reads. X, like the eyes of the dead in comic strips? Not a Japanese character, but still a message. Her heart hammers harder, until the beats don't separate. She sees Claude, the blood leaking from his hand like the silk rose from a magician's sleeve, his last question left hanging... about the ghost of the maid who broke the dish and endlessly counted to nine. How was she exorcised?

Jenna comprehends: "Not X," she cries. "Ten!" And as she hears her own voice, like ripping paper, the colors in the mirror whirl into a blinding, saturating brilliance that fills her core. Her limbs dissolve, and she is absorbed by her completion.

Author Bio

 GregoryWolos.com

Author of 100+ short stories, Gregory J. Wolos is published in *Glimmer Train, Georgia Review, The Pinch, Nashville Review, Los Angeles Review, PANK,* and *Superstition Review.* He **ha**s earned Pushcart Prize nominations and won awards sponsored by *descant, Solstice, Gulf Stream, Emrys Journal,* and *Gambling the Aisle.* His work follows Kafka's assertion that a literary work "should be an ice ax to break up the frozen sea inside us."

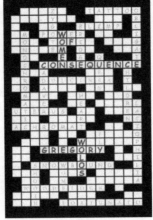

Wolo's full-length collections include *Women of Consequence* (Regal House Publishing), *Dear Everyone* (Duck Lake Books), and *The Thing About Men* (Cervena Barva Press), while his debut novel will be *Kika Kong vs. the Dead White Males* (Adelaide Books.)

Daisy in the Dirt

By Amanda Cecelia Lang

I've never been special or adored or wanted.

But, as we finish dessert, he studies me in the candlelight, inexplicably fascinated. His eyes—a devastating pale blue—hold me hostage and the edge of his grin sharpens with champagne and handsome amusement. I hope I'm not blushing. I hope he hasn't noticed I don't belong here. His penthouse boasts glittering views of the city and the distant mountains. The meal was delicious but intimidating, each course garnished with an edible flower: hibiscus, forget-me-nots, and a black dahlia. Each as surprising as the man himself. He leans in, and my heart riots through me, a full-body pulse.

"You're very rare," he says. "No siblings, no roommates. Nobody waiting at home for something so exquisite? I'm not sure I believe you."

"Tragic but true," I promise. "Perils of being the new girl in an old city."

I don't tell him why I never stay in one location for long. How it hurts to lay down roots in places where the people are grounded and hearty, their family trees like ancient oaks. Not me, a stray seedling with a quiet heart nobody ever claims. Not for anything good anyway. Girls like me are made to stay in motion, fleeing from foster home to foster home, and now city to city. I keep my roots in a plastic to-go cup on the dashboard. And when I meet someone new, I don't tell them how the isolation haunts me, how it chases me down each new highway.

I don't tell them how the angels I pray to never answer.

"I'm already imagining the possibilities," he confesses. "I can have you all to myself."

I blush. He says that *now*, but people never want me for long. This is only our second date, and only if we count the hour after he first said hello in the park. We shared a wrought iron bench and talked about the cherry blossoms, the fleeting loveliness of spring. When he took my hand, it felt like the most natural gesture in the world, as if he'd known me for ages. Our fingers tangled, and he asked if he could see me again. I gave him my number, never expecting him to call—not someone with eyes like that. But after six days of waiting, he did.

"Forgive me," he said, his voice in my ear. Even over the phone, he filled me with a hummingbird's heartbeat. "I was preparing my garden."

At the time it seemed a curious thing to say, but now I understand.

Holding my gaze, he tugs a petal from the dahlia on his plate and slides it onto my tongue. The flavor is purple and tart, like grape skin. When I reach for another, he takes my hand and presses my fingertips to his lips, one by one. Each kiss trembles down my arm, warming my core, waking every delicious nerve inside my body.

He knows what he's doing to me. I'm not so naïve that I don't see that. How many pretty girls have tasted his flowers before? But my lonely soul doesn't care about that—it shivers at his touch and words like "rare" and "exquisite." And how rare and exquisite it would be for this moment to be genuine. To finally discover what it means to be part of something greater than myself, something that deepens the earth and brightens the stars. This man is like a storybook, too good to be true, yet his eyes keep promising happily ever after.

Never letting go of my hand, he guides me to my feet. "Would you like to see where they grow?"

"Thought you'd never ask," I say, imagining moonlit kisses on a rooftop garden. His dahlia lingers on my breath like an elixir. "Tonight feels like a dream. I'm afraid I'll wake up. It's all too perfect."

"Yes, you are."

He bows his head, drawing in a slow, luxurious breath of my pulse-points, notes of cherry blossom and warm vanilla rose, then he glides his lips across my mouth. That's all it takes. We come together, twining bodies and heartbeats and passions, clinging to each other like vines. I whimper at the sweetness of him, and our kiss intensifies: famished, frenzied, real. We twist closer, so lost in each other that we collapse onto the table, toppling champagne glasses, cracking dessert plates, and— Oh God, what is he doing?

Stop! His hands! I choke and gargle and try to pull away.

His hands constrict my throat, clamping down, digging in.

My fingers fly to his, monstrous. He's become a nightmare of pure muscle. I thrash and buck, prying while his bear-trap hands squeeze and squeeze.

Let go, let go, let me go!

I bring my knee up hard, everything I've got.

He grunts, reddens, then grips harder, baring his teeth in a savage smile. Arms hard as tree trunks, he thumbs my hollows. He lifts me and slams me down, driving his weight onto my throat. Candlesticks and flower petals explode outward. My hands flail. I gurgle and squirm. My vision bulges and darkens on the edges, darker, darker. A gasping burning despair ignites every curve of my chest. Blood thunders, louder than the scream that can't escape me.

Inside my throat, bones grind against cartilage, turning to gravel.

He pushes his face in close, his breath coming fast and hot and cruel against my lips. Those bedroom eyes drill into me: shining, ruthless, invading the privacy of my soul. The strength wilts from my arms. I try to hold on—even as my bones sag and the fire in my chest climaxes.

"You love me," he whispers. "You love me not."

A brutal pop.

White light surges across my vision.

A ringing silence yanks me down.

Light and silence, they tear me away, sweep me weightless. I try to dig in but the pain scatters like leaves. My thoughts flutter, my life flutters. I remember his flowers, his hands wrapping around me. It's like a dream trying to fade, but I understand what's happened to me. Yes, I think I know.

Light is everywhere, an ethereal thing, a blinding white absence of the world. It envelops me, it permeates. I'm alone... yet, for the first time in my life, I'm not.

Hello?

At my silent call, a human shadow breaks through the radiance. My vision blurs and doubles as the silhouette leans in, filling my void, slowly bowing, as if greeting me from far, far away.

Me, the child of nobody, a toddler forgotten on the doorstep of life. No true identity, alone in my footsteps and tragedies.

But in this sudden aftermath, someone is here for me.

But who? Who could have possibly come such a distance? My birthmother? A guide... An angel? Whoever it is, I forgive them for abandoning me in life. I do, and I ache for them as I always have. Someone to take me home. Someone to tend my wilted roots. I try to reach out but don't seem to have any hands.

The silhouette draws nearer, and the dazzling light fades to a halo, shading in the contours of a face. And still, it takes a slow, shimmering moment before the light expires and I see: This is no angel.

It's him.

He releases my throat, then sits back and tilts his head as if admiring something... rare and exquisite.

I try to scream but nothing happens. He crushed my voice box, the maniac, the fucking monster! But it's more than that. My lips aren't moving. I attempt to sit up but can't. Can't so much as twitch a finger or roll an eyeball.

He straightens his shirt collar then raises my limp hand. He kisses my cracked nails and bloodied fingertips.

I feel nothing. Nothing. No icy chill of disgust. No nauseous gut-twist of disbelief. Did he snap my spine, paralyze me? Poison me? Where's my throbbing pulse? What happened to my fluttering lungs?

I am utter and complete stillness, beyond numb... a silence of flesh.

My soul screams.

Between kisses, he whispers something. I see his lips move, but his words are velvet mud inside my ears.

He stands and glides to my left, beyond my frozen line of sight. For a moment, my entire existence is the crystal chandelier. Then he pulls my arms over my head. The scenery shifts as I'm dragged off the table in a cascade of flower petals and broken glass.

Oh God, somebody help!

The dining room ceiling slides away, becoming the hallway, becoming the opulent bathroom. All the while, he is nothing but a shadow at the edge of my periphery.

He draws a steaming bath then wiggles me out of my clothing. The new dress and underwear I bought special for tonight. I sob and beg, but he doesn't hear me.

Does anyone? *Please!*

He removes his shirt then sweeps me up and settles me into the water. The tub is a jacuzzi, deep. My face slips easily below the pale blue surface. My murky hair floats like seaweed, but I expel no air bubbles.

I wait and wait for my breath to run out.

It already has.

But I'm not dead! I'm not, I can't be! I'm still awake! Still in here!

My vision ripples with the bathwater as he lifts my hands and loofas them clean. He scrapes the gore and desperation from beneath bent and torn fingernails. He clips them, one by one, taking loving care as my mind whirls.

Not dead, not dead, not dead! This isn't possible!

At last, he pulls me from the tub. I try to gasp, to suck in the fullest lungful of my life. Nothing happens. He deposits me onto the marble floor. My dripping head lolls to one side, and there I am in the full-length mirror.

The leftovers of a forgotten child, a foolish daydreamer. Look what I get for attempting to belong. Face spidery with filigree veins, throat jagged. I wear a necklace of amethyst bruises and a strand of crescent cuts where I tore at my own neck, trying to break free from him. My eyes are rubies, bloody where they should be white. I want to look away. Can't. Can't even shed real tears.

"Exquisite," he says. His voice is grainy and nebulous, nearby yet far, far away.

He kneels beside me. His attention flits across my eyes, but nothing behind them holds his interest. Not like it did when he was strangling me. His indifference diminishes me.

You were supposed to love me!

Silently, he produces a bottle of nail polish. He paints my fingernails a pearlescent white, kiss-blowing each one dry. He's hideously tender, hideously attentive, truer to me in death than in life. Each kiss kills me again and again and again.

Afterward, a cedar hope chest awaits me in the master bedroom. A beloved hollow where rosy-cheeked girls keep their wedding veils and lacy ideas of their future.

He folds me inside, tucking my head into my nude lap. Bones crack and pop from their joints, but he gets the lid closed with a snap, a metal latch, so darkness encases me.

No, no, no! Don't do this to me! I'm still in here!

Voiceless, I beg and scream.

Motionless, I scratch and bang.

Over the echoes of my desperation, I hear the distant, murky chime of his private elevator... a car trunk slamming... the otherworldly purr of a luxury engine...

The drive is eternal.

I know where he's taking me long before my casket lid opens, and darkness gives way to starlight.

He scoops me into his arms, a prince from the bleakest of fairy tales, and carries me beneath a lacework of treetops. At the end of a long path, the forest parts, revealing his secret place. He lowers my naked feet to the tall grass, cradling me like a dancer, spinning me so I can see.

His garden is magnificent. He didn't lie about that.

His plot fills the meadow. Dahlias and forget-me-nots. Artful tangles of primrose, lilacs, jasmine. Lazy, supple beds of slumbering bluebells and lungwort, impatiens, and blazing stars. Strands of tiny lights glitter between the leaves like fireflies.

He follows the cobblestones, breezing me to the center where his prize blossoms grow. If I had breath in me, it would be stolen.

"Daisy," he whispers in my ear, "meet Lily and Rose."

Daisy. That's not my name—but does it even matter?

Amid the ivy, two left arms protrude from the soil, fingers splayed like petals. Lily and Rose.

Lily is naked bone, snaked in delicate vines and bleached from summers in the sun. But Rose... Rose is fresher. The meat of her squirms with burial bugs, watery maggots, and beetles with iridescent shells. New polish glistens on what remains of their fingernails. Pink for Lily, red for Rose.

A gaping sorrow consumes my urge to scream.

The dinner, the flowers, I was right. He had other girls.

Who were they? What did they dream? Are they shrieking down there? A freshly dug hole waits between them.

He arranges me atop a bed of lavender then kneels before his victims' graves. I have no choice but to watch as he bows his head and kisses their fingertips. I pray to the sky. Pray to turn my head away, pray to sit up and return to the lonely highways and living panorama of the world.

Isn't anyone listening? Isn't anyone out there?

Too soon, he approaches me, and—just like our hour in the park—those devastating eyes promise a happy ending. I wanted someone to adore me, someone to keep me—but not like this!

Never like this!

"Daisy, thank you for tonight. It was a dream come true." He lifts me with a flourish and his garden whorls around me, my legs floating like a ball gown's hem. But how fleeting the romance. He lowers me, toes first, into the grave. I slump, my forehead bumps the soil, but I remain standing, paralyzed with death and Hell and heartache.

Dirt rains down around me. Shovelful after shovelful of crumbling darkness fills the gaps between my body and the walls of eternity. I thrash and shriek skyward.

But in death, as it was in life, I'm on my own.

When the dirt reaches my chest, he raises my stiffening left arm into the night. As he does, my head crunches backward on splintered neck bones. I'm granted one final barrel view of the sky—*Please!*—then dirt sprays my face. It fills my open mouth, my gaping eyes, obliterating the last of the light.

Why didn't anyone love me?

Why did my family abandon me?

Why was the most intimate moment of my life the final one?

I wail and beg and claw at the velvet of my own mind. Please, please, please!

I only want to go home.

Nobody answers me, not a soul, not here in the dirt—and never above it.

Isolation, my only friend, sews a gentle gloom and deafens me with indifference. Time distends over the edge of comprehension.

I writhe inside the void of myself, a prisoner of my echoing mind. Never worthy of family, never worthy of love, never worthy of a real life.

Not even worthy of a peaceful death.

Never should've been born, never should've searched for hope. Only girls with sturdy roots deserve to be found, deserve homes. The truth is stark and eternal before me.

I am nothing now because I have always been nothing.

Just let me end!

A hundred hours pass, or perhaps a hundred years.

Without moonlight, without sunlight... until all at once, it happens.

Not the end.

Something small—so very, very small—glimmers in the darkness.

A pinpoint in the abyss. Then another. And another.

My cries fizzle into silent awe.

All around me, slowly...

Grain by grain...

The dirt begins to glow.

Particles spark and flicker like underground stars.

Except I'm not witnessing this with my eyes.

I can see the soil beneath my toes, in the crease of my back, at the nape of my neck. Everywhere the dirt touches me, I see it. An uncanny, all-encompassing awareness of the Earth around me. The fertile soil twinkles with mica, glimmers with the vein-work of roots and tiny crawling things.

The beauty softens the edges of my solitude. It surrounds me—not quite a motherly embrace, though I succumb like a newborn, held within the mysterious, loamy arms of the Earth.

And slowly, sunrise by sunset, my body returns to me. Not as I had it in life, but as a tingling phantom awareness of organs and limbs.

I still can't move.

But sometimes, my toes itch down into the bone. Sometimes, I sense the feathered greeting of a bird alighting on my blooming hand.

Or the hideous caress of his lips returning like a nightmare to my fingertips.

And I feel myself decay.

Inside the moist, glittering ground, I bloat and burst and become a slurry of the pretty girl I once was. The earth tastes of worms upon my melting tongue. My final meal of hope and edible flowers seeps out with my organs, staining the soil around me. All the while, the tiny crawling things enter me and feast. The noises they make are chittery and squishy and intimate.

And, for a time, my screams do return.

One evening, an elderly centipede wriggles through my jawbone into the cavity my right eye once resided. It curls its skittering body into a ring, expels a final twitch, then dies.

Like me, it begins to decay. It nourishes the soil inside my skull. As it bleeds deeper, its voiceless voice chitters through me. I absorb its knowledge. I share its hundred-legged memories, winding through the sunshine and leaves and dirt. It was quite friendly with the dirt during its life, and it knows the buried secrets of the Earth.

Wise centipede. It whispers, it sympathizes, it inches around my vain and tragic expectations. These human yearnings to be loved and saved by someone who watches over. To stir the cold stars with my cries. To awaken the heavens and draw imaginary guardians down into my waving arms.

Such prayers are futile seeds.

Who am I to change the cycle of the seasons, the calling of every creature? We rise from the ground, we dance and stumble atop it, we taste of its blossoms and urges and fermented fruits, then we succumb to the grave, flesh and mind. In the dirt, it doesn't matter if we are loved or unloved. Here, we offer ourselves, our histories, our indulgences, and agonies to the collective heirloom memories of the Earth.

And indeed, as my mortal oils bleed blacker and farther out, I caress the wilting tiptoes of flowers and mingle with the dust and long-gone days of those who came before me. A vast field of minds echoing: spiders, foxes, flowers... They call to me.

His victims call, too.

Beautiful voices, phantom tongues, and tragic song.

Lily and Rose.

Those aren't their names, but in the dirt, names are inconsequential—as are the forlorn highways, the forbidden cities and homes that passed them by. Bleeding closer, I see their skulls in the glowing soil, their pretty faces in his candlelight and polished silverware. I witness the soft music and their screams, the promises he made as he stabbed and bludgeoned and adored them. I feel their lovely, undernourished bones, fingers gnarled in the shape of the futures he ripped away. Dreams indistinguishable from mine. Dreams of a family, of a place to belong, to be loved.

These girls, these perfect scattered girls, they lived and perished like me. Maybe up above we could've been friends... or maybe nothing more than passing headlights in the night, strangers avoiding eye contact in rest stop mirrors. It doesn't matter now. We've found our home. Here below, our minds entwine, gentle, thorny creepers twisting in the gloom. Each of us poets and daredevils and lovers who never were. With voices of gravel, we weep and whisper and daydream ourselves into something grander. We become sisters of the garden and daughters of the Earth.

Together, we sprout roots.

Together, we reach skyward.

We never do wake the heavens. Though sometimes, on overcast evenings, we imagine ourselves rising from the grave as rare and exquisite skeletons ornamented with vines and delicate flowers, lurching into the city to find and drag him under.

But no.

The call of the soil is stronger than visions of vengeance, and the wisdom of the Earth soothes us and reminds us to be patient. He'll join us one day.

One day, everybody returns to the dirt.

Author Bio

 AmandaCeceliaLang.com

Aspiring recluse Amanda Cecelia Lang of Denver, Colorado, writes horror laced with whimsy, magic, and mayhem. When she isn't plotting her next imaginary murder, she sleeps all day and plays all night—but probably isn't a vampire since she thinks hickeys are "seriously gross."

Lang's fiction haunts the best-selling anthologies *Night Terrors* and *The Year's Best Hardcore Horror,* as well as Dread Machine's *Mixtape: 1986* and *The Lost Librarian's Grave.* Her stories also lurk in the dark corners of the following podcasts: T*he Other Stories, Thirteen, Creepy,* and *Tales to Terrify.*

More From Outcast Press

International travels and ayahuasca, oh my! A novel about friendship dragged through the Amazon jungle and spit out through the stars with the aid of decades, DMT, and well-meaning debauchery.
Now available on Amazon, Kindle, SmashWords, Barnes & Nobel, & more!

Je Ne Sais Quoi

By G.C. McKay

Marie, *ma chérie*, our daughter's been sleepwalking again. In the middle of so many nights, I wake, thrust straight out of the phantom of you—of you and your departure—only to be confronted by the frigid stillness of our Antoinette, who always eerily seems to find herself stuck between the pillars at the end of our bed. Unaware, yet present. Out of you, I scream myself awake to be greeted by an abject silence, where, furthermore, a whispered shriek in the wind creeps through the window slit to meet the mannequin posture of our daughter.

Breathing over her porcelain skin, invisible hairs stand, and the creased folds of her silken nightgown appear to constrict, as if squeezing for dear life, unable to let go. She appears uncannily elevated, in what I consider to be a taunting apparition of you. An impression of which I'm afraid I shall soon have to succumb, one that haunts as much as it teases. She has taken—or should I say, *has been taken,* since her actions are not of her volition—to lurking about the house during the night, trespassing into what used to be the secrecy of our bedroom. Her safety is not of concern, since I've taken pains to ensure that no gaps in any windows can be breached further than the limit in which they reside. Naturally, I still find myself lost in worry though, not knowing what she might bump into or where she may fall, all alone in the dark, as vulnerable as a naked child. Sometimes, I wish she were still a child, instead of the spitting image of you, which now stirs a compulsion within me to a breaking point.

I find myself divorced from everything, Marie. The same urge that once overtook me with you is now re-emerging. Threatening to evolve into something sicker. A possession so unnerving that it seems to have deliberately unearthed itself from the unconscionable. You know what urge I'm speaking of, don't you?

It began, of all places, just over a year ago, at your funeral. Where Antoinette and I grieved together like any normal child and parent should. Where, blinded by my disorientation, it took me several days after your burial to realize that Antoinette, in an understandably regressive state, had been calling me Daddy the entire time. You may laugh, as I also did, until the uneasiness of it sunk in. Her being grief-stricken and consequently infantilized by your abandonment was not so surprising, but her addressing me as Daddy was something she'd not done for the longest time. And now, it's near enough the only word that ever leaves her lips, if, on any given day, any should leave them at all. Perhaps I did pick up on it during the proceedings, as we held hands, watching you descend into the ground forever, but the recollection's nothing but a whitewash. I wish I could say that I was too preoccupied by the void you'd entered and subsequently left behind (through no fault of your own, *ma chérie*) but... It was as if... as if Antoinette just stepped straight out of the shadow of you. Out of you in your immaculate prime.

Oh, Marie. Are secrets the source of femininity?

She has, I must say—sleepwalking notwithstanding— acted rather strangely to your passing. Perhaps even more so than I. Her tears and turmoil are really nothing out of the ordinary, but her behavior around me, I'm certain, has played equal part in my lusting. Whilst still being her father, I comforted her all night when three officially became two, never once allowing her to witness my despair, all in the hope of strengthening her resolve. The morning after, however, something had shifted. Having indulged in too much wine at your wake, Antoinette and I had fallen asleep together atop the sheets of our bed. I woke in a haze, where Antoinette greeted me with a tray in her hands, having prepared breakfast.

"There you go, Daddy."

Not only had you done the same thing the morning after we, or I suppose *I*, christened the bed in our new home, Marie, but our daughter had also decided to adorn the same silk robe you'd worn. The white one I had no clue was still lurking around, hanging in what may as well have been a different house, for its existence had only hung in the closet of my mind. I presume you must've given it to her... perhaps as death came closer. Why

Antoinette decided to wear it though, I've no idea. She acted as if it were normal. Nothing out of the ordinary. I'm still not sure whether that heightened its spookiness or gave it a certain allure, but as she passed me the cup of coffee she'd prepared, it slipped straight through my fingers. It was as if I, too, had been rendered transparent. You see, as she leant forward, the tassels of her robe slipped out of their bow, and there she stood (which she surely must've been aware of) in the nude.

Marie, my beautiful wife, for what felt like the longest ache of the cruelest time, I genuinely thought that our daughter was you, or that she had been possessed and therefore embodied by you, back from a long time past, at the time of the singular, standout struggle in our whole relationship. Only then, did I notice that our daughter is a little slimmer than you ever were, despite also being larger-chested, as I've regrettably come to acknowledge since the incident. I had not seen our daughter naked as far back as the age of... eleven, just as she was coming to terms with the body in her possession. Yet there she stood, as lacking in the awareness of self as she did in the days of yesteryear, still just as hairless in the region my eyes should not have been drawn upon.

Perplexed as I was by this overlapping duality of past and present, I spaced the next moment out, only to come back to my senses once Antoinette had begun mopping the spillage about my groin. The glint in her eyes as her head flicked up, as she brought her petting of the bedsheets to a halt, could not be ignored.

"Oh, Daddy."

We both knew what had happened. Then I heard her gulp. But her following eyelash flicker and crossing smile was as long as it lasted. Before I knew any better, she was in the shower, where I seemed to re-awaken from where I'd just woken, only with a wet patch around my groin to remind me of the truth of what had just happened. The sight of our daughter, caught somewhere between the ghost of us, had caused me to ejaculate.

We both knew that something had taken place, but nothing had occurred. After all, we'd barely touched. Days went by, then weeks. I began to convince myself that the incident had not, in fact, taken place. That it was my grief in reverie. Nothing but a silly dream. I started to wonder... if my mind saw it fit to mourn you via visions involving our daughter, what was really the harm? But since I'm reaching out to you now, Marie, addressing this once and for all, you should already know that my stirrings did not just stay there, under the sheets of our bed.

I tried to give you and Antoinette the benefit of the doubt, that if she saw it fit to wear your clothes to mourn, who was I, even, or especially as her father, to impose my will against her? This much I reasoned for the months that flew by, expecting things to change. But nothing has, Marie. Not one thing. Antoinette has done nothing but stay put, here between the walls of our home. Remember how you'd encouraged her to leave before leaving us yourself? Well, she barely ever leaves the house at all anymore. I can't see her ever departing. She spends all day and all night in her room, hardly ever uttering a word. Except Daddy, which slips out of her mouth during sleepwalks, as I take her by the shoulders to guide her back to bed, forever in the same, godforsaken robe, which I'm often obliged to tie back up.

If half-unawares myself, I find my fingertips poised over her skin, where my delirious temptation to feel her has me in the most agonizing paralysis. It's not uncommon for me to return to bed, hysterical, in need of an extremely cold shower, aroused to the point of tasting nausea at the back of my throat.

"Daddy, no... Daddy... Please, Daddy."

I suppose, no matter how detailed the illustration, I shall never be able to fully demonstrate just how torturous that noun has become. Just like with the mysterious reappearance of the robe, Marie, it seems that touch was too unsettling to be coincidental. Perhaps that's why I didn't register it at first, at your funeral. It had to get under my skin, to wax and stir and resurrect once its utterance ceased to be echoed about these walls, but where its resonance certainly remained.

It was during a day like any other. One so arbitrary that nothing else stands out about it. Only the event at hand. Wherever you were, in the house, it was not. I believe I was checking to see whether Antoinette was in her room, prompted by the quietude of the house. I headed straight there, not really considering the silence of my approach. Perhaps I called out her name. Perhaps not. The same can be said as to whether I knocked on her door. Since I usually would—more out of habit than anything else—I would find it odd to be informed that I did not, but well, oddity would soon find me, regardless.

Once inside her room, however, I wished that I had announced myself. I'd never seen Antoinette in such a state. She was on the floor. Her eyes closed. Legs open. Wearing nothing but a pair of socks, one side of her underwear caught around an ankle. Embarrassed at having caught her in the act, I coughed and went to turn, but all she did was open her eyes. A lot like when she sleepwalks, come to think of it. Yet she was certainly awake. No scream came forth. No sudden jolt or shake of surprise. She just continued playing with herself, Marie. Everything else went on exactly as before, as if I weren't in the room.

"Antoinette," I said, watching yet trying not to look, but nothing seemed to phase her in the least. She kept on exploring herself, now faster, biting her lip just like you, Marie. Though where you would've said, "Anton," Antoinette said...

"Yes, Daddy?"

Assuming I'd perturbed her, going by her change of tone and anguished face, I sort of froze, not knowing what to do since she sounded as if she might've been suffering whilst her hand quickened. She went red, I went red, and together, our locked eyes tightened in contact, despite us each shedding a tear.

"Fuck... Daddy."

How do I know if she actually orgasmed, you may ask? Why, the translucent, everlasting flow of liquid that so often erupted from you during our best years together, which, in honesty, I'd only ever experienced with you, was not only matched but *bested* by our Antoinette.

Like mother, like daughter.

It was, without doubt, one of the most ill and regrettably aroused states I've ever suffered—not necessarily because of what our girl was doing, for that was natural, but why she felt so at ease, even desirous, doing and continuing to do what she was, as if for parental approval... right before my very eyes. She gushed, over and over, half the woman she'd later become, the other still my little girl, who looked as if she wasn't so sure about what exactly she was flooding over the rug and carpeted floor.

"Daddy."

I turned though I was desperate to comfort her, rattling the door on my way out, for I'd struck a stiffened knee against it in my blind haste. As you may have guessed, that was, as nature had seemingly intended, the last time she'd cry, "Daddy," to my face—right up until the next time we held hands for longer than a brief passing, as we watched you descend into the ground.

Keeping this from you while you were alive was never my intent. It just so happened that that very evening, Antoinette woke us with a scream. You and I initially assumed it was the cry of a nightmare, which you insisted on tending to. You practically flew out of the room, which, as I look back on now, tells me you may have known otherwise. Upon your return, you made a quip about how our daughter, God bless her, had wet the bed. We both knew that was preposterous, right? Our Antoinette had barely wet the bed in her earliest years. Yet, believe it, we did. But just because you could not say it—could not bring yourself to admit that your daughter, in the throes of her earliest confrontation with ecstasy, would gush like you—did not stop it from being true. That was when I decided not to tell you about the incident earlier that day, when I saw first-hand what our daughter was capable of, what we both knew deep down she was up to in her room, soaking her bedsheets, crying, "Daddy."

I always found it remarkable how you jumped to attention the way you did. She had cried for my aid, my assistance, yet up you sprang and out you went, ignoring the trapped-mouth word of our daughter's ambiguous cry. Was I held in the eye of your suspicion around this time, the way the chilled hairs of your skin seemed to suggest? What was it about my behavior, or perhaps hers, that gave birth to such a radical change in yours?

You see, Marie, *ma chérie*. You kept to this story that our daughter had undergone a nightmare, that whatever lurked about her dreams had been so terrifying as to make her wet the bed. As if overcompensating for a truth you couldn't ever deny to satisfaction, only to have it backfire on you. For the weeks that followed, as you very well know, this unspoken truth found itself layered over again and again, just like the bedsheets you replaced and re-tucked night after night. I was beginning to suspect that you had gone mad. Antoinette seemed less bothered by her supposed night terrors than you did—though of course, the true terror lay in the fact that she was frequently and unabashedly touching herself. For reasons unknown, her playing with herself was the true nightmare.

What was it about it that unsettled you so? Did Antoinette happen to mention the little non-incident, perhaps? Did you then exacerbate this occurrence yourself, and turn it into something it never was to begin with? You didn't let me near her whenever she screamed herself awake. Did you think I was molesting her, *ma chérie*? You were always so panicked during the nights surrounding these days, forever on alert, and, in essence, living out the very nightmare you found yourself in constant anticipation of. To tell the truth, it seemed that you even lie awake at night, in hope of hearing our daughter's cry for help rather than otherwise.

I suppose, in a sense of the ironical, fate decided to intervene, and make light of this during the six or so weeks that followed, where her nightly masturbatory screams came to a sudden though partial end, on the eve of her twelfth birthday. You suspected it would come around sooner than it did, but our poor girl was introduced to womanhood the night her screaming ceased. Lo and behold, that's when her sleepwalking began.

No scream provoked you that night though, Marie. You just went on a feeling, prompted by the very lack of a shriek, by the absence of your expectation. You said you were sure you'd heard something, but I assure you, you heard nothing! You found her standing in the middle of my office in her nightgown, with blood streaking down her leg. And do you remember how you told me? Well, "told" is actually the wrong word, but you know what I'm getting at. For some reason, you saw it fit to show me instead. Upon returning to our room, you flicked on the lamplight—no, all the lights in the room—as if preparing to interrogate me, but instead wordlessly displayed your bloodstained fingertips before my eyes, as if the blame lied with me! Nothing to do with our baby's nature. What on earth possessed you to do such a thing? Were you trying to communicate something, or were you simply absentminded, petulant about the whole affair?

You slept like a baby that night, as if you'd been awaiting our girl's first period in duress. Bloodstains aside, why would such a thing as her sleepwalking provide you with so much relief?

It perturbs me to look back now, and the months which followed this change in our daughter, to realize how peculiarly comforted you were by it all. Though her sleepwalking ended as she adjusted to this biological adaptation, you never seemed quite so content in all the years that I'd known you—except maybe the days before the date of our marriage was set in stone. Be it speculative but empirical, that's when I believe your tumor truly began to take root. It wouldn't blossom until Antoinette reached her late teens, but that's when it first appeared—took you under its influence! Even still, tumor be damned, you thought I was fucking our daughter, didn't you, Marie!? Forgive the crass acidity of my tongue, but I cannot come up with any other conclusion, no matter how often I rearrange the fucking equation. The sight of our Antoinette bleeding gave rise to a sense of relief in you because it meant she hadn't been impregnated. Of course, this doesn't dismiss the notion that I could have been making our daughter perform oral sex or touch me with her hands, or simply helped her "wet the bed" instead. How could her not getting pregnant put your mind so at ease if you so strongly suspected me of fondling her to begin with?!

Forgive me. I haven't slept in days. And my missing of you, especially this eve, aches like always, if not worse. Most including our daughter, it seems, don't believe in the concept of "the one" anymore. But, Marie, as difficult as this may be to believe, that is exactly what I felt, what I knew, from the moment I met you. I'm not sure if I ever told you, but everything you said during our introduction to one another was never anything more than a blur. An intoxicated excursion of ecstasy, where life took on a sharpened iridescence, an evolved effervescence even, that I hadn't ever dreamt possible. Of course, as you very well know, I did not so much as dare to lay a finger on you. Confronted by such an unknown quality—entity, even—I felt nothing short of full-fledged fear. Fear of the man a woman like you could make me, of what a monstrosity you could so easily turn me into. Being a man of reasonable self-control comes with the knowledge of knowing what he is capable of. It is a fate so cruel that it haunts him for a lifetime.

I sometimes think that I died along with you. That my bestial imaginings are nothing short of a desired suicide via the sexual, defined by what it perpetually struggles to deny. For ever since this wretched universe took you away from me, I wake each morning erect in my own personal Hell. I'm now forced to see my Antoinette for the woman she's become—rather than the daughter I once had. And *ma chérie*, I'm struggling, for that woman is you. I really don't know what to do. I cannot even allow my glance to lay upon our daughter for one minute without coming under her possession. My saying it will somehow help, I hope. Marie, please believe that this never happened before, but right now, in this moment, you are right: I have an uncontrollable urge to fuck our daughter. And these thoughts infest me everywhere. Each memory born from the times we'd shared under this roof—the very roof we spent all those years constructing into a home—has been infiltrated by her very presence.

I'll say it, too, she's prettier than you ever were. Far more sensual. And she puts your body, even in its best era, to absolute shame. Antoinette has your scent. Your demeanor. Your very *je ne sais quoi*. I don't know what! I can't concentrate or focus for a single fucking minute without feeling this incessant, repulsive impulse. And it's occurring so often that my subconscious seeps into waking thoughts, telling me my urges are just fine, that I should do something about them, take action! And the fever of this sickness only grows with each unendurable night, where no matter how or why I'm awoken—either to find or be confronted by the sight of our Antoinette—as absent of mind as she is in body, stuttering the word of her first exile into ecstasy, utterly oblivious to the overwatching father, as he desperately struggles to keep his quivering hands to himself.

This begs the question: Is it really so wrong for a father and daughter to come together... if, Antoinette, is in fact my daughter at all? You see, Marie, since we're digging up our past... your behavior in and around the time of our moving in together has never been forgotten. We simply buried it. And now that I've been burdened with life without you, there's a shovel in my head, unearthing histories left unspoken and the tumorous rot they inevitably passed on to the years we had not yet lived... not to mention the little baby girl whose origins surrounded one.

You'd made mention of a rendezvous with your ex. A flippant one to which I was expected to treat with likewise triviality, and, dutifully, I did. All I remember you ever saying about this man was that he was your first lover out of however many it was, the one old enough to be your father. The one the Devil tells me you used to call "Daddy" in your time before me. After the date, 27th April 1993, to be specific, not one single word about the affair ever left your lips. In fact, for weeks afterwards, you barely uttered anything at all, as if some light in you had gone out. There in body but elsewhere in spirit. Pale in comparison to the Marie I once knew. All the while, I tried to give you the benefit of the doubt. Tried to understand that whatever your reasons, your meetup with him was personal. Yours and yours alone. We were never possessive of one another. Not until then at least. The silence on the subject was another matter altogether though. Do you remember how we breached the subject on the morning of that fateful night?

"There's something we need to talk about, isn't there, Marie?" I'd said, as dead in tone as your infrequent replies about this period. You said nothing in return. Merely nodded, childish in your knowing discomfiture, a gripped fist creasing the bedsheets as you shriveled into fetal position. A solitary tear fell across your cheek that you would've normally wiped away in shame. That morning, however, you left it there for me to observe. We'd been married close to a year by then. Yet, I could hardly conceive of knowing the woman in the bed before me. As I headed toward the door with my feet harshly brushing the fresh carpet, I thought I heard you whisper an apology. A sorry I can't be sure I ever heard, but to which I chose not to cast my doubt.

That evening, I drove home from work later than usual, though only to collect my thoughts and essentially avoid the same subject I'd finally addressed, and it rained something apocalyptic. Once parked, I sat for a while, watching the windscreen wipers futilely swipe back and forth, never quite clearing the view through the glass in time, despite my lack of intention to go any further. I didn't think you were home as I let myself in. No heartbeat of another, of you, my love, could be detected. I thought you'd just up and left. Abandoned me with the same sealed lips of the past fortnight. Drenched to the bone, I found myself taking a shower before even thinking of going into the bedroom. It was almost scalding, so hot that it felt cold... or so cold that it felt hot. That much I remember, though I barely felt anything at all.

In nothing but a towel, I sat in our living room, the only room that still had several unpacked moving boxes. After filling and draining the same tumbler glass I'm drinking out of now, five or six times, I stood and took to the stairs. Out of nowhere, I was struck by the sense of your physical presence. In that moment, it was quite possibly the most convinced I've ever been of anything. As if in alignment with my thoughts, the brightness of the room took me somewhat aback. What I hadn't anticipated, however, was your nakedness. Underneath my foot, the silk of your night gown caressed my sole, lain in a clump before you, directly centered between your coyly opened legs. Your perfumed scent— the very one you wore for your date—tore through the flared nostrils of my explicitly heavy breaths. You lie not in the bed but half-over it in the middle, your feet slightly elevated from the carpet. Knowing that I'd come across you in this position, a position I'd not seen you display ever before, you must have known if I simply wanted to go to sleep, I would've had to lift you up...

That's how I knew. Your signal glared at me, along with the unusual illumination of the room itself. You presented yourself to me like that, not only in a premeditated taunt, but also by way of confession. Before I knew what hit me, I joined you in the place of your absence, into the emptiness of which you'd been thrust, to bring you back to me again. I almost didn't do it though, Marie. In a blink, I saw your vulnerability and went to move you instead, but you protested my disturbance of your slumber, fighting back my parental attempt to comfort. When I stopped, I huffed, exhausted. "Marie?"

To that, you tossed and turned, mumbling your no-no-nos until...

"Daddy."

I wish I could recall more of the instincts which took over, but I can only ever recollect in *medias res*. I fucked you both intimately and with savage remorse. You'd betrayed me and so then, in acceptance of your sorrow, I betrayed you. I'm positive that I must've awoken you, not through my agonized penetration, but with the tears I could not stop shedding. I'll never know now whether you were in fact asleep, awake or somewhere in between, but I like to think that in the latter is where we both ended up. We entered the void that was keeping us apart, knowing, in some abstract sense, that it was the only way to bring us back from the dead.

Would you have felt as guilty as you clearly did during the aftermath had you cheated on me with consent? I think not. In fact, I'd go as far as to say that the ex-lover, the daddy who forced himself on you in a roundabout way, actually saved our marriage. The ghost you became right before I raped you in your sleep went away with your pregnancy, erasing its existence in the first place. Two wrongs, in this instance, had indeed made a right. For 27 years at least. You never had to breathe a word about your betrayal, whilst I never had to shed light on mine. It was our Faustian pact. But now that you're gone, the Devil has returned, inside a silken robe I'd long thought gone but has been adorned once more, asking for it all the time in perfect, intolerable silence.

I have no access to your mind for your mind is nevermore. I'm not sure what I'm aware of any longer but know this: I am more than positive that you told Antoinette the story of her origin, or at least my contribution to it. Whether you told her I raped you, took advantage, or overwhelmed you by force makes no difference. I just wonder, did you happen to make mention of what you were getting up to, in and around this time? Did the name of your ex-lover happen to crop up, or did that particular blemish remain concealed? It seems to me, what with our Antoinette's eagerness to be seen by me, naked as the day she was born, you may have left the slightest hint behind, that I may not in fact be her biological father.

Over the past few days, I've found myself in her room at a midnight hour, half-unaware of what motivated me to go there. Most times I thought I'd heard a disturbance, only to find the silence I walked into most paralyzing in its contradiction. The first night, I plucked a wayward strand of hair from her scalp, to maintain the perfection she's come to represent in my eyes. On the second, I scooped the fall of drool she'd omitted during her slumber with a tissue. Yesterday, a sanitary towel, used, that she'd let slip from her hand during her slumber, presumably having needed to change it during her sleep. If memory serves, you did the same thing a few times over the years. For you see, the smell would always wake me. Through no choice of my own, its scent shall forever remain in my blood.

All those items of retrieval now rest in an unsealed envelope, inside the drawer of the writing desk where I speak to you now. What will I do, if not a trace of my DNA is to be found inside her? I'm not sure what would be worse. To find out that she isn't my daughter and have the urge that makes Hell out of my days remain, or to discover that she is indeed mine, and have it stay put regardless, driving me, day by day, as mad as your tumor made you, *ma chérie*.

I'm tortured by the physical manifestation of our union, of our noble though terrible secret, our spawn of silent evil. I do not want to act upon the urge that curses me so. Antoinette is my daughter. Our daughter, Marie. Did our silence seal our fate of losing her? You've taken shelter in death and left me for dead in the same breath. I wanted to confront you when, out of the blue, your demeanor took a turn on me. Your entire behavior regarded me with the highest suspicion. What was it about our daughter's womanhood that frightened you so? Was it all simple projection? Don't think that I'm not aware of the absurdity, the sheer nonsensicalness of my reaching out to you now, but I am desperate. At a point of no return. Like a coward, I threw myself into my work just to avoid the subject, and before I blinked, years had gone by. Then your tumor emerged, setting the stage for the next few years, as everything you once were to me began to decay, atom by atom. It hardly seemed right for me to bring up your infidelity, my taking of you, and all the repercussions that inevitably fell upon our Antoinette.

Did we ever truly look at her? Let's face it, look at what she's become. She's a shell of a human being, *ma chérie*. Shy to the point of barely existing, absentminded as if permanently on drugs. Extracting a word from her is exactly as the cliché goes: like getting blood out of a stone. And I hate you for leaving me with her. For implanting ideas of which I have no access. What disturbs me most is the vague though undeniable intuition, that you convinced our very own daughter that I'd molested her. And now, my Antoinette glides about the walls of this rotten house, as if your carcass were still here, feeding off the fumes that make up her flight. What have we done to her? 27-years-old but mentally barely 11. I must remind her to eat, to bathe, and to go to sleep. She's just not there, Marie. We used to say that her depression was a phase, that she'd grow out of it—not *in*. That's all she is now and all she has ever been. Depression itself. She's the walking embodiment of every word we never shared. Unable to look at me unless half-conscious.

  I remember reading an introductory piece by a fellow psychologist once, stating how it is the secrets of a family that bring about their dysfunction. That every unspoken and therefore phantomized truth that floats between the walls of their home will lay the foundation of each trauma, mental illness, and episodic psychosis in their possession. But what a lot of these so-called psychologists either fail to realize or refuse to admit, is that at the end of every extreme, the same result applies. That's the syllogism. The same secrets that break a family apart are the exact ones that keep them together. It seems to me, *ma chérie*, that the secret that kept us devoted to one another is suffering the severest neglect. I do not want to do what it is that screams to be done, nor do I plan to, but Marie... The longer your ghost insists on haunting me like this, the closer I'm tempted to the void.

Author Bio

@GarethCMckay

YouTuber and author G.C. McKay co-hosts *The Bastard Sons of Oedipus*, a podcast with *A Thin Slice of Anxiety*'s Cody Sexton. Welcoming a morbid fascination with sexual taboos and a deep dive into deteriorating mental states, McKay's work spans three novels.

You can buy these books, including *Heather*, another speculative *Lolita*-esque piece, direct from his website: GCMcKay.com

@SliceOfAnxiety
Anxiety Press & Outcast Press partnered to release the Kindle e-book, *Misandry*, by Louise MacGregor. With artwork by *A Thin Slice's* founder, Cody Sexton, this small story collection focuses on women sick of fetishization—to the point that they sometimes kill.

Dollhouse

By Simon Broder

I comes out the casino with a packa Cravens and three-thousand bucks. I normally don' smoke natives, so the Cravens is kinda a big deal. In the parking lot, Amanda squeezes a can a PBR in my pocket, but it done spills all over my jeans so I swears at her. She says she stole it from the bar and then she gets to laughing. I hate it when Amanda laughs. She gots bright red hair and these thick freckles and sometimes, when she laughs, ya can't tell if she's gonna cry or rip your throat right out, and then—just like that—she's all normal again.

"Jimbone's all right and proper now, eh?" she asks.

"We gots perfectly good beer in the car," I says.

In the car, we drinks our beers and I tells Amanda if it's real late at night when you start drinking, you gots to push through and see the sun, and she laughs like she gots no idea what I'm talking 'bout.

"If it feels good, do it," she sings, cranking the radio. I thought I knowed the tune but I ain't.

Next morning, I leaves the Cravens on my dresser and hike down to the beach where the lake comes right up to the casino, right where they gots this "No Swimming" sign that always makes me wonder what kinda poison they puttin' in the water. Time I gets up to the side road that leads into the dumpy parking lot, I'm done fiending for a cigarette, so instead I buys a tallboy from the store and pounds it out when I see the accident.

Girl's like seven- or eight-years-old with that bleach gold type hair that changes color 'round puberty. I sets down on a cinder block and chews my fingers while I watches her. I don't gots the heart to go over and tell her everything's gonna be all right, 'cuz it ain't—front fender's all crushed in and the chick in the driver's seat ain't moving. But she's a smart girl I guess because it don' take her long to figure out she ain't gonna get her mama out the car. She starts to walking towards me and suddenly I gets real nervous like everything's my fault and I wish I coul' just disappear into the ground.

"Hi," she done introduce herself. "I'm Doris. That's my mom in there."

I stares at her for a long time, thinkin' bout all the trouble I'll be in. I already gots plenty a troubles in my life. "I can't help ya," I says.

"I don't need help," she says. "My mom says little kids always want to run away but they're not allowed to."

"Well, suppose I could help ya run away," I says. "Where ya gonna go?"

"I don't know," she done say. Then I see some tears in them baby blues and damn if she ain't coming right towards me, warm, little fingers yankin' my arm. "I wanna go home, mister."

"Now how you gonna run away if you're home?"

"Because," she says, and that's about when I figures an eight-year-old just can' be reasoned with.

I picks her up and carries her into town and, when they done ask me for a credit card at the Ritz-Carlton, I slips the clerk three bills and that shuts her up right quick.

"Now you stay where you is," I tells Doris.

I'm still fiending so I goes back to the store for a fresh packa Cravens, but, soon as I put a dry one in my mouth, damn if some asshole don't offer me a buck for it. I just gives him the whole pack and then I goes to see Amanda. She been waitressing this shitty breakfast joint for a creepy, old dude named Albert, who always just sets outside, listening to his fancy-ass headphones and evil-eyeing anyone who done tries to pick her up. 'Cept me. He never says a word to me, just stares through me like I ain't nobody.

When Amanda done asks me for the fifth time what I'm figuring to do, I says, "I'm gonna quit smoking." She done rolls her eyes at that, so, even though I ain't hungry, I order runny omelets and an Irish coffee to keep her talkin'.

"You lose your money yet?" she asks. I tell her that ain't fair, but she just shrugs and says she only making conversation.

"I been thinking 'bout nice things and how I don't never notice they're nice," I says, running my finger along the edgea the table where it's all raggedy-like. "What kinda wood this be?"

"It ain't wood," she says. "It's fake. You don't know the difference?"

"But what if it's real?"

She starts into that dangerous, goofy laugh and hits me and, for a minute, I done feel stupid. Then her eyes goggle up real big and she done press her face right up against the table. "Hey there, maple tree, you got any sap for me?"

"For real, though. You could see your reflection."

"What does it matter?" She pulls my plate over and starts forking into my cold messa eggs.

"Just look."

She squints. "Okay, maybe I see myself. Like a tiny bit. So what? Maybe it is real. I don't fuggin' know."

She ain't taking me serious, so I shoves the plate and done walk right out. On the way past, I done flips Albert the bird and see an angry flash in Amanda's eyes like it sometimes show.

"Jim, sometimes I don't get you at all."

Jerry's the kinda guy who's loaded at 4:30 on a Wednesday afternoon so he never asks nothing 'bout where I found Doris or what I'm doin' with her. We takes her down to the beach and teaches her to skip rocks and Jerry tells tales about huge river sharks and a fantasy land across the lake. Doris done stares up at him, all wide-eyed, and afterwards we eats fried perch and Jerry puffs a cigarette as we splits the mickey between us. Doris done screws up her nose at the smell and we laughs like we ain't never laugh before, but then she wants to know if we gots any marshmallows and I figure she's 'bout to start wailin' when we says we ain't. Instead, she puts on a brave face and stares right on into the fire. Pretty soon, Jerry done passes out in the sand.

"Are there really sharks out there?" she says, real quiet-like.

"Maybe a couple," I says. "Not too many."

"Can you swim?"

"Nah."

"Are you a dad?"

I grabs her 'round the waist and tosses her as far out into the water as I can. She done comes up, shrieking and flappin' her arms 'round like a banshee and I think maybe I done a real bad thing, so I go on out after her. Once she done stops screeching, I dunk her down again, all the way down to the bottom then back up for air. She's screaming again and then she's laughing and, when I lets her go, she pads over to the slick rocks.

"You so can swim," she says. "Liar."

After we comes out the water, I shows her how to lay her clothes out on the rocks so the sun can dry 'em out and then we dries ourselves off with some leaves. She fades off to sleep on Jerry's fat belly, but I sits up with the lasta the whiskey, listening to teenagers hollerin' on the other side the water.

I weren't planning on sleeping but realized I musta been when something warm drips on my arm. When I opens my eyes, it's a shivering Doris wearing nothin' but her little undies and lookin' real scared-like.

"Mister, where'd he go?"

I seen Jerry's piss puddle still glistenin' in the morning light, so know he ain't been gone long. The sun's up but not high, so I sets up with a pounding head and tells Doris to check if our clothes is dry yet. Hers is but my jeans is still soaked, so I carries her back to Amanda's apartment, wearing nothin' but a pair a boxer shorts, and soon pass right out on the couch.

Time I gets up again, it's past two and Amanda got Doris done playing backgammon. I pours myself some orange juice and coffee and figure I'm feeling pretty good 'bout myself since I never had no responsibility like what I got for Doris. I calls Amanda "Mama Bear," but she don't like that too much.

"Well, what we supposed to do with her?"

"Feed her, I guess."

"You should take her to the cops."

"Fuck the pigs." I laugh, but Amanda ain't join in.

"You found her."

"Yeah," I says. "I think it's a sign."

"I win," Doris squeals.

"Good job!" Amanda high-fives her, but she sounds so fake cheerful that it just reminds me how raggedy she been lookin' these days.

"I don't want to play this anymore," Doris says.

"What you want to do, sweetie?" Amanda's voice is all quiet and serious, like I never heard it in my life. "You want us to take you somewheres?"

"Disney World," Doris shouts.

"Disney World?" I says dumbly. "I ain't know 'bout Disney World."

"Disney World!"

She shouts it louder and damn if it don't make me flinch.

So that night after it done gets dark, I takes Doris down to the casino. She looks up all wide-eyed at the shimmering neon sign and asks if they got rides.

"Rolley coasters," I says. "You falls off and you ain't never walk straight again."

"I wanna see."

"They's adult rides," I says. "You gon' have to prove you's a grownup first."

Doris flexes her biceps and says she's a big girl, so I takes her by the hand and walks her to the store, where I buys a six-pack a beer and talk myself outta buying more smokes. Then I figures I ought a buy her a Nestle bar or something.

"I don't want ice cream, stupid," she says, all condescending-like. "I'm an adult now."

I gives up on that idea and head back out front, where I sets Doris down on the cinderblock and lets her drink the lasta my beer while I cracks another. They done towed the car since yesterday and all that's lefta the wreck is a few glass fragments in the light. Doris scrunches up her face at the taste of booze, but after she done drink it down, asks for more.

"Now the way this game works," I says, "is you chooses red or black. Then when the Ferris wheel done stop, you either win a prize or you gots to try again. And when you wins, it ain't a teddy bear. It's real cash money!"

"I'm gonna win," she says. "I'll win every time."

"Maybe," I says. "It ain't always that easy."

"I so will," she says. She scrunches up her face like she thinkin' real hard. "I'll do it right now. I pick red!"

I go on inside and puts the resta my winnings on red, but Doris ain't as lucky as she claims and I gots to come up with a different plan.

"Come on," I says. "I gots a new game for you. If you win this game, we's gonna get a nice prize."

"What prize?"

"We's gonna buy you lotsa teddy bears."

See, Amanda done told me in winter that Albert can't afford the heating bill, so she gots to climb onto a big ol' ladder and stuff up a big ol' vent with towels. I don't gots a ladder, but I gots Doris. I shows her how to shimmy up the wall of Albert's breakfast joint, then I tells her what to do once she gets on the roof.

"It's like hide-and-seek," I says.

"You're kinda dumb, you know?" she says, and, after that, I done keep my mouth shut.

She gets up on the roof all right, 'cept she has to belly-crawl along the shingles and her shirt gets all black from the dust. She gets the money out the register all right, too, but then she just can't figure how to open the door. I tries to show her to twist the lock, but she just stares at me with these sad, doey eyes. We still just standing there, looking at one another through the glass, when the alarm gets to blasting and I know we done fucked up.

It be almost evening next day when Amanda rustles up the bail money and comes pick me up. I ask what they done with Doris, but she ain't know.

"Foster care or juvie, probably." She shrugs and hands over a Native. "Maybe they even found her family."

"Guess so," I says, taking the smoke and feeling like a failure. "I done miss her already."

"Whatever you say," she says, looking through me like I ain't but nobody once again.

I figures she must be feelin' bad though, 'cuz she picks up Jerry from his hobo corner and buys us a couple forties. Then she drives us down to the beach, where Jerry builds a big ol' fire as we pass the bottles back and forth. When we gets down to the dregs, I says something 'bout how we's gonna have to replace Doris with one of our own someday.

Amanda hits me and peels into that belly laugh once more—'cept this time it don't bug me so much. I just puts my arm round her shoulder and lift the bottle to her lips as Jerry sits there across the fire, watching the sun comin' up on the water.

Author Bio

🐦 @DougieJays f /SimonBroder

A freelance writer from Toronto, Canada, Simon Broder features in *Blank Spaces, Chantwood Magazine,* and *EconoClash Review.* His award-winning middle-grade book, *Running The Point,* is now available on Amazon.

For more updates on his publications and blog, visit SimonBroder.com

A Fire Inside

By Sebastian Vice

Fire is passion. Fire is lust. Fire is creation in reverse.

Surrounded by pictures of burnt buildings and blackened corpses, a forest fire rages in my cock. Human skin burns at 118 degrees. At 162 degrees, tissue is destroyed and, beyond that, you become an aborted Icarus.

Industrial lubricant drenches my member. Blue, green, and red flames surround me. Fireality works to achieve orgasm. Images of enflamed deities swirl in my head.

Agni begs me to cum.

Logi chants battle hymns against Thor.

Sengen cries out.

My volcano erupts with the force of a thousand suns.

Once a sad orgasm defeats my erection, my windows glow. I see the house across the street burning like an effigy and my penis fills with blood. Women and children swarm the streets, peeping toms dwarfed by flame, staring at the house as if it's the second coming of Christ. Cops bumble around as firemen shoot their load all over the house.

My doorbell rings, and I throw on a crusting bathrobe.

"Hey, Maxi-Pad," Alexis says. "Join me for a closer look?"

My face cracks in disgust at the nickname. "No."

"You might see a dead body, though." She pauses, scratching her ass. "I got a joke. Been working on my comedy act and all that shit." She doesn't wait for my response. "Why did the priest fuck the nun?"

"Why?"

"He thought she was an altar-boy." Her laugher pierces the night, and she socks my arm. People turn to look. "C'mon, Maxi, that's funny."

During forest fires, trees sometimes explode. The water boils deep within its roots and turns to steam.

"Really? The joke fell flat?"

"I mean, it's alright. Kind of simp—"

"Whatever, Maxi-Pad. It's a good joke."

Given a reliable heat source in conjunction with stable oxygen and fuel, a house fire can double in size each minute. The right accelerant can increase its spread exponentially.

"Okay, Max, another one. Why was the nun's face covered in cum?"

"I'm sure it has something to do with a priest."

She grabs her stomach, laughing before the punchline. "The priest bent over and farted."

The Great Chicago Fire gets all the notoriety as the biggest reverse creation on October 8th, 1871, but the Peshtigo Fire in Wisconsin consumed 1,200 lives—not a puny 300.

"C'mon, Maxi," she says, "it'll be fun. Let's watch."

"Well, I would, but my dick is sad."

My life is one of quiet masturbation. On days my case worker fails to show up, or my court-appointed therapist forgets to shrink my head, there's no need to hide lighters, or oxygen tanks, or pretend I no longer purchase butane and glycerin. On these days, rainbows of flame and ash are mine, filling my basement with the fireworks of the gods.

Today, my case worker sits across from me, drinking coffee, but, knowing her, it's probably spiked with Irish cream. Her name is Karen and making jokes about it only riles her up. She doesn't see the irony in making the phrase "Karen" a slur like you hurl during a hate crime. She hates it even more when I ask how often she sucks cock.

She goes over my file, speaking of me in the third person. Sometimes, she gets off on tangents about failed boyfriends, or how her kids don't listen. The ear molestation gets old and all I can do is imagine her doused in gasoline.

"I'm required to ask if Max Cunningham started the house fire across his residence on Bradbury Street," she says.

Around 4,000 Americans die from fires each year, and most within the home. Those over 65 are especially at risk.

"Amateur hour," I say.

For violet flames, dissolve three parts potassium sulfate and one part potassium nitrate in alcohol. These are common enough ingredients found in fertilizers and stump removers. You can make your own too, or—if you're lazy—buy them from pyrotechnics stores.

Take the mixture, let a rope or candle wick soak it up, and let the gods sing when you set it ablaze.

"Given your history," Karen says, "You realize it looks suspicious."

Given my history, it's understandable she'd question me. However, my MO isn't house fires like this. A lackluster flame? No fun for me. Unless it paints the sky with a midnight rainbow, she's a castrated dog humping the wrong tree.

"You didn't do it?"

The house in question was built in the '70s, before highly flammable synthetic material. The woman who lived there was in her late 80s, and preferred slower-burning materials like cotton over polyester. It's estimated the house took 15 minutes to burn down. If she'd been younger, more with the times, it'd have been around three minutes.

"Max, this is serious. Did you—"

"A flame like that has Karenhood written all over it."

"You little shit."

"Kill yourself, Karen. The best part of you ran down your mother's leg."

She bursts into tears.

"If you need help, let me know."

My shrink moves through life like a rusted whale, hunched over his desk in a tan suit and a dye-job offensive to the color spectrum. Our sessions consist of DSM diagnostics, akin to a mechanic changing oil.

He is my hoop.

I'm his ring of fire.

He asks if I've had any dark thoughts lately.

I say, only of him engulfed in flames.

He asks if I'm religious.

I say, "Hell must be a nice place with all pyrotechnics."

My DSM list grows. One day, I'm depressed, another an anti-social personality disorder, whatever cocktail he can muster to submit to insurance companies.

The DSM, an instruction manual funded by the pharmaceutical industry, is useful for stripping citizens of their rights. Anyone could be DSMed if the shrink tries hard enough. Then again, his field is responsible for eugenics, a systematic denial of child sexual abuse, lobotomization, and—until the late '70s—classifying homosexuality as disturbed behavior.

Psychiatry, a 21st century Spanish Inquisition. I may not get the rack, just pills or electro-convulsion therapy. They say frying the brain is better than drilling holes in it.

"How are you managing fire abstinence?" he asks.

Psychiatric hospitals amuse me. Humans are social animals, as hardwired into us by evolution and documented in thousands of peer-reviewed articles and books.

Psychiatric facilities regularly isolate patients. Human rights organizations condemn solitary confinement in prisons, but it's seen as therapeutic in medical contexts.

"How's the wife?" I ask. Deflection is key.

"She left me, man." He pauses. "At least I got to keep my 100-inch plasma TV. Silver lining."

"How many more of these?" I ask.

He shifts in his chair. "You're not opening up to me. How's the medication?"

As long as I take the pills, it doesn't matter how I'm doing. Last month, he gave me Effexor, with the side-effects of confusion, tiredness, and erectile disfunction. Most anti-depressants lead to reduced sex drive, or an inability to achieve orgasm. He has me on Loxitane, ever since he DSMed me with schizophrenia. Possible side-effects include confusion, seizures, and irregular heartbeat.

These folks love drugs more than Keith Richards. The only difference is that Keith Richards holds societal value.

When dealing with educated morons, it's best to stick to the scripts, then wash the pills down the drain. These folks like comfortable illusions. He'd like to think most people never contemplate suicide, as though life is one of talking owls and cotton candy houses.

"The medications?" I ask. "Work great. Couldn't be better."

"That's wonderful news, Max." He's convinced I wet the bed, as that matches a condition that he DSMed me with.

As with medication, placation is best. "I haven't wet the bed all week."

"Mr. Cunningham," he says, "that's more great news. Our session is almost over. Any final thoughts you'd like to share?"

"I got a joke," I say. "Knock, knock."

"Who's there?"

"A washed-up quack who should've been aborted."

He scribbles on his pad. "And this joke is funny to you?"

"Hilarious," I say. "Seriously though, kill yourself."

The news says suicide rates are high. I say, not high enough.

Alexis greets me outside, dolled up in a Sunday dress. This means a tent revival has sprung up somewhere. This means she wants me to join her. This means I'll go from one babbling idiot to another, both selling delusions.

"Maxi-Pad," she says, "come with me."

"Why?"

"It's nice to have company." She pauses. "Hey, check this: Why did the priest retire?"

"Erectile disfunction?"

She laughs. "Not bad. But no. He ran out of altar boys."

"Do I really—"

"Just come with me. What else ya got planned? You'll probably just yank your dick. Do that later. C'mon, it'll be fun." She pauses, patting her side. "I decided to start carrying a gun."

"Why?"

"It's the 2nd Amendment."

"Just because you can doesn't mean you should."

"Shut up, Maxi-Pad. It's good for the soul. Let's go."

Folks at the tent revival spasm and twitch like a nonconsensual orgasm. The preacher rants and raves and reads out-of-context Bible verses. The crowd is mostly obese, gapping like braindead fish.

Alexis moves with the crowd, but insists we sit at opposite sides of the tent. I'd say this is my worst date, but that award goes to my grandmother, who took me home for cookies and a candle-lit blowjob. She said her lack of teeth made all the difference. I'd always stare into the roaring fireplace while she sucked.

This happened weekly—until she took a stumble down the stairs during a house fire. My parents cried at the funeral and cried during the eulogy. When asked to speak, I told the church she said she was the best cocksucker in town, and I hoped the Devil would rape her for all eternity.

My father gave me the belt when we got home.

Then the wrench.

"In Jesus' name, wash away the sins of this wicked world," the preacher says.

"Amen," the crowd answers.

"Preach, brother!" a gelatinous man says.

In college, Alexis majored in comparative religion, but to my eye she specialized in comparative sex. She'd ask the professor about the "erotic" parts of the Bible. She'd hunt for sexual passages in the Koran, Torah, and other holy books. One would think she'd be attracted to *The Kama Sutra*, but she said the book was boring.

Each session brought more questions. She asked why incest was immoral since Adam and Eve's offspring would have to fuck. She'd ask if the Red Sea was red from all the women having their periods.

"The gay agenda," the preacher howls, "wants you to believe sodomy is natural. Politicians saying otherwise are stooges of the Devil. God doesn't have mercy on sodomites. He will rain fire from the Heavens."

In *Biological Exuberance*, it's shown over the course of 700 pages how homosexuality can be found across most if not all animal kingdoms. The author even includes drawings of animals engaged in sodomy.

Alexis carries a leatherbound journal she dubs *Alexis' Bible*. She never shows me the inside, but tells me it's like any other Bible, except it only contains the best parts.

The revival ends prematurely when a snake bites the preacher in the face.

"Pretty wild, no?" Alexis asks, palming my genitals.

"Grabbing my penis?"

"No, ya goof. The preacher."

"Think he'll make it?"

"I hope not, but hey, there're always miracles."

Alexis says miracles happen every day. One day a man is broke, the next supermodels are blowing him. One day a preacher is denouncing faggotry, the next he's snorting coke off a gigolo's dick. God works in mysterious ways, so she says.

"You don't believe in miracles, I get it. But last week there was a 30-car pile-up and everyone died."

"How's that a miracle?"

"They all died, Maxi-Pad. How's it not a miracle?"

Alexis' God isn't one from the pulpit, or even one theologians defend. You won't find her God in the New Testament or Maimonides. She brags about getting into Harvard's Divinity School, but never explained why she dropped out. Maybe she didn't like their God, or maybe they didn't like hers.

"This is boring," Alexis says. "Imma go see when the next revival is."

Parrot fucker theory, shorthand for rule 34, states that for any fetish, there are at least 10 websites devoted to it. The same cannot be said for adult bookstores. Those places might not be the best way to satisfy an unusual fetish, but the sexual knowledge is invaluable. The films show what women like, what positions and toys they want. Given Alexis' increased interest in me, and my lack of sexual finesse, research is required.

Giant dildos line the wall of the store, as well as a few rubber fists and plenty of midget wieners called butt-plugs. Some bondage gear hangs from the wall, in addition to blowup dolls.

My grandmother said toothless blowjobs were the best, but the rubber fuck-my-faces contain teeth in the throat.

Women love cum on their faces, as the store contains volumes 1-7 of *Bukkake Bitches* and similarly drenched DVDs. Odd, but who am I to argue with pornographic knowledge?

The clerk pops gum. Piercings pepper her face.

"These dolls any good?" I ask.

She peeks from her magazine. "Buddy, how the fuck would I know?"

Upon leaving the store empty-handed, I see a poster stapled to a pole:

Doused in Flame: A Rammstein Cover Band
8-9:30PM, Matthew's Bar and Grill
And YES, there WILL be a fiery finale!

Rammstein doesn't do much for me. They're too German and therefore too Nazi, but I own all their DVDs. If you fast-forward through the German bullshit, the finisher will make you cum with the force of a thousand forest fires.

Returning home, I phone Alexis. "I got a date idea."

"Another pyro convention?"

"No. A Rammstein cover band."

"Oh, I saw the flyer. Lame. There's a tent—"

"Jesus fucking Christ."

"Hey," she says. "Let me write that down. A drawing of Jesus fucking a guy named Christ. Oh, I might also draw—"

"This is important to me."

"But the tent—"

"Oh, fuck the tent." I throw the phone.

If she ever saw my therapist, he'd DSM her with a conduct disorder, or maybe female sexual arousal disorder.

Most people know about kleptomania and pyromania from the DSM. My primary diagnosis is the latter, but my fireality stems from sexual arousal, and it's not about impulse control. My being, my fireality, is a philia.

Watching the opening bands makes me order extra drinks. The first two acts dress as women with too much hair spray. If they had pyrotechnics, the shows would be much better. Perhaps they could've become human candles.

While downing my fifth beer, Doused in Flame enters, looking like skinheads. The singer uses autotune, so he doesn't need skill. He's already riding off the original Rammstein, who "inspired" the Columbine massacre.

Doused in Flame gained notoriety several years ago by being booed off stage and lighting the drumkit on fire. They paid a fine, did a brief stint in jail, and bars forgave them. It's not a school shooting, but controversy, like death from smoking, is paid in installments.

Towards the end of their set, the lead singer puts on a flame-retardant suit. My penis hardens like an oak tree. He becomes a wicker man.

There's panic, the trick not going as planned. People push passed me as sprinklers soak the room. Through the screams, and delicious smoke, someone shouts, "He's burning alive!" If controversy is paid in installments, perhaps this is their final one.

Heading for the bathroom to rub one out, I'm stopped by a security guard who orders me to evacuate.

Flooding the street, retard screams pierce my ears.

Alexis calls for me. "Sorry I'm late. What happened?"

Sperm fills my pants. My shrink would DSM me with premature ejaculation disorder. "Why'd you show up?"

"Well, Maxi-Pad," she says, "you've been a champ coming to the tent revivals. Figured I'd surprise you."

"Okay."

"I got a joke. Why did the priest cross the road? To stop the altar boy from going to the cops!"

"For a religious woman, you sure have a lot of priest rape jokes."

"Who said I'm religious?"

Alexis prowls for tent revivals like a junkie looking for a dirty needle, and when none are available, she settles for a church. Usually then, I pass the time DSMing the Pentecostals. Reptile fetishists suffering from psychosis. That's my best guess.

Each time we go, it feels like a date, but she insists we sit apart. At one, I was sandwiched between two morbidly obese men, their necks blending in with their torsos. Sometimes, I'd pitch a movie or dinner date, but Alexis always insisted on these religious meetings. For someone not religious, she'd be DSMed with a fetish of sorts.

"Hey," she says, "there's a midnight mass at St. Thomas Cathedral."

"I'm tired, and not in the mood after Doused in Flames."

"I'll make it worth your wild." She pulls on my hand. "Trust me, you'll thank me after. Things will start making sense."

The church reeks of incense and death. Alexis makes a joke about the crucifix looking homoerotic. I know the drill. She sits at one end, me at another.

As I go to my side, she says, "No. Sit by me today."

We head for the back, away from the elderly folk, as the priest drones on in Latin.

When the time comes where everyone kneels, she whispers, "Hey, Maxi, this is the perfect cocksucking position."

I hardly hear her, focusing on the priest. He looks familiar, but different. Older. Once my eyes land on his facial scar, memories surge back: My folks took me here as a boy, and Father Francis made me an altar boy. My parents were pleased when he took an interest in me and bragged to the neighbors. My father never said, "I love you," until he saw me as an altar boy. He'd say, "I'm proud of you, son."

The altar boy dates were probably the worst. I showed Pops my bloody underwear. He gave me the belt and told me not to be so disgusting or spread rumors of faggotry. He said to be grateful the priest picked me, and that the church helps the family.

More memories: The coroner's report listed my father's death as accidental, specifically, death from autoerotic asphyxiation. It would have been suicide if I hadn't burned the note, inserted a dildo up his ass, and threw a *Playboy* at his feet. My mother couldn't take it and drowned herself in alcohol. On my 18th birthday, I found her dead, pill bottles littering the floor. She left me the house in her will. Paid in full.

Alexis grabs my hand, slides it up her dress. Her vagina radiates heat. Images of house fires swirl in my head. "Finger me."

I recoil, but she clutches.

"Please, I need this."

As my fingers rub her clit, she moans, louder with each stroke. First gentle, then harder. People look, but she coaxes me on. She cums with a howl and throws my slick hand back.

"Excuse me," the priest says, "what's going on back there?"

"Not committing sex crimes," she says.

"Excuse me, miss?"

"You heard me! Did more than that. Raped me on the altar and threatened to kill me if I told." She pauses, looking around the church. "I was seven, you fuckin' cocksucker." She stands. "Listen y'all, this fucker is a pedophile. He shamed me. Made me feel dirty. Took me 15 years to come back here. And I know I'm not the only one."

"Young lady," a woman says, "this is a respected—"

"Fuck you, cunt. I want everyone to know he's a rapist."

"He did the same to me," I say. "For over a year." As if possessed, I run up to the altar, grab him by the throat. Before either of us know what's happening, I break his nose. "Called me a faggot, remember?" I punch him again, grab a crucifix, aflame with a once-extinguished dream. "Bend over. Drop your pants."

It takes an effort and several gasps not just from him, but the crucifix fits his ass perfect. He cries and begs, "Please."

"Who's the faggot now? Take it like a man. Remember telling me that?" I jam deeper. "Remember threatening to burn my house down? You ruined my fuckin' life."

The church-goers who aren't scared stiff by the scene are by Alexis's gun. The miracle of the 2nd amendment. "Don't even fuckin' think about it," she snarls. "Sit the fuck down. Y'all had no problem letting this happen to us or the thousands the Vatican shrugged off. Y'all made your bed so *lie in it*."

They watched, and I took my time. For the first time in 13 years, I felt alive. I wager it was the first time his ass fell out, too.

The church empties as we sit outside, the priest unable to walk. Alexis says miracles happen every day. Maybe she's right.

"I love you, Max."

Flames can be born from ice. Smooth a slab of ice into a lens and use it like a magnifying glass. This trick has prevented many Donner Parties for those stranded in cold climates.

"Max, I love you."

Fire in crematoriums burns between 1,400-1,800 degrees. An oxyacetylene welding torch, on the other hand, composed of concentrated oxygen and acetylene, burns at over 5,500 degrees. If you don't wear protective gear, the light from the torch will burn the eyes from your sockets.

She hugs me, bringing her lips to mine. "I love you. I'm sorry for what he did to you."

"Did you know?"

"I knew you were an altar boy," she says. "Not a hard deduction."

"Nobody believed me."

She pulls me closer. "I know."

"I love you, too... Hey, Alexis," I say.

"Yeah?"

"Please don't call me Maxi-Pad anymore."

She laughs. "Sure thing, man. Let's burn this motherfucker down."

"I think the priest is still alive in there somewhere."

"I know, pretty cool, right? I keep saying: Miracles happen every day."

With the church ablaze, painting the sky, Alexis reads from her Bible while I eat her pussy. She yanks my hair and bucks her hips as she comes. We retreat to the woods to watch the fire trucks follow cop cars.

"Alexis," I say, "I got a joke. I think you'll like it."

Alexis kisses my cheek. "I cornered the market on pedophile priest jokes, yo."

"Nah, you'll like this one." I clear my throat. "It's called The Nun and The Bus Driver. I heard this back in middle school."

"Okie dokie."

"A man enters a bus and notices a hot nun. He sits next to her and says he wants to fuck her. She slaps him, calls him a pervert, and changes seats."

"I like where this is going."

"So, after a while, the man is about to get off at the last stop. The driver stops him and says he knows how to bang the nun: to show up decked out like Jesus, at her convent at midnight. 'If she thinks you're Jesus, who she's been saving herself for, she'll fuck you.' Now, the man is skeptical, but—"

"Good lord, how long is this?"

"Alexis," I say, "please."

"It better be good."

"Anyway, midnight rolls around, and the man's dressed like Jesus. He's got the robe, long wig, and fake beard. He raps on her chamber door and announces he's Jesus, there to rapture her in the flesh. She invites him in, but says she's a virgin and taken a vow of celibacy. However, she's open to anal sex. So, the man rams her asshole and, midway through, rips off the beard and wig. He goes, 'A-ha! I'm the guy from the bus.' Then the nun takes off her mask and goes, 'A-ha! And I'm the bus driver!'"

"Holy shit, Max!" Alexis laughs, "That ain't bad."

We can never return home after this blaze of glory, yet my only regret is that the fire is a bit boring, too small and lacking in casualties, something a Karen might do.

Alexis says she stole the communion plate money and knows a guy who forges passports. She says, "Mexico sounds nice. Mexico could wash away memories."

She cracks a few more one-liners and we laugh as firemen snuff the inferno. In that moment, peace ensues, as if the world has devolved into smoke, leaving only Alexis and me with the gods.

"C'mon, Max," she says. "We got a forger to meet."

Author Bio

@Sebastian_Vice /OutcastPress

Founder of Outcast Press (through which this book
is published), Sebastian Vice specializes in transgressive
fiction and dirty realism. His poetry and short fiction can
be found in *Punk Noir Magazine* and *Close to the Bone*.
He is currently working on his debut novel, *Heaven's
Tourist* expected to release in 2022, and his second novel,
Driver for 2023.

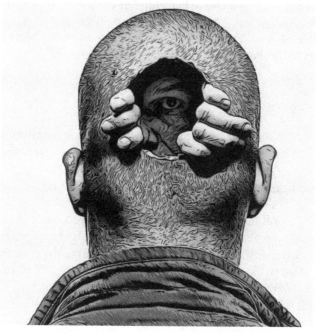

His short story, "One Last Good Day," as featured on *A
Thin Slice of Anxiety,* has been nominated for Best Of The
Net 2021 (Fiction)

The Secret Smile

By Emily Woe

I'm not sure when it all started. But I remember this day vividly. It was the first time Jess truly annoyed me.

I was just... tapping my pencil on the desk while studying her dark, glistening hair from the back of the classroom.

With one arm raised, Jessica The Prissy Bitch was correcting the professor on his use of the word "effect." It was the third time during his lecture on ecological processes that she'd interjected. The professor was becoming irate. I could tell by the way he flexed the fist in his pocket and pressed his lips when she spoke. He must have wanted to grab her by the throat, knock her on the ground and choke her until her eyes went still. I fully understood where he was coming from, because Jess somehow evoked those feelings in me that day, too. My body became tense every time she spoke, and my heart was... racing.

"God, I hated her for making me that uncomfortable, but how could I possibly hate someone who I barely even knew?"

Vance, my would-be lawyer, put down his pen and leaned back, arms crossed. "Did you tell anyone else this?"

"You mean tell the cops? Why in the fuck would I do that?" Lord, fuck me! This guy was old and couldn't have been more than a year away from retirement. If I had any money, I'd probably stand a chance. "Listen, am I wasting my time here?" I stood up in the dingy, cold, blue room and paced. "I researched your record but couldn't find any wins in a case such as this. Do you think there is any shot at you winning?"

"You think I'd waste my time coming here just to ruin my record?" Vance rubbed his silver eyebrows. "Listen, kid, I already know four lawyers have passed on your case, and your case is extremely high profile, so even a loss means something, but... the only way I can see winning is if you tell me the story in full detail—the REAL story, even if the details make you seem guilty." Not only did Vance's voice give away his age and his smoking habits, but his weight, too.

"What if the details prove what a shit hole I am?"

"You think I give a flying fuck?" Vance coughed. "You tell me everything and I will try to find clues in your story that may help. So, again..." Vance grabbed his pen and let the notepad rest on his lap. "Explain to me why you hated the bitch."

I had the story memorized by now, but not the real one. Perhaps, for once, I just needed to get it off my chest. Vance looked like the kind of lawyer who had seen it all. I could have murdered the bitch, skinned her alive, then fed her remains to her family at Sunday brunch and he wouldn't have flinched. He was exactly the kind of lawyer I needed. A low-life asshole who only cared about one thing: winning.

I pulled the chair back, sat and rubbed my face as I prepared to tell this stranger absolutely everything. "H-Have you ever met a person—or a girl—and you just knew they'd be trouble?"

Vance gave me a dead stare.

"That was fucking Jess. There was always something off about her, something that bothered me. I thought it was the fact that her family was rich, and she was a preppy, irritating bitch but there was... I don't know, something else. She always wore sweaters with skirts which always seemed odd. I mean, was she always hot *and* cold? Was she a prude or a flirt? Who the fuck knew with her. What I did know was that she was an extremely presumptuous, self-righteous, manipulative bitch, and that," I pointed at Vance, "turned out to be true."

The class dismissed, finally ending my misery, and Jess gathered her books and satchel. I stayed seated, my pencil still tapping away. Usually, I wouldn't even notice her. I had no time for such obnoxious girls, but she wouldn't stop doing... *it*.

Suddenly—and this is important—Jess looked over her shoulder and held my stare. It only lasted a second, but it burned deep—and then she walked away.

That! I asked myself. Why did she keep doing *that*?

"Doing what, exactly?" Vance asked, puzzled.

"I don't know. She would just stare at me, smile, then walk away or ignore me. I didn't know what the fuck she wanted!"

"So, you're saying she was flirting?"

"NO! It's like— She was coaxing me into something."

I always waited 'til every student left the classroom to gather my things. Then I'd make my way to the next stop in that glorified daycare: statistics.

I would sigh every time I turned the corner because I knew what to expect. As always, Jess would be there, surrounded by her Summa Cum Laude friends and her strait-laced boyfriend. He was a law major, had to be. His father was some asshole politician, a good-for-nothing liar. They all are.

Anyways, it disgusted me to be anywhere near them. So, I developed this weird habit, a tick of sorts. "One. Two. Three," I'd whisper as I walked by them, as if to remind myself that the discomfort would only last that long, but—like clockwork—Jess would look up at me and smile, then tuck a lock of hair behind her ear.

I always ignored her and kept walking, always. I thought I knew what the game was about. She wanted me or my attention, but she wasn't my type.

"Wait, why wasn't she your type?" Vance lifted an eyebrow, confused I wasn't attracted to everyone else's plastic idea of beauty.

I shrugged my shoulders and scrunched my face as if the idea of fucking her didn't intrigue me in the slightest. "I don't like gathering attention, and she was popular, extremely popular. It wasn't my scene. Plus, I've always found that crowd to be fake, judgmental, and lacking in depth. Not to mention extremely aggravating."

Vance cocked his head and rubbed his double chin.

Whatever. Think what you want, dickhead. "Regardless," I continued, "I became curious about her intentions. So, during a class one day, I said, 'Hi, Jess.' But you know what that bitch did? She simply looked at me, rolled her eyes, and walked away."

I waved my cuffed hands.

"You know what pisses me off the most, though, Vance?" I slammed my cuffs and arms on the metal table. "It was how surprised I was by her reaction. It fucking irked me that for a moment I was convinced she liked me—as if gold-diggers like her are even capable of such feelings!"

A month later, however, I went to a party—some frat house. Again, not my scene but there was someone there I took an interest in, someone *my* type. A dirty faux-redhead named Alia. Rumor had it, she'd been around the block a bit and was also hot, so I watched her. She was extremely drunk or high, likely a combination of both, so when the party was dwindling, I got lucky. She was leaving alone.

Alia grabbed her car keys and went out the front door. I walked out after her and onto the porch when *guess who* fucking cockblocks me? Fucking Jess. She finally decided to say hi. I don't remember what we talked about, but it was some goddamn annoying shit about homework. The conversation lasted a total of maybe two minutes and—as soon as a friend showed up—Jess gave me the cold shoulder. If she wasn't so well-known, I would've broken a beer bottle, shoved it into her face and pushed her straight off that porch. Try smiling through stitches, bitch.

Anyways, when class started up again, it was the same routine with Jess. Her over-the-shoulder stare after class. Then "One. Two. Three." The same secret smile in the hallway.

You know, after a month of that she was driving me mad, and my anxiety-triggered twitches became worse. However, I kept my cool, doubled up on meds, partied, fucked, and made life tolerable again.

Months later, however, midterms came around and I needed to study. My scholarship required me to maintain a 3.0 GPA or above so, as you know, I took my grades seriously.

Dorms were always a messy distraction, and the campus library was massive, so I made my way to a quiet table towards the back.

I was there for maybe two hours, and the words were beginning to blur together when, straight across the library, guess who I saw? Jess, with her preppy argyle sweater and pleated skirt. She was sitting next to a girl I knew, a girl I recently fucked. My marks still clearly visible on her neck.

How sweet, I thought, the cold bitch is tutoring her whore of a friend.

Tutoring didn't seem like her style, which once again made me question her actions, but I couldn't let her distract me.

I tried to continue studying, I really did, but knew *it* was coming... It was only a matter of time before Jess would acknowledge me, and—not to sound cocky, but I did look my best that day. I had worn this dark blue sweater, which women have mentioned really worked off my eyes, and the black jeans that matched my dark hair... and heart, a few have said.

Anyways, around 10, I looked up and Jess was gone. I sighed but wasn't sure if it was from relief or disappointment. Either way, I made my way out of the library, knowing they would soon be closing, when—out of nowhere—I felt the heat of her stare on the nape of my neck.

My heart raced and my feet became like lead.

I looked over, and down at the end of an aisle of bookshelves, Jess smiled at me. She tucked a lock of hair behind her ear and walked away.

I threw my head back, incensed. I knew I shouldn't, but this... whatever the fuck game this bitch was playing? It was Going. To. Fucking. End.

Jess was searching through romance books when I found her.

"Hey!" I called, indignant, but she ignored me. I approached and decided to shift gears, flirt a bit: "You know, Jess..." I placed an arm on the bookcase in front of her, blocking her. "...saying something would get you further than just staring. I don't bite... Well, usually." I grabbed the book she was looking at and, seeing it was terrible, placed it back on the shelf.

"Why?" She looked up at me, full of contempt. "I have absolutely nothing to say to someone like you." And trust me, her harsh words did not match her flirty demeanor.

"Someone like me, eh?" So, she knows. "I'm confused." I squinted. "Don't you have a boyfriend?"

"Yes. So? Go away." She shot me a smug look. "I said, shoo!" And then she swatted me away like a fucking insect!

God, I was mad! But I rolled my eyes and simply walked away. Told myself she wasn't worth the trouble.

However, the warmth of her stare was on me, gouging and singeing a hole through my fucking back. My eye twitched and my breathing became labored. I swung back around to meet her equally determined stare. Okay, Jess, you want to play? Let's play.

Jess ran back for her purse on the table, but I swiftly placed a hand over her mouth and dragged her a few feet back, away from view and behind a bookcase.

She gave a pathetic yelp, but I hushed in her ear and when she noticed the cold metal of a pocketknife on her neck, she went silent.

"Yes, quiet, Jess," I whispered, "you wouldn't want to ruin that expensive sweater now, would you?" Hungry to feel her frantic heartbeat, I dragged my hand just under her naked breast. Her heart was pounding, and it was... magical. "You're not even wearing a bra, Jess. Is this what you wanted?"

She shook her head.

Aw, too bad, Jess. My hand, the one with the knife, traveled down her trembling body to her smooth legs and then up her skirt. "I saw the way you two looked at me. You and your promiscuous friend." I whispered, "So you know about my reputation on campus and *yet*, you choose to play with fire. *Why?*" I spat.

Her eyes watered but she stayed silent.

"Is it 'cause you're jealous, Jess? Wondering why I want to rape everyone but you?"

She moaned.

"Just so we're clear, princess." I pressed the knife harder against her porcelain skin yearning for blood. "*I* do the hunting. I'm not hunted. Understood?"

She barely nodded.

Without warning, I dragged her into a private study and locked the door. "Sit," I instructed as I undid my jeans.

"Wait! ...No, please, I'm a virgin!" She put up her hands and pleaded for mercy, but there were no tears in her eyes. She was fucking lying, and it was then that I promised myself— regardless of the location—that I was going to make her cry.

I approached her and put my hand around her neck. "That's a pity, princess, because this... This is going to hurt like Hell!" Gripping her neck, I slammed her down on the table.

Her eyes teared up as I ripped off her underwear.

Of course, they weren't cheap, or easy to tear through, so surely, the force left a mark. A beautiful pink mark.

"Stop!" She screamed when I forced her legs open.

"I'll make a deal with you, princess," I said, leaning over and whispering into her ear. "If you're quiet, I'll be gentle. You start making too much noise though, and well, I'll have to silence you. So, unless you want to die tonight, you have to be quiet." My eyes bored into hers.

Her wide eyes finally expressed the fear I was hoping for. It was clear she wasn't expecting me to kill her, and I'd never killed before, but she could be an exception.

"You can do that, can't you?"

She didn't respond, just laid back, barely shaking.

No, no, no I thought, *no*. This was too easy; it was hardly a fight! Infuriated, I used all my force to ram straight into her. She muffled a scream and I said, "*Whoops*. I thought I asked you to be quiet, princess." Ha.

"And you find that shit funny?" Vance broke his silence.

I wiped the grin off my face. "Honestly, yes. The bitch deserved it... and it's what she wanted."

Vance had seemed interested in my story up until now.

Pity, for a moment, I could have sworn he was enjoying it too.

"Did she ever say she wanted it?"

I rolled my eyes. "Do bitches *always* have to spell it out for you?"

Vance looked down at his notes, then rubbed his chin. I could sense he was done here, just like all the others.

"Now I ask you, Vance, do you want me to continue, or do you want to find another client? You wanted honesty and that's what I'm giving you."

Vance took a deep breath and unbuttoned his old gray suit as he contemplated.

I put a hand up. "Hey, if it helps, I promise you I'm getting somewhere."

Vance grabbed the remote off the metal table and pressed play on the mounted TV. The video was silent, but there I was... in the small room, grabbing her by the hair and lifting her off the table only shove myself into her from behind.

Vance didn't react. It was as if he'd seen the video a dozen times before.

Completely emotionless, he paused the video, and pointed at the TV to ask, "Here, what are you saying here?"

He pressed play and I watched carefully, remembering the moment. The smell of her hair, her wetness dripping onto the table, and the salty taste of her tears when I licked them after.

"I was saying, 'This is what you wanted. This is what you begged for, what you deserve. You stupid... fucking... cunt." I cocked my head and grinned as I watched him study me in action.

Clearly, he was interested in that particular part of the video.

"Fucking virgin, my ass."

"How soon after this were you arrested?"

"That's what I'm getting at, Vance."

After the midterm, the professor picked up everyone's exam and yet I sat there, in the back of the classroom, waiting for *it*.

Then, there it was again, Vance, the same over-the-shoulder stare.

Then in the hallway walk.

The same secret smile.

But her smile was different that day. Full of satisfaction. Grinning from ear to ear like the fucking Cheshire cat!

I walked outside, knowing something was wrong. I had always been careful and, for the first time, I was worried that Jess had caused me to slip, but, just as I debated leaving campus...

One.

Two.

Three.

"Sir, you are under arrest. You have the right to remain silent..."

Vance sat quietly for several seconds.

I was expecting him to say something, anything!

"Don't you see it?" I banged my fist against the table.

"See what, exactly? That you raped this girl and many others on campus?"

"No! She— She set me up! She knew about the camera!"

Vance stood, put his hands in his pocket, and shook his head. "No one is going to buy that. Perhaps your defense should be about your meds or stres—"

"But it's the truth! There has to be video surveillance at the school proving everything I just said, how she taunted me into doing it, how she smiled the next day in class and the hallway! She did this on purpose!"

"On purpose?" Vance stopped pacing and looked at me, dumbfounded. "You expect this to be your defense? That a young lady from a good family would risk her life and coax you to rape her? For what exactly? We need a motive!"

"I don't know, to avenge her friends or— or for the fame? Her Instagram exploded! She's had numerous reporter interviews!"

"True." Vance stood with his back away from me, thinking.

"Vance," I said calmly, "I just need you to find evidence of this."

Vance came back and sat. "Even if I do, there are a slew of women who are willing to testify against you."

"All of which have pasts, Vance! They were all known whores on campus, women who no one would take seriously! All of them riding on the fame Jess mustered up from all this."

"God, you are insane," Vance muttered under his breath as he rubbed his ringed eyes. "I don't think blaming the victim is the right angle here."

I stood and paced. Somehow, his words had bothered me. I placed a hand on the wall and lowered my head, thinking: Was there really a way out of this?

No, there wasn't.

It was fun while it lasted. The game? Jess won. This was checkmate. But I refused to lose without a fight, at the very least, I needed to let Vance know I wasn't delusional about my circumstance. If I couldn't win them all...

"Listen... I don't expect to walk." I stared at the walls of my new home. "I'm guilty of a lot of things. If the evidence is strong, I'll admit to them, but Vance, I need you to help me make the world see the truth here." I looked back at him. "Jess framed me; this is the truth. And the world needs to know that she's lying her ass off!" I walked toward Vance. "I will proudly go to jail for things *I have* done." I pointed at myself. "But I refuse to let that fucking cunt play the victim on TV another day!"

One.

Two.

Three.

Vance: "There was no camera in the classroom. And the hallway? A blind spot."

One.

Two.

Three.

TV reporter: "The alleged Dempson College serial rapist, Cal Thompson, was found guilty earlier today for the rape of Jessica Kennedy. Though Thompson admitted to sexually assaulting at least eight other students, he proceeded to proclaim his innocence after sentencing, exclaiming that he was framed. Thompson then tried to lunge at the victim but was immediately restrained by police. Today, students at Dempson College and their families can rest at ease, knowing that the culprit is now behind bars."

Author Bio

🐦 @MLeeWoeber

Emily Woe ran away from an abusive, religious household at the tender age of 17. Today, she is co-founder of Outcast Press (through which this book is published) and owns InterestCircle.com (an up-and-coming social media site where writers and artists can gather and collaborate.) "The Secret Smile," featured in this anthology, was born out of her obsession with serial killer documentaries.

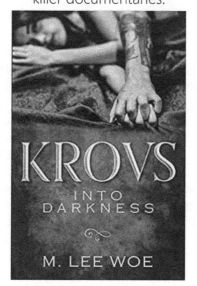

Woe is also the author of *The Krovs Trilogy.* If you're interested in a dark and twisted romance, book one, *KROVS: Into Darkness,* is available for purchase at: www.M-Lee.us

Sunder

By Craig Clevenger

John Doe #17 lands staring up at the blue yonder he'd just fallen from, getting his eyes cooked and awaiting whichever Boatman draws the short straw to rope up, drop down, and hoist him from the gulch floor. Ever you think the dead might ought to consider your sorry-ass backache during descent, you just begging Mr. Tick Tock to clock-block you at the top of your shift, so you're on sloth time for the next nine hours. Turns a brush fire into a lava lamp and you can count a hummingbird's wing beats, you lucky enough working the River to see anything that's alive or that pretty. Which you won't. Believe elsewise, might as well believe you're on water for real, forget this place ain't been but dust and drought since God split light from dark. Making peace with that piece of truth next yesterday is the only way to stay sane on the River.

Working the River is half search-and-rescue and half crime scene hunt-and-gather, but the first half's coming too late and the second won't ever see trial. Shit, a Boatman could string that yellow barricade tape double-wise around the equator, make the whole planet off-limits during investigation, and tell every man, woman, and child on Earth not to leave town. Day comes we got flying cars and Christmas dinner in a pill, Sheriff still won't have no leads. And after the last living parrot squawks the last human word, the sun goes black, and the Earth turns to ice, every John Doe and Jane Doe file will still be open.

Worst of the job is how locals take you for a windowpane, look right through you. Like it's a question of when some bird bashes full throttle into your chest. Best, you a sore sight for bright eyes or worst, you straight up invisible. Not worth the swipe of a hat brim 'less they getting an itch scratched back of their head with a gun barrel. Truth up, nobody wants to touch a Boatman or wants you touching them. You handle the dead with them hands. Chalk it up to some sanitation fixation, on account of they don't get how germs work. But us Boatmen? We all eat with these hands, brush our teeth, live. Until one day it hits you, can't recall the last time anyone offered a hand. Backtrack in your head for scraps: handshake, backslap, shoulder punch, anything. 'Less it's from another Boatman, you come up empty.

That lead block in your chest is hunger from your skin-starved skin, your own blood-leather rotting for contact. Ain't just for want of a good fuck like everyone says, though you won't hear any complaints. But you need eyes and breath and a heartbeat, reminders that we all cut from the same God, because working the River is daily evidence elsewise.

No surprise then, there's mingling among the crew. Any other gig, that's a one-way ticket to a human resources sit-down, next stop: the door. Above board, the Shop ain't no different since we're on the county payroll. Reality's another story, a point of fact unspoken but one we all know. You get partnered with someone, everyone looks away, and nobody whispers or makes jokes. Truth up.

Take Leigh. She rides shotgun with me, a real pro. We'd been together a couple times, just weren't together. A couple of nights (one early morning, still dark, it makes any difference) when that black weight was the same for both of us, knotting up limbs in the dark, pulling each other closer, like maybe we squeezed hard enough, we could touch hearts. Matter of time, though, any Boatman will tell you, when being together won't be enough for one of us.

Keeping your wits on the River means keeping to the Boatman's Code. Break the Code and *you* break, simple as that. Code says treat every Passenger like they're alive. Leastwise, you handle them like they got loved ones going to queue up to pay their respects, which you know they don't. Not in this universe. All the same, you respect their humanity, but you can't give them names. Ain't on us to tell them who they are, who they were. Stake your perimeter, take your pictures, then come boarding time, you and your partner do a three-count with the Passenger onto the gurney, another into the van, another back out, and one last time onto that metal table before bidding them safe passage: "Thank you for falling to your death from out of nowhere in Puerta Roja County. We hope you enjoyed your screaming plummet to the ground. The furnace is now at a cruising temperature of 1,700°. Please, keep your arms and legs inside the afterlife at all times. Your Divine Creator will be along to explain Him- or Herself shortly."

Check it: We are not monsters. Passengers are straight-up due recognition. You christen a Passenger off the books, good on you. Means you got something elsewise than engine coolant pumping through your veins. But truth up, a Passenger's got more coming than what one Boatman can bring to the embalming table. And slapping a Beauregard or Cheyenne on a John Doe or Jane Doe comes too easy, even with some make-believe toe tag what's only in your head. Rookie Boatman liable to think the rest just as quick.

It ain't. But make it a habit, give yourself warm feather pillow memories what ain't never happened, then you got to keep soundless about it, elsewise locals think your right mind made up some story about going out for smokes, left you alone at the kitchen table for good.

First one of us to break the Code was the very Boatman who wrote it, I shit you negative. And truth up, that same dude was the one who nicknamed us Boatmen, christened our desert the River. First generation, he trained the rest of us. But day came when deputies dragged his bare ass from the crematorium, kicking and screaming. Boatman said he was authorized, said he had a key. Which he did, you count a crowbar. They'd found him on his hands and knees, sorting uncrushed bones barely cooled from the day's burn. Said he had to separate Phyllis from Darrel, or they couldn't rise on Judgment Day.

We cleaned out his locker, turned up a banded stack of John Doe and Jane Doe head shots thick as the Word of God. Backside of each, he'd a name: Stephen. Donald. Patrick. Rhonda. Samantha. Marjorie. Carl. Danny. Diana. Anything and everything but John Doe or Jane Doe.

They threatened to shut us down after that. County suits flexing their cufflinks, all press conference and no bite. One of us bound to ask, "You think the dead just going to stop falling? Or guess you figured out where they been falling from, that it?" Then maybe we graph the numbers, plot the curve they all pretend ain't real, ain't climbing to that event horizon predicted by none other than Hopper Zero himself. Crazy-ass half-gimp hermit crunched the full Hawking with them first three Passengers who fell from the clear blue, reckoned the coming day when the sky would sunder—his word, *sunder*—and the dead would rain down on all us.

They backed off right quick.

They can go fuck themselves. To comport oneself as a chaperone to the afterlife, treating each Passenger with respect and accepting them as unknown but not unnamed, is the upper limit to what any of us can offer. Ain't enough love and compassion in one Boatman's lone heart to make everything right for one Passenger, much less the coming legions. Believe elsewise and you'll be sorting ashes bare-assed yourself, hoarding bootleg morgue snapshots like some Manson family Christmas album. Or worse. So, it's Jane Doe or John Doe. Never Jane and John Doe, unless you got evidence that they're a couple. Which you won't, not ever. Passengers always arrive alone.

But we all slip. The best Boatman's still human, same as any civilian. Like the afternoon we'd been dispatched to a Passenger—that year's Jane Doe #6—and it was Leigh's turn to write it up (working for the county means our forms got forms, like you need to request permission in triplicate to request permission). She's doing the legs-not-back squat with maybe some underthinking thrown in to check for ligature marks (routine but always negative, same as tox screens and any trauma, pre- or post-), and she brushes the backside of two fingers against Jane Doe's room-temperature ankle.

Common sense calls for some latex between your hands and your Passenger, never mind how your own blood-leather gets skin-sick for want of being wrapped in somebody else. Last thing anyone as sad as a Boatman needs is miswiring his or her own circuits with the touch of another who's already breathed their last. But Leigh hadn't gloved up yet, so we're talking blood-leather *on* blood-leather here and truth up, you never felt cold like a human being gone 72°.

A touch like that'll make a proper civilian recoil, but skin-sick blood-leather like what ails us Boatmen, could be contact with a Passenger gets you thinking that's what you hungry for. That's when brushing your teeth means staring at a perfect stranger, like maybe you shrink-wrapped inside the wrong human so tight you can't breathe, so you got to cut your way out of that stranger who's squeezing your outsides and that's what you do.

But Leigh, she plays it like she don't notice—who knows, maybe she doesn't—so I go along. But come to load Jane Doe #6 into the van, we catch eyes on the down drop and that half-second pause where we pretend nothing happened, it stretches in lava lamp time. We ain't fooling nobody, least of all each other. Drove 70 miles back to the Shop (nothing's close to anything around here), both of us wordless the return leg. Like the radio dial was wired to shock anyone who touched it. Whole way's like watching a house on fire, frame and floors getting weaker, the place near to collapse. But ain't a house, and it's all happening inside Leigh's chest and whatever I mutter from misfired goodwill is just more weight on what can already barely hold upright.

That was the first time I stayed the night with her. And truth up, it's been more than a couple times. Having someone not recoil at the sight of me, at what I do, that changes my world. Same for Leigh. Folks try to hide it, but we all know. Like when you cross paths with some civilian coming opposite, they step aside, hold the door, and give you their sweeping upturned palm. "After you." Making polite what's really straight-up fear and repulsion. Four-way stop sign, maybe a dozen altogether inside the county line, and you got a blind man's chance in a burning corn maze of ever seeing another driver.

But, if you do, they sure to wave you on if they know what you are. We all learned to park out of sight with the county rig, keep civilian threads on hand. That taco stand cashier whose voice ain't yet dropped but thinks he can dupe the schoolyard girls he got a mustache? You don't want that kid clocking the patch on your shoulder, the chisel-topped rescue knife at your belt. Times like that, you forget. You say, "Lemme get a number two carne asada, side of rice and beans," and the kid's looking like he sees a ghost, when all he sees is you.

Like the time one of our crew hit up the Spur. Tried to, anyway. Told me on the downlow the black weight was getting too much, and Homeboy just wanted another flesh-and-blood on the longside for a time. Any civilian makes that pitch, your bullshit radar can't scream loud enough. But a Boatman, you know it's their word. And Homeboy, he and his partner riding shotgun had been a thing once or twice, but she'd gone dark after a slip, forgot to glove up, and hadn't been looking herself in the eye, never mind Homeboy.

"Hourly rate at the Spur is a knockdown from a double-thirty," Homeboy tells me. So, the upsell sells itself but party would be shot in 12 minutes tops, civilian time. Yet Homeboy guns his black weight for the full 60, maybe longer. Says he's happy to pay full freight for a breath and heartbeat.

So, Homeboy—all paycheck and breath mints, in his civilian ride and street clothes—rolls up just outside the neon range of the Spur. Double-wide jackrabbit clap shack on the outside, discount disco-ball hillbilly Moulin Rouge on the inside. Spike-heeled Girl Friday at a dollhouse front desk—they got to look respectable—and the main attraction rank-and-file wilt about the leopard-print cushions, all half-dressed for a wet-dream pillow fight, but faces like they stuck in detention. Homeboy parts the plastic beads for three seconds of pouty, robot come-hithers before one clocks him for a Sweeper (what civilians call us Boatmen). Who knows how, just happens. Signal spreads at the speed of light and twice as quiet. Their smiles short out and a dozen nursing students scatter.

Next thing, Homeboy's standing in a ring of vacant love seats and blood-red 40-watts like some post-nuke Bourbon Street basement when their enforcer comes calling. Short-handling a ball bat should negotiations break down, he tells Homeboy to find another stack of hand towels. Says he can't go bringing Death 'round here, says they got mouths to feed.

Homeboy steps off. Ain't no alpha dog, but not like he's ever had to back from a fight either. Nobody wants to cross a Boatman, and Homeboy reckons the enforcer for cotton-mouthed and pissing frost, same as the anyone else. Most days, Boatmen resent that fear. Just a big wall of nothing between us and everything else—but this time, Homeboy gets it. Last thing on the enforcer's list is bringing his life to a gunfight, with no less than one of the Reaper's bagmen. Was never part of the deal, but the job's how he earns his keep, so he steps up.

Because those mouths to feed, they're his.

Homeboy makes a reverse rooster tail. No need to try his luck and libido elsewhere. No longwise spoon-and-cupping, rib-to-ankle, lie still and breathe in lava lamp time. That dose of life through another human's eyes is proof he hasn't lost himself to the River, and it sustains him for a time. Until it doesn't.

Cut myself bad shaving not too long ago. Hadn't slept in 21 days, so it's like reaching around a stranger's head, lathering up and doing the blade while looking through eye holes on the wrong face. Don't quite recognize my own looking back, truth up. Lost more weight, too much. Think maybe my hair used to be lighter, or my eyes darker. Maybe. Circles and lines where there weren't any, last I checked.

Nights, I shut my eyes but know the drowning's coming, like being buried under wet cement, but there's nothing I can do. Can't sleep, can't stay awake. Pretty soon, I'm talking cave painter singsong gibberish, seeing lights where there ain't none, halos where there is. Skin's too tight, like a smaller man's outsides stretch over mine. But, no lie, slit my chin and take the first full breath of air since John Doe #17 came calling.

When Homeboy tells me about it, what I mean to say.

Doze off in the rig during lunch. Is all Leigh can do to rouse me again. Make another cut that night. Not my face. Take a breath deep enough to feel my lungs stretch. Sandman comes 'round, sends the nightmares packing. Keep at it, a little more each night. Stop seeing lights and halos, back snug inside my blood-leather, looking out of my face instead of a stranger's. Deep under, I bleed through and stick to the sheet, rip it away when I roll over, snap myself awake. Wake Leigh, too. But she doesn't say anything, never does the whole time.

Before all this, Homeboy and Shotgun, they got a Passenger waiting. Civilian called it in, floor of a steep gulch near the base of Shunning Falls, so no heads-up whether the Passenger was John Doe #17 or Jane Doe #12. Procedure—that unwritten mystery manual rookies take for cut-stone gospel—says to winch the stretcher up top and not to sweat the canvass below. And Homeboy on the ravine floor gets a close-up with the Passenger, shouts up to Shotgun, "It's a boy."

Already been a long day, and now he's hopping rocks, scraping his shins and knuckles, and every rattlesnake story he's ever heard is playing in his head. Heat's touching triple digits, dry air turns the inside of mouths to sawdust. But turns out Homeboy and Shotgun got to radio the Shop 'fore one of them rigs can spool upwise, so they got to wait. Maybe inside their own rig, air-conditioned, while the Passenger cooks under sun.

#17's no older than 12, Homeboy reckons. Youngest Passenger by far and light enough to handle on his own. Homeboy on the downlow—not this Boatman, like I been saying, but somebody else, a pro—he wraps the sheet burrito-wise around little #17, watertight, no blood-leather on blood-leather to short out the man's own longing for contact. Homeboy does a solo legs-not-back three-count and, with nothing but the dust as his witness, scoops the boy up cradle-style, then calls up his inner mountain goat to scuttle up the rocks on his own two smokejumpers. Figures on setting #17 in the dirt up top, like he was there when they rolled up. Call that Crime Scene 101 snapped over the knee bigtime, truth up. But after long enough on the River, you learn most of that's pissing into a hurricane headwind, anyway.

So, he's cradling the boy, and he lowers him gentle onto his next-to-last resting place, when he catches Shotgun's eyes, a sliver of time transparent-thin, and their back-and-forth radar says, *This stays between us, it's all good.* They wrap up, no need to radio another rig, and Homeboy—what he tells me on the downlow later is he thinks they got to rooster tail pronto, because they got Johnny 17 hanging in the touch-and-go. Words marshaling on his tongue, ready to make with the sounds when he checks himself. His non-words ghost out while Shotgun's 'round back of the rig, so Homeboy's standing in solitary dead quiet, his watch set to lava lamp time.

A solo cradle-carry, that's for the living. No matter, you kept your blood-leather separate the Passenger's, your good sense just shot out the jet plane flush-hole. 110° in the shade but a slip like that makes the sun go dark. Ain't Homeboy's fault—what I tell him, 'cause he's somebody else, not me—way he's wired on account of being a good soul. What human beings do is we cover each other's backs. Ring around the living, safeguard against the big, dark nothing waiting to pounce 24/7. Like the kind of soulless black void what jettisons the nameless dead out of a clear blue afternoon into a town so small, they got maybe four gas pumps and the only work you can find is cleaning up the dead who just keep coming.

But Homeboy reckoned Johnny Seventeen could be saved when he was dead, hours before we got there. You famished for blood-leather when you cradle the living in your arms, then find they ain't alive after all? Like the stars and sky get peeled back to what ain't nothing but scaffolds and rats behind. And every love and loss and joy and ache you ever know turns out is just current running through your circuits. What you think is your soul is just a bunch of invisible switches what came out of a clean room.

You snap out of it, maybe your partner walks back from 'round the rig, says ready up for a three-count so you can call it a day. But you ain't the same. Johnny Seventeen is past rigor, gone full sandbag with his feet knocking about my leg like I'm carrying my baby brother off to sleep. Or my own boy. Was saying before, we all slip. Even us pros.

Leigh's breathing slow and steady, eyelids thrumming like hummingbird wings, but I count every beat. Come daylight, she'll open her eyes and she'll see me, I'll see her. No invisible windowpane, neither of us, not to each other. For now. I hope in her dreams she's far from the River, just for the night. My little Shotgun. Been bringing me back here, mattress on the floor and a tiny kitchen with just forks and spoons. The knives, she told me, she wraps in a garbage bag with my razor and buries it in the desert. Hides the keys so I don't go walkabout while she sleeps.

I lie back down longwise, shoulders to shins, heart pressing against her spine that stipples paper-thin skin, arms around her feel that she's all bones. Needs to eat. So do I. But we won't, no time soon. No matter. Slow-motion rise and fall of her ribs sends the nightmares packing, and I look to nights like this one, not yet gone, and I breathe with her, my little Shotgun, and time slows. Lava lamp.

Author Bio

🐦 @CraigClevenger

Craig Clevenger has written three novels, most notably *The Contortionist's Handbook*, which Chuck Palahniuk, author of *Fight Club*, praised as one of the best books he's read in 10 years. It's about an on-the-lam con artist/forger facing a constant battle of intoxication and incarceration in a mental hospital.

In addition to penning contemporary fiction, Clevenger also regularly puts on workshops to help other writers tap into the darker truths of their storytelling.

Isaac and Me

By Don Logan

Part 1  Tom

Highland Park, Illinois

June 5th, my wedding anniversary. A beautiful summer day. The day my world changed. The day I came home to find suitcases at the front door. Melissa, my wife, handed me the papers and told me to sign. Told me enough was enough, that our sham marriage was over, and it was time for me to go.

Said she never loved me, not for a minute. Said the kids weren't mine either. Laughed when she said it. The kind of soul-piercing laugh that makes you feel small. The kind that hurts the most. The kind you can never take back.

So, I dropped the roses and put a bullet in her stomach.

Friends disappear when you're on the run. All the ones I thought were our friends turned out to be her friends. Even the ones I'd made rich. Sure, I could beg and plead and shame them into letting me spend a night on the basement couch. I'd lie there and listen to the hushed arguments through the ductwork. Morning would roll around, and so would the weak smiles. An offer of a shower and a hundred bucks if I was lucky. A threat to call the cops if I wasn't.

Homeless shelters? Forget about it. Predator central. A bologna sandwich and orange Kool-Aid, followed by a sermon about the evils of sin. "Jesus was the answer," the preacher would say. He'll take care of everything. Then the lights would go out. Jesus wasn't around then.

Summer on the streets wasn't too bad—plenty of places to sleep, to stay warm, to hide. I got lucky and found a sweet spot in a railway tunnel, a utility closet a few hundred yards in. The lock had been jimmied by the previous occupant. All he left behind was his initials scratched onto the wall and a lingering stench.

My teeth ached when the train brakes screeched, but I grew accustomed to it. The room was small, not much bigger than the inflatable pool raft I shoplifted from the dollar store. I didn't need much. It had ambient heat. A bare bulb to read by. That was enough.

There was a bookshelf in Union Station. One of those take one, leave one deals. Dog-eared paperbacks with cracked spines and cheap, yellowed paper. Soppy romance novels mostly, but other stuff too. I read them all.

In the dark, empty hours, I'd reminisce about my old life, the one that had slipped away. I'd try to conjure the good times with Melissa and the kids, only to realize there weren't many. What I remembered as good times were when I was on the road. Those were the moments when I was truly happy. When I was really me, not the harmless suburban guy with the backyard pool, who barbecued on the weekend.

At work, they called me a Fixer. Who were they kidding? I was a hatchet-man, a gun for hire. Dig up dirt on a CEO? I'm your man. Steal secrets? Sure thing. Plant evidence? Deliver a beating? No problem. I did whatever my bosses wanted. Corporate raiders, hedge fund pricks, destroyers of worlds. They were the modern-day robber barons, and I was one of the fucking Pinkertons. So, what if a factory or two closed? As long as I got paid, it didn't matter.

Lying there in my cold, dark, concrete box, I was overcome by the impact of all the things I'd done, the totality of it. It hollowed me. I didn't deserve redemption. I earned every bad thing that happened to me, and every bad thing that ever will.

When I couldn't read or sleep or think anymore, I'd exercise in that coffin of a room. I had a routine. Down on the floor for push-ups, up to the drainpipe for pull-ups. Burpees until my back ached and my thighs burned. Had to stay in shape, had to stay hard. Never knew when I'd have to run. When I'd have to fight.

I promised myself that I wouldn't become like them, the ragged, filthy bums sleeping in doorways and pissing themselves on the subway. I stayed clean, washed in public toilets, or the deep sink in the all-night laundromat. A few hours of panhandling would get me into the YMCA for a hot shower and a shave.

I'd fish clothes out of the Salvation Army donation bin in the Supermercado parking lot over on Damen. When hunger struck, I'd walk the streets, go on the hunt. Sometimes all night. People ate out a lot in summer, plenty of dumpster scraps.

It was always a relief to sneak down the tunnel to find that my little shelter hadn't been discovered while I was away. That it hadn't been taken over. That I wouldn't have to kill for the dusty tomb I called home.

Autumn in Chicago lasted a week. Winter came fast and hard. The streets froze, but I didn't. I had to stay inside, hibernate, protect my claim. Leaving my spot meant cold, and cold meant hunger and desperation and fear. Cold meant death.

I could make a can of beans last three days. Spam four. My supply dwindled to nothing, and the mystery of how long I could hold out was answered. 15 days. I made it halfway through February on dirty icicles and nothing else. One mystery remained: Why hadn't the Union Pacific workers come around?

And then they did.

A cardboard box over a steam grate on Lower Wacker became my new resting place. Not that there was much resting going on down there, especially at night when the hardcore homeless came out to search for money, food, blankets, shoes, whatever. If the knives and boot-kicks didn't get you, the cops or sanitation trucks did.

With the café umbrellas tucked away until spring, I'd hit the Union Station food court for scraps, maybe hustle a few bucks from commuters. Or I'd go to Starbucks at closing time. I'd just guzzle milk or cream straight from the carafe. Other times, Stephanie, the barista, would take pity and give me a cup of burnt coffee and the leftovers from the pastry case. Stale crap destined for the garbage.

Until someone complained.

My days were spent in the Harold Washington Public Library. Reading, keeping my mind sharp, trying not to descend into madness. I'd huddle in the stacks with the periodicals—not many people ventured back there. I managed to stay hidden for a whole night once. The quiet was deafening, but I slept, really slept, for the first time in memory. Then the pig-faced dayshift security guard found me, and that was the end of that.

I moved further south of downtown, in search of better hunting grounds. Like a wild animal, I adapted, blended in, became invisible, part of the landscape. Studied faces, watched people come and go. Found new places to stay warm, new places to scrounge.

And that's when I met the kid.

He sat by himself inside a fried chicken shack on 26th and Wentworth. One of my usual spots to get warm. 17-years-old, give or take. Asian, probably Chinese, given the proximity to Chinatown. He couldn't have weighed more than a buck ten, even with the cast on his arm.

After a while, you learn how to spot homeless people. Not just the long-timers. The dirty-ass crazies, they're obvious. No, I'm talking about regular folks, the down-and-out. The hard-luck stories. The newly evicted or foreclosed. See, it's in the eyes. Frightened, shifty, head on a swivel. Heads jerking at every movement, every sound a danger.

That's how I knew he was a newbie. That and his clothes. Fresh, clean, no grime. But when he offered to share his food, that sealed it. No way did he know hunger. Not like I did.

He pushed a fried chicken leg forward. I tried to hold back but couldn't. My teeth tore the meat off the bones. I felt his eyes on me. "Thank you," I said. It was the first time I'd spoken in weeks, and the words came out like a croak.

"What's your name?" the kid said.

He was American, or at least spoke like one.

I sucked the grease from my cold, dirty fingers, eyes shifting between the remaining wing in the basket and his warm smile. The kid nudged the basket forward. Tentative, like he was feeding a stray dog that might bite.

"Tom," I said, digging in.

"Tom what?"

I had to think. First, to remember my last name. Then, to wonder why he asked. Was it just an innocent question, or did he know something? No, he couldn't. Paranoia came easy on the streets. "Ryan. Tom Ryan."

"Nice to meet you, Tom Ryan. I'm Isaac Kim."

Korean, not Chinese. I tossed the stripped wing in the basket and dabbed at the wax paper. "What's your real name? The one your parents gave you."

He blinked. "In-su. It means—"

"Wisdom." I licked the salty crumbs from my fingers.

"How do you know that?"

"I read a lot. How long you been on the streets, Isaac?"

His black eyes grew wide.

I answered for him. "If I was a betting man, I'd say a week, max. Takes practice, but I can tell. You want my advice? Go home, Isaac The Wise. The streets are no place for a kid like you."

"I can't," he said. "And hello? I've been out here for over a year."

"Bullshit."

"It's true. Listen, do you have a place to stay?"

I shook my head and huffed. "I knew it."

"Knew what?"

I glanced over my shoulder. "Where is he?"

Isaac laughed, a giggle. Like I was playing a game. "Where's who?"

"Your pastor. You're trolling for souls, right? Probably from one of those Korean Baptist churches. Thanks, but you're wasting your time."

That one really got him laughing, a girlish giggle hidden behind a manicured hand. "I can see why you'd think that, but no. My God, I haven't thought about those churches in forever." Then his eyebrows met. "But why would your soul be a waste of time?"

"You don't wanna know, kid. Let's just say I've had to do some things to get by out here."

Isaac held up his arm, the one in the cast. "Tell me about it."

I smirked. "Oh, yeah? What did you have to do?"

For a split second, his face cracked into a torn expression of pain. Real pain, the kind that only the needle can erase. I felt like a dick for being so obtuse, so dismissive. For judging him without knowing the first thing about him, what he'd been through.

"Tell you what," I said. "Why don't you get us another three-piece special and tell me all about it."

He did. And then he told me his life story. It came out like a burst dam. He talked, and I listened. It was strange, conversing with another human being again—especially one so young, so lucid. It was like he spoke a different language. Shorthand quips, abbreviations, pop culture references that meant nothing to me.

But I got the gist. Turned out I was right about the church thing. His parents took him, made him go. Dressed him up, combed his hair, and marched him in every Sunday. Some leafy suburb 30 minutes and a million miles away. He resisted. Feigned illness when he could but mostly went along. Figured he'd bide his time, go off to college, and then be done with it. Done with them all.

Everything changed the day he got caught with a cock in his mouth.

I never understood how a parent could kick their child out of the house. Love them, raise them, worry about them every second. Only to condemn them to the streets. To hardship and misery and harm. Why? Because of who they were? Because of who makes their eyes light up, who makes their heart flutter?

Then again, I shot my wife. So, yeah... What the fuck did I know?

But Issac wasn't finished with his story. He finally got around to the cast on his arm.

"Okay," I said. "Tell me about this guy again. What did you call him?"

"Ramone." The name stuck in his throat when he said it.

"Is that his first name or his last name?"

"I don't know, everyone just calls him Ramone. One name. Like Madonna, like Cher, like—"

"Where did he find you?"

"Roscoe and Halsted."

"Boystown."

"That's right. I was doing this and that, whatever I could to get by. Omigod, I was a total charity case. I worked part-time in a nail salon for a while, or I'd catch a few shifts waiting tables. Translated a menu once. Stayed with friends, couch-surfed. You know, here and there. I'd get a hotel room when I had the money. After a while, I could get into bars and clubs, depending on who was working the door, or who was inside—if you know what I mean."

I knew what he meant but didn't want to think about it.

"All right, so back to this Ramone character. What happened?"

Isaac let out a heavy sigh. Wistful, not tired. "Well, he practically begged me to move in with him, didn't he? I was like, 'Okay, he's cool and cute in a Ryan Gosling bad boy kinda way, and he has a spare room, and it's close to everything.' So, I did. It was nice." He scratched the crown of his head and looked away. "And then it wasn't."

I'd seen plenty of kids around, street urchins who roamed in packs. There were the tough ones, the muscle, the leaders. They'd roll drunks, snatch purses, break into cars. Do whatever was necessary to protect the weak, the small, the dope sick—the ones who sat on the curb, head down and hand out.

Then there were the in-betweens, the pretty boys and girls. The ones like Isaac. The ones who sold themselves for whatever they could get. Whatever bought enough poison for a few hours of escape.

I saw them all. The sad thing was that I didn't really see them, at least not for who they were. What I saw was competition for food.

Then Isaac dropped the bomb.

"Move in with me."

"What?"

"Think of it like I'm paying it forward. Look, you need a place to stay, and I need someone to watch my back. It's a win-win."

"You don't know me. You don't know anything about me. I could be a killer. A monster."

That was being a little too honest.

"But I do know you. Not your name, you just told me that, but I've seen you around. You have sad eyes. I trust those eyes."

If this was a scam, he'd picked the wrong guy. All I had to my name was an old army jacket and a pair of worn-out boots with paper towels stuffed in the soles. The money in my pocket wouldn't buy a chicken leg.

"That's not enough of a reason."

"I saw what you did to that guy," he said. "The one who tried to rob that woman."

Well, that took an unexpected turn.

I'd stopped a mugging a few days before. Happened in broad daylight. Young woman, late-20s, well-dressed. Professional. On her way to the Orange Line platform. Walked too close to the alley. A junkie attacked her with a kitchen knife.

Don't know why I did what I did. It wasn't like I was on a crusade for justice. It just happened. More of a reaction than anything else. She screamed for help, and I jumped the guy. We struggled, and I took a pretty good gash to the shoulder. He fared a lot worse. I handed over her handbag, and the woman gave me five bucks for my trouble.

Isaac stared back at me with pleading eyes, biting his bottom lip, waiting for an answer.

"Look, Isaac—"

"C'mon, please. You don't know Ramone. He's..." His voice trailed off, eyes downcast. Shoulders hunched tight, face pallid. All alone.

Shit.

I eyed the cast on his arm, the blue fiberglass tape fresh and new. And then I looked out the window at the black, frigid night. The snow had turned heavy, big flakes, swirling sideways through the glow of the chicken shack sign.

Fuck it.

"All right, kid. We'll give it a shot."

Part 2  Isaac

Chicago, Illinois

Freshly showered, Mister Hairy Legs stepped out of the bathroom with a hangdog face. A lost stray in from the rain. My largest kimono was like a boy's robe on him.

He was adorable.

"Nice abs," I said. "Feeling better?"

He grumbled something, took the clove cigarette from my hand, sniffed it, then dropped it into my teacup with a sizzle. "You're too young to smoke."

"Whatever you say, Dad."

Tom stood in the middle of the room, dripping wet, taking inventory. "What is this place?"

"It's an apartment, silly. You know, pay rent, complain about the heat, listen to the neighbors fuck. Want me to cut your hair?"

It took a moment for it to sink in, then he ran a hand through his wet mop and grumbled something that made me smile. I led him into the heinously small kitchen and pressed him down into the creaky metal chair. His brow pinched as he shifted his butt, tilting from side to side in concentration to identify the short chair leg.

"I'll fix that later," he said, Mister Helpful Handyman.

It was hard to take my eyes off him as I snipped. The way he stared at himself in the mirror, like a ghost whose secrets were staring back. I moved in with the scissors, and he jerked his head away, grabbing my wrist with his big hand.

"What're you doing?" he said, the grumble-growl returning.

"Hold still, Batman. Or, if you want, I can braid those nose hairs for you."

He opened his big tiger paw to release my tiny kitten arm, and snip-snip, I was finished. "*Voilà*, all done." I held up a hand mirror. "Whaddaya think, handsome?"

"Why do you do that?"

I raised an eyebrow in the mirror. "Do what?"

"Talk to me like you're a girl."

I put on my best butch voice and slapped him on the shoulder. "Sorry, sailor. Should we go watch a hockey game? Or maybe get drunk and pick up chicks?"

"You know what I mean."

Unfortunately, I did. But I'd finished pretending a long time ago and wasn't about to start again. Not now. I left him and his baggage draped in a sheet, surrounded by a pile of four-inch split ends.

"Think what you'd like. It's a free country—at least for you," I said over my shoulder, not wanting to look at his face.

I plopped onto the loveseat and lit up—a big, fat joint, this time. Cabinets opened and closed in the kitchen, probably him scouting the place, cataloging what he could steal. Then the sound of broom meeting dustpan made my heart flutter. Or maybe it was the onion rings from the chicken place, I couldn't tell.

"Listen," he said, eyes down, standing in front of me now. "I'm sorry."

"Wait, let me guess. Is this the part where you tell me about your gay cousin, how much you loved Elton John as a kid, or that you couldn't possibly be a homophobe because you jerk off to lipstick lesbian porn?"

"No." Tom set his big square jaw. "It's the part where I admit I'm an asshole and that I shouldn't have said what I did."

Well, that was embarrassing. "Apology accepted."

"It's just—"

"Maybe we'll just leave it there, shall we?"

Tom nodded, raised a hand to his lips, and turned an imaginary key.

Nicely done, Batman.

We sat there for a while, two strangers in a crappy studio apartment, staring at the exposed brick and wondering what the other was thinking. Or at least I was wondering. He might've been thinking the snowstorm would've been his better option.

The silence finally got to me. "I'm such a terrible host. Can I get you something to drink? I have green tea. Oh, there might be a few bags of oolong left. Shit, I bet you're a coffee man, though. Strong and black, am I right? Jesus, I'm rambling. That's me, always talking too much. Please say something."

"Tap water is fine."

I smiled. "A man of few words. We're going to get along just fine."

Back from the kitchen, I handed him the glass, which he drained in one long gulp. He set it down, nodded thank you, and then went back to taking inventory.

"How did you get this place?"

I took another toke and held out the joint, which he refused. "It's a sublet," I said in my stoner voice, breath held, lungs bursting. I exhaled a silver stream and continued, "I found it on Craigslist. The guy who lives here—a real Type A—is off on some work adventure. Sao Paulo, I think. Somewhere like that. He's not supposed to be back for six months, and let me tell you, he will not be happy with what I've done with the place."

Mister Grumbly Grumble was back, sitting there, eyes shifting up and down, side to side, taking in his new habitat like a caged silverback fresh out of the jungle.

My cellphone buzzed and rattled on the coffee table. I checked it and thumb-typed a quick response. "Duty calls." I rose from my warm spot. "Will you still be here when I get back?"

"Hang on," he said, struggling up from the beanbag chair. "You're leaving?"

"Some of us have bills to pay." I held my arms out. "You think a palace like this is free?"

"I'll get dressed and come with you."

I tugged an earlobe. "Um... that's gonna be kinda difficult."

"Why?"

"Because..." I sucked through my teeth and winced. "I tossed your clothes in the furnace while you were in the shower. Don't worry, I'll go shopping—"

"You did what?"

"Oh, come on—they were disgusting. I had to put on gloves, and let me tell you, it takes a lot for me to wear latex."

Tom dropped into the beanbag and pressed the heel of his palms into his eyes. After a long beat, he looked up. "I don't understand. You said you wanted me to—"

"Watch my back, I know. But this is different. It's a service thing. Very private, very safe. It'll be fine." I made a show of checking the phone. "And quick. Trust me."

"How does it work?"

I stared from under my brow. "Do you really have to ask, cowboy?"

"Christ, not that. I mean..." He tossed a hand at the phone. "The... whatever you called it. The thing, the fucking service thing."

Arms crossed, I looked skyward and sighed. "I really wasn't planning on having this conversation, but since you asked, I'll show you." I patted the loveseat. "Come on, I won't bite."

Tom waved for me to scoot over and took his seat. I pulled the laptop out from under the coffee table, brought up the website, and tilted the screen to show him. "See, it just looks like your average, everyday softcore tits and ass. The kinda stuff you get on late-night cable. Ho-hum, right?"

"Okaaaay," Tom said.

"But then I do this," I said, doing the secret squirrel series of clicks. "And it brings up a log-in screen."

Tom's eyes grew wide at the black screen with sparkling gold letters that spelled Samantha's Playhouse.

"Who's Samantha?"

I shrugged. "Fuck if I know. To me, it's just a chat room in case I have any questions. My guess? Samantha is probably some Russian guy on the other side of the planet. Sounds kinda cool, right?"

"No, it doesn't. For all I know it could be kiddie porn. Turn it off."

"I thought you wanted to know how it works?"

He stood and turned his back. "Changed my mind."

"Okay, Mister Prude. Jeez, it's just a website."

Tom swung around. "Does this have anything to do with what's-his-name, Ramone?"

"It has nothing to do with him. That's why it's safe."

He stood there, an XL white guy in a Japanese medium kimono, hands on his hips, eye twitching like a broken kewpie doll. This morning he woke up a dirty, hungry, homeless man—and now he was in the apartment of some Korean boy-queen he met in a chicken shack.

"Listen, Tom. I shouldn't have burned your clothes. That was a really lame thing to do—even though they made me break out in hives. Still, you're warm, clean, and fed. Not to mention, you have a fabulous haircut. If you ask me, you've stumbled onto a pretty good thing here, but I can't make you stay if you want to leave."

"I don't."

"I have a little money I can give you... Wait, what?"

"You're right," he said, glancing around. "You have no idea how much better this is than where I've been."

"I have a pretty good idea."

"No, you don't."

"All right, fine," I said, indignant. "We can play the game of who's more tragic, you or me. Wait a minute, was that a haiku? Hang on, I need a pen."

He pinched his temples with those Gulliver hands and gave his head an I-can't-believe-this shake.

"What's wrong?"

"Nothing," he said. "It's just a lot to take in, that's all."

"What part? The not freezing to death part, or the not having to eat out of the dumpster part? Sorry, I'm a little confused."

"Who's being the asshole now?" he said, arms crossed.

That one stung. "Okay. I deserve that."

"No, it's fine," he said, dropping his arms. "When you said you wanted me to watch your back, I had a different idea, that's all."

"I see. So, you thought it meant you'd hover nearby while I gave back alley blowjobs, is that it?"

"Jesus Christ."

I was on a roll. "Well, it's not like that—it never has been. Okay, maybe once, but that's not how this works, and that isn't what I need. What I need is for you to be here in case Ramone finds me, finds this place. Because if he does, he'll kill me. And before you say I'm a drama queen," I held up my cast, "this was just a taste of what he's capable of."

Tom sat there, lips tight, blinking at me. After a long moment, he said, "And what if he finds you when you go out on these... dates or whatever you call them."

"Service calls."

"Right," Tom said. "What if he finds you out there, and I'm in here? What then?"

I tossed my head from side to side. "Okay, good point."

"If you want me to do this, to live here, then we need some ground rules."

"If you're talking about sleeping arrangements, you have nothing to worry about. I have no expectations."

"Stop it."

"Are we back to this again? I thought we covered the subject quite well in episode one."

Tom stood and gestured at the loveseat. "Does that fold out?"

"Unfortunately, no."

He kicked the bean bag with his size-twelve. "Fine, I'll sleep on the floor. But that isn't what I was talking about."

I held in a hit from the joint and spoke with a clenched throat. "Pray tell, what might that be?"

"I'll need a key."

I blurted an exhale. "Um, sorry, but I don't give out keys. It's one of my first date rules, and I don't have many of those."

"Would you rather that I leave the door unlocked?"

I pictured an empty apartment. "Okay, a key. What else?"

"New clothes."

"I'm already shopping in my head. What are you, a 42" long?"

"This isn't Pygmalion. I'll make you a list."

"Pig what?"

Tom sighed. "*My Fair Lady?*"

"Mmmm. Nope, sorry."

"*Devil Wears Prada?*"

I clapped. "Ooh, I love that one."

"Now, there's one more thing," he said, Mister Serious now. "After tonight, I go out with you on these service calls."

"I don't need a pimp, and believe me, if I wanted one, there are plenty of people willing to apply for the job."

"Well," Tom said, "you can scratch me off that list. I don't know shit about the game, and I don't want to. The whole thing turns my stomach. In fact, I'd prefer that you not do it at all, but it's your life, and I suppose it's better than working a corner." Then Mister Sad Hero with a heart of gold shook his head at his bare feet, his feet of clay. "I was in a bad place, and you took me in. If I can pay you back by making sure you're not murdered, then that's the least I can do."

I grinned until my cheeks hurt. "You had me at 'After tonight.'"

Part 3 🐾● Tom

Chicago, Illinois

Alone in Isaac's apartment, differences surrounded me. Everywhere I looked: different smells, different sights, different sounds—same old loneliness. The apartment wasn't anything like my old tunnel, yet somehow it was the same.

Plus ça change...

Television seemed strange. Sure, I'd seen it while I was on the streets—quick flashes through the windows of bars and restaurants. Places I couldn't enter. Silent images of basketball or baseball or football, games changing with the seasons.

It used to be the soundtrack of my life. Always on, always present. Eat breakfast to one set of talking heads, dinner with another. Stocks in the morning, news at night. I'd forgotten what it was like. The droning voices. The serious men with curly earpieces and the green-eyed blondes with shiny legs and perfect teeth. The red-on-white flashing chyrons, screaming BREAKING NEWS, feeding the beast, quenching the thirst for information.

I flicked through the list of Isaac's favorite channels. A show about alien visitors. A statuesque transvestite running some kind of torturous modeling competition. A raucous talk show, music videos, cartoons, a cooking show where weed was the main ingredient.

I turned it off.

No books. It seemed Isaac wasn't much of a reader. He had a few magazines fanned out on the coffee table like palm fronds: *People, Cosmopolitan, GQ*, a computer magazine. I skipped the gay porn at the bottom of the stack and read the others. They were like candy. Sweet and tasty, but left me unsatisfied, hungry for something more substantial, something savory.

The urge to scavenge came back strong. Why? I was safe. There was food and water and light and warmth. Jesus, there was even toilet paper.

Was this forever me? Jittery, anxious, wondering where my next meal would come from. Worried that someone else would find the good scraps before I got there. Scouting places to sleep. Mentally assigning scores based on exposure to the elements, to danger, to the chance of discovery.

No, it was something else. It was me trying not to think about Isaac. About where he was, who he was with, what he was doing. I don't know why I cared, but I did. He'd been gone for hours. Each tick of my internal clock ratcheted up the level of concern.

I liked him. I liked his carefree, irreverent style. I liked his wit, the way he spoke, the way he laughed. Even the way he looked at me, at times warily, like I was a wild beast in his midst. At other times, trusting, like I was a wise uncle dishing out gold nuggets.

But most of all, I liked that he had made a place for himself, how he had beaten the odds, beaten the streets. I didn't like the way he did it, but truth be told, I admired him for it.

Sleep came. Restless at first, then deep. No dreams, no cold sweats, no waking up to sore throat screams. I blinked at the morning light. Listened, smelled, listened again. Nothing.

Two pots of coffee in, the first sounds came: keys rattling at the door. Isaac breezed in, loaded down with shopping bags, already rambling away. "Fucking Uber guy took forever. Car smelled like tikka masala, then he got lost, said he didn't, but hello? GPS. He was lucky I tipped anything. Wait until I rate him, then we'll see who's laughing... What's wrong?"

"Where have you been?"

He held up the shopping bags. "This should be your first clue, Detective."

"Goddamnit—"

"Aww, were you worried? Never fear, your baby boy is back. Safe and sound—and bearing gifts," he said, grinning.

The next hour was spent trying on clothes, modeling each ensemble while Isaac looked on. He'd drum his chin and twirl a finger to have me spin around. My catwalk routine finished, he separated the clothes into piles, matching colors, and scowling at his choices, only to do it again.

I thanked him, grabbed the things I'd actually wear—boots, jeans, a flannel shirt, and an expensive goose-down jacket—and waved at what remained. "You can take those back."

His face fell. "What? Why?"

"Listen, I appreciate it. Really, I do. But it's too much."

"If it's the money, don't worry about it."

I shook my head. "There's that, but it's also just too much stuff."

"I'll clear out a drawer for you," he said, glancing around. "Er, that might be a challenge. How about that corner over there?"

I rubbed my forehead. "If I learned one thing on the streets, it's not to become attached to things. Ever seen a bag lady pushing a cart full of crap? It becomes an anchor, and an anchor weighs you down. An anchor makes you a target."

"Wow," he said, lost for words. Maybe for the first time since I'd met him.

As I shoved the clothes back in the designer bags, Isaac blew out a breath and dropped his head. Then he twisted out of a black turtleneck and flopped back into the loveseat. That's when I saw the red marks on his neck—not hickeys either. Bruises. Deep ones. I put a hand on his chin and turned his head.

He jerked his head away. "It's nothing."

"Bullshit, nothing. What happened to you?"

He hemmed and hawed for a minute, avoiding my insistent gaze, telling lies about it being a rash, an allergic reaction to detergent, and swearing to find a new dry cleaner. I poked at the purple blotch.

He slapped my hand away. "Ouch. Jesus."

"Detergent, huh? Fuck you, tell me."

Tearful words poured out, an agonizing play-by-play. The Uber ride to the Four Seasons. The knock on the door. The pudgy man in a white robe and black socks. A change of plans, a negotiation. The belt snaking around his neck. A safe-word ignored. The panic, the struggle, the pleading apology, the payoff.

Isaac snatched a handful of tissues and dabbed his swollen, red eyes. He blew his nose and cried some more. Cried until the hiccups came. I brought him a glass of water and put an arm around him. The first human contact I could remember, at least one that wasn't in anger.

"Why did you go along with it?"

He jerked his chin at the designer shopping bags.

My heart sank, and I felt something I hadn't felt in a long time: shame. When I first hit the streets, it consumed me. Shame for shooting my wife. Shame for leaving my kids, even though they weren't mine. Shame for having dirty hair, dirty clothes, dirty nails. For relishing half-eaten food. For shitting on railroad tracks. For checking for blood with every cough. But most of all, for losing at the game of life.

Shame never completely ran dry. You learned to suppress it, push it to the back of your mind. Even learned to just say 'fuck it.' But it liked to pop-up once in a while to stab you, to remind you. In fleeting looks and searing stares, hushed voices. The sting when young mothers lowered their children's pointing hands, tugged them aside, pulled them close.

And now it was back.

Isaac looked over with sad eyes, and raked his hair, tried on a smile that didn't work. That's when I noticed it. "Where's your cast?"

He glanced down at his arm and flexed his fingers. "Oh, yeah. Well, after the thing with the guy, I went to Rush Presbyterian. You know, thought I could score some pain meds. They saw my cast, X-rayed it, said I was healed. So, they cut it off." He made a sound like a buzzsaw and wiggled his fingers. "See? Good to go."

Something didn't sit right. I hadn't been to an emergency room in forever, but I remembered how they worked. "Let me get this straight," I said. "You get attacked, go to the hospital for your neck, and then they decide to check out your arm instead. That about right?"

He blinked a few times. "Don't you believe me?"

"Did they call the cops?"

"No," he said in his of-course-not, silly voice.

The story would never fly at Cook County Hospital. You went in there looking for pain meds, they'd kick your ass to the curb with the other junkies. But even there, if you told them some guy tried to strangle you, sure as shit they'd call CPD.

A flashback came. I used to go to hospitals like Rush. Took my kids there for bellyaches and bumps and bruises. Bright and clean, efficient, every possible medical device under the sun. Need an MRI? A CT Scan? No problem.

Maybe Isaac was telling the truth?

Still, something bothered me. I studied his face, looking for tells. Nothing. My gut still said no. "All right, here's the deal," I said. "Let's go to the Four Seasons and pay this guy a visit. I'd like to have a word with him."

Isaac shook his head. "Can't. He's gone."

"Whaddaya mean, he's gone?"

He shrugged. "I don't know, he said something about having an early flight."

"A flight to where?"

Isaac scrunched his button nose. "Are we playing 20 questions now? Jesus. Look, the guy was an asshole, all right? He requested half-and-half. That's—"

"I know what it is." A phrase learned from a saucy train station paperback.

He grinned. "Okay, Mister I-don't-know-anything-about-the-game. Anyway, like I said, he paid for one thing and then switched it up when I got there. I should have known better. Should've checked him out with Samantha, but I didn't. It's my fault." He waved it off with a nonchalant sigh. "Lesson learned."

"I'm going with you next time."

Isaac thought about it for a moment. "Fine. But we need to work out a system."

And we did.

For the next few weeks, I accompanied Isaac to his appointments. It became a routine. He'd get a text message, check the website, summon an Uber, and away we'd go. I'd sit in a five-star lobby and wait. The doormen shooed me out the first few times, but the clothes Isaac never returned fixed that.

Things settled into a rhythm at home too. If we were both in the apartment, I would read books. New ones, bought with the stipend he paid me. Isaac would spend most of his time on the computer. Headphones on, probably watching YouTube or listening to whatever the hell he listened too. Sometimes, he'd go out early and be gone most of the day. Said he went to work out, or window shop, or catch a movie.

That was okay by me, the place could get a little claustrophobic, us bumping into each other all day. When lunchtime rolled around, I'd venture out to Whole Foods, to the

French Market, to butcher shops. In the evening, I cooked. Introduced him to food, to literature, to Jazz, to the Criterion Collection.

My life changed. I traded dirty floor push-ups and deep sink baths for health club workouts and steam room showers. Faces on the streets transformed, too. Scowls became smiles. Women's looks, once diverted, now lingered.

Then someone hurt Isaac again, and my comfortable life unraveled. I begged him to stop. He refused. I insisted on talking to the johns. I waited outside the suites. Tricks bailed and guests complained.

"This isn't working," Isaac said. "I'm sorry, but you need to go."

"Come on, we can figure something out—"

"You're smothering me."

"Please. You don't understand..." I let my words trail off, painfully aware of the desperation in my voice.

He shook his head, adamant. "End of the week."

We didn't speak much after that. When we were in the same space, it was nothing more than grunts and nods, followed by ferocious silence. The idea of being back out there occupied every waking moment, and the images flooded back: the cold streets, living hand-to-mouth, hiding in the shadows. I had to prepare myself. Get back into the mindset, the old skin. The one I had shed.

The day arrived fast, like a thunderstorm in July. Isaac looked on as I packed, as I examined each pair of underwear, socks, and pants. Every shirt and sweater. Judging them for necessity and weight.

"Jesus," Isaac said. "It's like watching one of those black-and-white movies of yours, the Swedish ones about death or whatever."

I stopped.

Isaac rolled his eyes, inhaled deep, and let out a reluctant sigh. "All right, you can stay—but we need new rules."

I didn't want to seem too eager but was sure it was written all over my face. Still, I paused before speaking. "What kind of rules?"

Isaac pulled his legs up underneath him like a pretzel and leaned forward, elbows on his knees, using the finger of one hand to bend the index finger of the other as he counted off. "First, before I go out on dates, we have a conversation about when you come with and when you don't. Look, sometimes it's cool, and I like knowing you're out there, but hotel people talk. Trust me, they're like fishwives—if fishwives were gossipy gay men. Can't have it. It's fucking up my groove."

"Not great, but fine. What's next?"

"Number two, when you do join me on a date—"

"You know I hate that term. They aren't dates."

Isaac did his nasal sigh thing again. "Do you want to hear these or argue about semantics?"

I nodded and dished my hand to give him the floor.

"I'm going to give you a cellphone so that when you do join me, we can stay in communication. You know, send texts or whatever. We'll work out a code. That way, you'll know if I'm in trouble."

I jerked my head back, mildly surprised. "Why didn't we do that before?"

"Um, because I just thought of it?"

And so, it began anew. He gave me an old cellphone of his, a burner. We discussed his clients. He'd describe them, lay out their profile, their mannerisms, their wants—sometimes giving me a little too much info.

We compromised on my role. For those he felt were safe, I'd camp out in a nearby coffee shop. I'd wait in the lobby for those he wasn't sure of. He was happy, and so was I. Things worked out well.

Until they didn't.

Early evening, meal prep time. Isaac burst into the apartment, frantic and terrified. I turned from the kitchen sink to find him stuffing clothes in a backpack.

"What's wrong?"

"We need to go, leave. Like, right the fuck now."

I grabbed his wrists. "Stop."

"Eww, your hands are wet."

"Shut up. Tell me what's wrong."

He yanked his hands away and resumed packing, rambling on, incoherent. Something about knowing he shouldn't have gone there, how everything was ruined, fucked, that he thought he was going to die, then wondering if he should go to Miami, or New York, maybe San Francisco.

He reminded me of Melissa when she was off her meds. God, I hadn't thought of my wife since I was in the hole. I shook him, just like I used to do with her.

"Goddamn it, calm down and tell me what happened," I shouted in a way I never had. It shocked him back to reality.

"Ramone. He found me. Says he's going to kill me—"

"Hang on," I said, squeezing his arms, my eyes pressed shut. "Hit rewind and tell me everything."

"No, fuck that. I'm leaving. And you should too if you want to stay alive. He's a fucking maniac."

I shook him again. "Does he know where we are?"

"No, but—"

"Then we're safe, right?"

"I don't know. Maybe for a little while, but he'll find us."

I let go and crossed my arms. "I'll go talk to him. Straighten this all out."

Isaac tossed his head back and laughed at me. The same kind of laugh I'd heard a long time ago. "You're insane, you know that?"

"You're being paranoid. Now, tell me where he lives, and I'll go pay him a visit. It's what I'm supposed to do, isn't it? It's why I'm here."

"Jesus, now I know you're crazy. What, you think you can just march in there and talk to him? 'Hi, Ramone. My name is Tom. I'm a homeless guy here to convince you not to murder Isaac.' Is that your plan? Say 'pretty please' and it'll all be over?"

"I'll be persuasive, trust me."

"He has guns. A lot of guns. You know, the things with bullets in them? They go *bang-bang*, puts holes in people? He'll shoot you in the head and dump your body in the river. Then he'll hunt me down and do the same, maybe worse. No, not gonna happen."

Isaac resumed packing, and something clicked in my head. A tingle, way in the back, a warning. A little voice telling me the story didn't jive. "Why does he want to kill you?"

"What?"

"You heard me."

Isaac blinked but said nothing.

"See, I've dealt with guys like Ramone before. Maybe not him, but people like him. People out for revenge, out for payback. It's what I used to do, a lifetime ago. Before all of this. And one thing I learned is that there's always a reason. So, I'll ask you again. Why does he want you dead?"

Mouth open, eyes searching mine, Isaac dropped onto the loveseat. He lowered his head into his hands. "I ripped him off."

"I knew it. How much?"

He sniffed back a tear. "Fifty grand."

I wasn't surprised. Things began to fall into place: the apartment, the clothes, the seemingly endless supply of cash.

"Where does he live?"

He brought his gaze up. "You're not serious."

"I told you, it's what I do. Or at least what I used to do. Tell me where he lives, and I'll take care of it."

"Yeah, right."

"I will, and then you'll give me half of whatever's left, and we go our separate ways. I can't live with a liar, not again."

"Hello? Did you hear the part about him having a shitload of guns? The part about him being a crazy motherfucker who doesn't care about anyone or anything?"

I snorted a laugh. "I'm not afraid of crazy—or guns."

"Yeah, well, I am," he said. "Forget about it."

I knelt in front of him. "Listen to me, I've been on the run. Don't ask me why, because you don't wanna know, and even if you did, I won't tell you."

"We can go together," Isaac said, pleading now.

"What, like *Thelma and Louise*? Bullshit. It's about as far from a Hollywood movie as you can imagine. Night sweats, constantly looking over your shoulder, every face a cop, or worse. Doesn't matter where you go, it'll catch up with you. I know because I was the one who caught up with people."

"No." Isaac shook his head. "You'll die if you go in there unarmed. Then what do I do?"

I smiled. "Who said anything about going in unarmed?"

Part 4  Tom

Highland Park, Illinois

The commuter train pulled into the station and came to a stop. I stepped down onto the platform, and inhaled a deep breath, filling my lungs with clean suburban air—the place of my escape.

I hadn't been back since the day I left. Memories came flooding back. City Hall across the way. The library just up the tree-lined street. The pancake house where I used to take the kids for Sunday breakfast. Downtown, with its wide boulevard and Tudor storefronts. Brand new cars, Mercedes and BMWs and Jaguars, parked on the diagonal in front of yoga studios and hair salons and bakeries. The sushi place would be packed. Same with the coffeehouse, the one with the ironic name I couldn't remember.

An idea popped into my head, more of an urge to be honest. I could pay Melissa a visit. Not to reconcile, that wasn't gonna happen. Shooting someone in the gut tends to take that off the table. I just wanted to see her face, to tell her how sorry I was. That, despite everything, I still loved her.

Ten steps in the direction of my old house, and I stopped cold.

Another memory came, a more recent one. I had called the house once. It was a stupid idea, one of many in my life. I took the Blue Line all the way to O'Hare and called from a payphone. My son answered. Told me he hated me, that he never wanted to see me again, and prayed for me to die.

I snapped my head to rid the memory and brought myself back to the moment. I wasn't there to reminisce or take a stroll through my past, through a life lost. I was there to get my gun— the one I used to shoot my wife.

My heart raced as I strode along Hazel Avenue, fists clenched in my pockets. The station parking lot loomed, and for an instant, I wondered if my car would still be there, right where I parked it. No, of course, it wouldn't. It would be locked away in an impound lot across town, or maybe she sold it along with everything else I owned.

But the gun would be there. Double-wrapped in plastic shopping bags and buried beneath the wooden fence, in the corner at the foot of an oak tree. My eyes scanned, sharp glances up and down. Nobody. I tore at the gravel and dirt with my hands, digging like a dog in search of a bone. My fingers hit plastic, and I pulled the bag from the hole. I took the piece out and hefted its weight. It felt comfortable in my hand.

Hello, old friend.

Chicago, Illinois

Isaac stared at the gun like it was a venomous snake. He stumbled backward, hands up, his butt hitting the kitchen counter. "Keep that thing away from me."

I released the magazine, pulled back the slide, and caught the ejected round in mid-air. Then I shoved the grip toward him. "You want to hold it?"

"Hell no." Then he tentatively stuck his chin out to peek. "Is it loaded?"

I slapped in the magazine and racked the slide. The snap made him wince. "It is now."

"Jesus," he said, smiling, eyes wide.

"This isn't a fucking toy, understand?" I tucked the weapon behind my back.

"You don't need to tell me, Dirty Harry."

"Now," I said, putting a hand on his shoulder, "tell me where this Ramone fuck lives."

He did. Then we went through the plan. Isaac made tea. I had him draw a map of the house and describe each room. I peppered him with questions: How many people live there? What kind of security system did he have? Did he remember the code? Where did Ramone keep his weapons? What were the best points of entry? Exit?

The cold reality of the discussion seemed to give him pause. "What time are you, ya know, gonna do it?" he said, unable to make eye contact.

"Late. The middle of the night is best. Sneak in, wake him up. He'll be disoriented, easier to handle. And don't assume the worst. I don't know what I'm going to do yet. Probably just sit him down, have a chat, maybe tune him up a little. Put the fear of Christ in him and be on my way. Why, what's the matter?"

"I don't know," Isaac said. "I don't think he scares that easy."

"Trust me, I'll be persuasive." I finished the tea, settled into the bean bag chair, and placed the gun on the floor behind my head.

"What are you doing?"

"What does it look like? I'm gonna get some sleep." I grinned. "Got a busy night ahead of me."

That one really blew his mind. Isaac sat on the loveseat, melting into it. After a moment of staring out at nothing, he slipped on his headphones and buried his face in the laptop.

I had to admit, I was looking forward to being back on the hunt. The thought of it gave me a thrill, one I hadn't felt in a long time. I laid there, eyes closed, trying to sleep, trying to picture Ramone's house, trying to fight the urge to just get up and go.

No. I'd wait. Stick with the plan. Then I'd do what I had to. Grogginess set in. Just a few more hours... Then I'd be done.

Loud pounding shook me awake. Was it in my head? More pounding. No, not a dream, someone was at the door. My mind couldn't get in gear. Everything seemed slow. I blinked at the light streaming in the window. What time was it?

I buried my eyes in the crook of my arm. Another knock. "Isaac, get the fucking door already. Jesus."

Nothing.

I sat up and sniffed in a deep breath. Turned to the loveseat. No Isaac. Another bang. I reached for the gun. It wasn't there.

A voice boomed from outside the door. "I can hear you. Open up."

What the fuck?

I tried to concentrate, but the synapses wouldn't fire. Who was at the door? Where was Isaac? I managed to get to one knee before the door burst open.

Three men.

Cops, not Ramone.

Shit.

It wasn't my first time in the box. The interview room was small. Maybe ten-by-ten. Gray laminate table, two metal chairs. Fuck them. I could do small and dingy all day long.

A detective entered the room, paper bag in one hand and a blue folder in the other. He set the bag on the floor next to his chair and slapped the folder on the table.

Tall and lean, mid-40s, face like rain on opening day. He wore dark gray suit trousers and a white dress shirt, pack of Marlboro Lights in the pocket. His cornflower tie had a stain right where the hot dog mustard landed.

"Mr. Ryan, I'm Detective Frank Sullivan. I'll be conducting the interview today."

"How long have I been here?"

"I'll ask the questions."

Dick.

And so, it went. He'd pace. He'd lean his hands on the table and ask his rote setup questions. He'd sit. He'd sip from his Styrofoam cup. He'd glare. He'd shift positions. He'd ask another meaningless question. He'd glare some more.

Usual cop shit.

He opened the blue folder and wrangled his drugstore readers into place. "How do you know Mr. Kim?"

"Mr. Kim? You mean Isaac. We're friends."

"Is that right? How long have you known him?"

I shrugged. "Not sure, a few months, I suppose. What's this about? Is he okay?"

"He's fine. We'll come back to him in a minute."
Sullivan checked his folder again. "What about Ramone Diaz?
What's your relationship with him?"

"I don't have any relationship with him. I don't know
anybody by that name."

"Where were you this morning at 3AM?" he asked,
skipping the fat and getting right to the meat.

"Sleeping. Right where you guys found me."

"Did you go out? Leave the apartment? Go for a drink,
cigarettes?"

"I don't smoke, and no, I didn't leave."

"So, you weren't in the six hundred block of West
Addison, near Pine Grove Avenue?"

Ramone's address.

I shook my head. "Nope. Never been there."

"And you're sure about that?" Sullivan said.

Truth be told, I wasn't sure. My head throbbed, and all I
could remember was flashes, fragments of time.

"Yes, I'm sure."

He reached into the paper bag and tossed a plastic
evidence bag on the table. "Recognize that?"

"It's a cellphone."

"It's your cellphone, isn't it?" Sullivan said. "We found it
in your jacket."

"Then I guess it is mine. So what?"

Sullivan squinted, chewed the inside of his cheek, then
licked his front teeth. A nasal sigh came next, the kind that says
I'm-gonna-tell-you-a-story.

"We live in a digital world, you and me," Sullivan said,
nudging the evidence bag. "Funny thing, these phones. Tracking
them, I mean. Used to be a real pain in the ass back in the day.
Now? No big deal. I give a phone to one of the propeller heads in
the back and *click, click, tap, tap*. That's all it takes. Something to
do with the cell towers, GPS, whatever..."

The pit in my stomach was the size of a bowling ball.

"So, here's the deal," he said. "We've got you there, at
the home of the dead guy, Ramone Diaz, at 3AM."

Dead? Ramone was dead? I swallowed. "I wasn't there."

He tilted his head and flipped a page in the blue folder. "That's not what your text messages say."

"What the fuck are you talking about?"

He brushed a finger over the sheet. "It's all here. Want me to read them? There's a shitload, but here's my favorite: 'Fuck you, bitch. I'm coming for you.' To which Diaz, the dead guy, replied: 'Bring it, motherfucker.' I guess you did."

"I didn't send those. I never sent any text messages to anyone. Isaac gave me that phone."

"Uh-huh."

"Look, something is wrong here—"

"Fuck yeah, there is. You murdered the guy in his damn house. Tell me what happened."

"I told you, I was never there."

"I'll ask you again," Sullivan said. "What was your relationship with the deceased? Couldn't be good. You shot him six times."

"What?"

He pulled out an 8"x10" photograph and flipped it around. "See?" He tapped it. "One, two, three, four, five, plus the one in the back. Jesus, you must've really been mad. What did he do to you?"

"He didn't do anything to me. Listen, he threatened to kill Isaac—"

"So, you planned it? A revenge type thing. That's what we call aggravated murder, my friend. The DA loves that shit. Juries? Not so much."

"What? No. Just check with Isaac. He'll tell you."

Detective Sullivan glanced at his notes again. "Isaac? You mean Mr. Kim?"

"What the hell are you talking about, Mr. Kim? He's just a kid. We live together. I mean, not together-together, I just stay at his place."

"Thing is, we have spoken with Mr. Kim. He's very distraught, as you might imagine. He told us that, yes, he did let you stay at his apartment once. Said he found you living on the streets, took you in during a storm."

"No, that's wrong. I was his bodyguard. His friend."

"Is that right?"

Sullivan reached into the paper bag again and lifted out a plastic bag. Dirty clothes. My old, dirty clothes. The same ones Isaac said he had burned.

"We found these in the trash two doors down from where you killed Diaz. Now, I'm no evidence tech, but I'm pretty sure that's blood spatter right there. My guess is you changed into his clothes at the scene. You're about his size, and you're wearing the same kinda stuff we found in his closet."

"I didn't do it. I wasn't there. Talk to Isaac, he'll tell you."

"Like I said, we did. According to him, you were a stalker. Says you used to follow him to business meetings, wait for him in the lobby."

"Stalker, my ass. And what're you talking about business meetings? He's a male prostitute. Works for a web site, Samantha's Playhouse. He's just a kid, for Chrissakes. I'm the one who took him in."

"So, it's your apartment? The one where we found you?"

"No, it's a sublet. Isaac said he found it on Craigslist. I didn't kill anyone. Please, you gotta believe me."

Detective Sullivan studied me until his gaze became uncomfortable. Then he pressed up from the table and let out a heavy sigh, the kind that says I-think-you're-full-of-shit, but-I'll-check-anyway.

"You need anything? Water? Toilet?"

"No, just the truth."

I sat there in the small room, shackled to the table like a field mouse caught in a trap. The fog in my head cleared, and the puzzle pieces came together. I was fucked, no doubt about it. The only thing that wasn't clear was how badly.

Detective Sullivan returned. He'd been gone for hours, either to let me stew or to build a better case.

My guess was for the latter.

"We found the gun," he said. "It's been sent off to the lab for prints and ballistics, but I think you know how that's gonna go."

Of course, I did.

"And we showed your picture around to a few hotel doormen. I'm pretty sure you know how that went, too. One other thing. Highland Park PD called. We told them to get in line."

Yep, knew that was coming too.

Sullivan crossed his arms over his chest. "Here's what I don't understand. Why'd you do it? Was it a rip-off? Did you have a beef with Diaz? What?"

"I told you. He threatened to kill Isaac. He was the reason the kid was hustling in the first place."

Sullivan huffed. "Yeah, about that. I checked on this Samantha's Playground of yours. Thing is, it doesn't exist. Never did, as far as the techs can tell. And the only person who we know threatened Mr. Kim is you."

"What the fuck are you talking about now?"

"Mr. Kim filed a report a few months back. He didn't give his name, but he said a homeless man strangled him. The ER docs at Rush confirmed it."

My stomach rose, and the cold ball exploded in my skull again. I snapped my head, trying to shake it away. "What's with the Mr. Kim shit? He's a fucking kid."

Sullivan made a sour face like I was nuts. "Sure, he looks young for his age, but the man is 27-years-old. He owns that condo you were in, and he and Diaz were business partners. They ran a tech company together."

I was stunned. Then I started to laugh. Not a maniacal laugh, more of a take-your-breath-away belly laugh. The kind of laugh that makes your shoulders convulse, that hurts your stomach, that makes your jaw and cheeks ache.

"What's so funny, asshole?"

"Nothing, man." I shook my head. "Take me away."

Bravo, Isaac. Bravo.

Part 5  Isaac

San Francisco, California

There are a lot of great places to people-watch in San Francisco. Dolores Park, Hayes Valley, Embarcadero. Even the Castro.

Not for me. Like most of the city, those places have gotten too gentrified. I'll take the Mission, or the Tenderloin any day. The seedier, the better. It's not hard to locate a good spot. All you gotta do is find the rundown hotels, the dive bars, the weed dispensaries—anywhere the sex workers and drug addicts call home. Find a nearby donut shop or cheap Thai place and settle in.

It wasn't as good as Chicago—that place was a fucking goldmine. But what can you do? Silicon Valley called, and I answered. Yes, once I collected the business insurance, I bought out Ramone's sister and flipped the company. Doubled my money and moved west.

New city, fresh start. Same old me.

I do miss Tom, though. He was the best, my all-time favorite. Hall of Fame. Usually, I'd get bored after a few weeks, after they got comfortable. Or once I got them hooked on heroin, or back on the booze. That was always fun.

But he was different. I saw the hero complex and knew he was it, the one who I could mold, get to do whatever I wanted. Sure, he bought the whole "gay hooker" thing a little too easily, but when he told me about the gun? Jesus, it was like all my birthdays came at once.

Whoa. Hang on, who is this beautiful specimen? Not too dirty, doesn't have crazy eyes. Hungry too, by the looks of it.

I pushed the steaming bowl of pho forward and smiled. Offered him the seat. Come on. There you go, big man. Dig in, get it while it's hot.

"Hi, my name is Isaac. What's yours?"

Author Bio

 @PseudonymUnk /DonLogan "Full Circle"

Don Logan is a Chicago-based crime novelist and screenwriter. Winner of the Mystery Writers of America Holton Award, his work has appeared or is forthcoming in many literary publications, including ExpatLit.

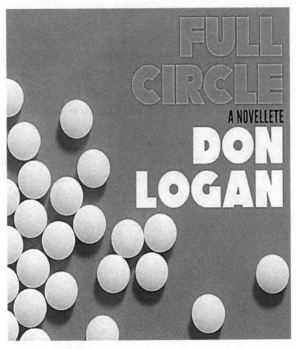

He writes stories about white boy pimps, trailer park hookers, carnies, cam-girls, Dixie mafia shot-callers, corrupt cops, and Juggalo tweakers. Sometimes, he writes about bad guys, too.

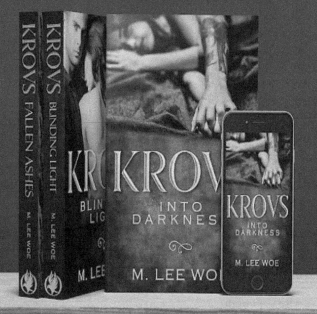

Gunselle

By Russell Thayer

Safe at last in her quiet apartment, Gunselle squinted into the bathroom mirror, the bare bulb above the sink roasting her face with a pulsating glare. Her eye had nearly swollen shut and would be plum-colored by morning. Both cheeks had been torn into like freshly tilled earth, and her jaw ached from the harrowing of fists that followed. Running hot water over a washcloth, she held it against the sizzling rawness, hoping to prevent infection. She'd bitten the inside of her lip near through when Mrs. Valentine headbutted her.

She fought harder than her husband said she would.

"An easy rub-out," he'd declared at his office, shoving five C-notes into Gunselle's breast pocket.

She should have known that the woman reduced to blubbering on her knees—her beautiful face turned up at the coming truth—would pounce like a tiger, knocking the pistol from Gunselle's hand. After all, Mrs. Valentine had been a gangster's wife, a savvy showgirl patted and probed up the ranks to appear nightly at his casino, then at his bed. They'd married. Created a daughter. The perfect happy postcard. Still, it hadn't been hard to lure her to a hotel. To get her naked. Defenseless. The woman's appetite for softer flesh was undoubtedly the reason she was meant to die.

Gunselle stepped back from the mirror to get a full vision of her damaged face and disheveled auburn hair. She knew she was pretty. It was the best tool in her arsenal, and she could wield it like a sap. She hoped her looks weren't ruined over that lousy $500.

After opening the tap to run a hot bath, Gunselle examined her stinging elbows. They were rubbed raw from rolling on the jute rug next to the bed, her arm around Mrs. Valentine's throat, rocking from side-to-side as they struggled, biting and spitting until the younger woman won out.

Mrs. Valentine had fought hard to live. Gunselle respected her for that.

Tough as nails, she was. After sitting up to catch her breath, watching the defeated woman sob on her back, Gunselle found the pistol, checked the threading of the silencer, then shot Mrs. Valentine through the forehead.

It was the husband's special request. There was another crisp hundred waiting for her if she took a pretty picture of the hole above his wife's eyes and mailed it to him at his alibi in Honolulu. Gunselle could use the extra C but had no idea where to get a photograph like that developed.

Following her target to a club, then buying her a drink, Gunselle had touched Mrs. Valentine's knee under the table, suggesting they go to a diner for peach pie.

"Where did you find that lovely blouse?" Mrs. Valentine asked after closing the door to her hotel room. "And how soon can you get out of it?"

"City of Paris," Gunselle answered as she worked the buttons with a knowing smile.

Now, as the bathwater ran, Gunselle looked the blouse over for blood, admired the subtle lace trim, then hung it neatly in her bedroom closet. She'd send it out with the rest of the laundry on Monday. The strap of her black brassiere had broken during the struggle. It wasn't a favorite. She'd dump everything else she'd worn that night into the building's incinerator after her bath. The pistol had already gone into the bay at Fort Point. No one knew her real name or where she slept.

After settling into the steaming tub, a bottle of red wine on the tiled shelf along the wall, Gunselle poured water over her breasts, creating the sound of a mountain stream, and imagined the little dress shop on Divisidero, the one for sale right now. She'd banked fifteen Gs from various jobs, enough to lay down cash for the place, but she knew she'd have to move to another city to live that dream.

She'd grown up in Wallace, Idaho, run away with a truck driver as a teenager, eventually killing him with a heavy wrench. That was after the third time he sold her. She'd tried her looks out on L.A. but hadn't made a difference until she hooked up with an escort agency and met a sketchy assistant director who suggested, after a tired wallowing, the idea of a simple blackmail job. As pretty as she was, the dough she made from selling herself barely covered the high fashions escorting required, so she said yes to extortion, then yes to the next thing. Being that corrupt had been a challenge, but one thing led to another. And now she hurt all over.

"I'm sorry, Emily," Mrs. Valentine had whispered just as Gunselle placed the silencer against her forehead. "My little baby."

Gunselle wished her own mother had cared for her as much, but then realized—safe and warm in the tub—what a horrible thing she'd done to a little girl. She would stare down the barrel of that truth one day—unless she found another life. She was finished with this one. She wouldn't even collect the other half G she was owed for tonight.

Gunselle's lip burned as she drank, but Idaho had made her tough. Tough as nails. Tougher, she thought as she soaped the ripped skin of her elbows. She'd never go back home, though. Maybe Montana? She liked the western styles always in fashion there, thanks to the enduring popularity of Dale Evans. She'd heard there was money in Billings. Oil money. Maybe a cute little dress shop on a sun-blind street. Cater to tourists in the summer. Winter on the beach in Havana.

Filling the glass again, Gunselle decided she might just be ready for the cleansing sun, the pressure of being on the square. It all sounded swell. Hard to resist. Like warm pie.

Author Bio

 @RussellThayer10

Russell Thayer writes period crime centered around San Francisco's Fillmore jazz scene of the '40s. His work appears in *Pulp Modern, Tough, Close to the Bone, Punk Noir Magazine, Hawaii Pacific Review,* and *The Phoenix.*

Thayer received his BA in English from the University of Washington and worked for decades at large printing companies. He lives in Missoula, Montana, but you can also find him lurking on Twitter at the handle above.

Palette's Colors

By Elyse Russell

My eyes opened more slowly that night. He was back; I could hear him trudging up to the door, rasping and rattling the air out of his ancient lungs. His steps sounded heavier than they had when he'd left. I trembled.

He's brought her back then, I thought.

The one next to me whimpered as the door opened. Frigid air whooshed in to trail its jagged fingernails along our naked skin. I took in the wrapped, limp form slung over his shoulders, then hurriedly cast my gaze to the ground. I didn't want him to catch me looking. If he did, he'd start talking. Somehow the process was much worse when he was narrating it in that scratchy, monotone voice of his.

He huffed, stomped the snow from his boots, and made an effort to set his burden on the table as gently as possible. He never treated them with such care when they were alive.

His coat and hat were carelessly flung into a corner. He was only meticulous about his work. His "art."

A fresh, blank canvas yawned at me from the easel. I imagined it had teeth.

I still didn't know what he was. He looked like a man, until you met his eyes. Then you knew: This was no man. This was something else, from somewhere else. It became even more evident, his alienness, when you saw what he could do.

And where were we? It looked like a cabin. That seemed to be snow melting off his boots. But I knew better. We were somewhere... other. And he had brought us here.

It was an old woman, this time. She had never spoken to me, but she used to rock with her knees drawn to her chest, muttering in Spanish. I had been calling her Abuela in my head.

It was foolish to name any of them, but I couldn't help it. They were people, after all. Some of them even told me their names. Most, though, were silent before he took them out there and brought them back lifeless. I had been here longer than the others. He was saving me for something different. I could feel it.

This one, though, the old woman: She hadn't been here long. Perhaps two hours. Now she was laid out on that table of his, next to the easel, and he was arranging her with such tenderness. I tried not to look at the private parts of her shriveled body, but I noticed that her breasts sagged over the sides, resting on her arms. There was a birthmark on her hip. Her lips were thin and had turned a deep purple with the cold. Her eyes were wide open and stared straight up at the ceiling. Her face was bland, expressionless. He had combed her hair, and it hung in a soft gray waterfall off the end of the table.

A barking cough startled me, and—before I could stop myself—I looked at him. We made eye contact, and I felt terror lick down my spine. Such cold, cold eyes. He cleared his throat, then continued with his preparations.

"My little watcher," he croaked. Snarled fingers fastened the ties at the back of his apron, and he peered at me over the rim of his glasses. "This one will be different, I think. You'll see. I may finally have it," he continued. He pulled a tall stool over in front of the easel and settled onto it with a creak. The back of the old woman's head was near his elbow. He reached for the jar of paintbrushes he kept fixed to the side of the easel. There was a series of tinkling sounds as he searched for the exact brush he wanted. Finally, he made his selection and sat back with one that had long, soft bristles. He absently rubbed his fingers over it, back and forth. He ran the bristles over his chin as he contemplated the canvas, then the old woman. "First, let's get the basics. I'll start with the focal point, here."

Then he did it.

The first time I saw him do it, I thought that I had gone mad. Then I gagged and clapped a hand over my mouth to keep a shriek from escaping. *That's impossible*, I thought, *this isn't real*.

But I had seen it often since then, and only slightly grimaced this time as he held the paintbrush over the old woman's face, then slowly dipped the tip into her left eye.

It sank in as though diving into a pool of water, and, when he drew it back up, it seemed perfectly clean. But when he brought it to the canvas and tentatively daubed, color came off, as though he had been using regular, normal paint.

I heard a retching sound next to me, then smelt the foul odor of vomit. The new one, I thought. I hoped she wouldn't do this every time she saw it.

He, however, took no notice, and sank the brush back into the iris. Fleshy tones manifested themselves upon the canvas.

"What is your name, little watcher?"

I jumped. He had never asked me a question before, nor treated me as anything that could respond.

When I didn't speak, his head turned so slowly in my direction that it seemed to take hours before his face was perfectly lined with his spine, his head sitting backwards upon his neck.

Terror prompted me to squeak, "Palette. My name is Palette."

His eyes widened and he let out a barking laugh. "Really? How poetic. How fitting. How delightful."

Then his head started its slow swivel back to its natural position, and he reached again for the old woman's eye.

Poetic. It certainly is, I thought, contemplating my fate.

"What do you think I'm doing here, Palette?"

I waited a long time to respond. Too long—he twitched and started to turn my way again. I couldn't bear to see him do that fucked-up owl trick again, so I blurted the first words that formed on my tongue: "You want to see the afterlife. You're wondering if they see it at the moment of their death, if it's the last thing they see."

A deep rumble. It took me a moment to realize that it was something like a "hmm" of approval.

I chewed the inside of my lip until it bled.

"What an interesting theory, Palette."

He leaned to twiddle the tip of the brush in a jar of water, as though washing off color. The water remained clear. At least, it did to my eye. Who knew what it looked like to him.

I had read somewhere that humans could only see a small fraction of the color spectrum. That there were colors we couldn't even conceive of. A mantis shrimp apparently saw more than we did. A shrimp. When I read the article, I remember thinking it funny to be jealous of a shrimp.

I had no doubt he could see every color imaginable. I didn't think he was painting with only color, though. Something else was bleeding off his brush onto the white expanse before him. Was it their souls? Their emotions? Their pure fear as he ended them?

If you thought about anything for too long, you would go mad. The more you contemplated something, the less sense it made. Existential crisis awaited down that rabbit hole. And that was just in the "real" world, the world he took us from. Here, a whole different set of rules was in play. A whole different reality.

A headache was beginning behind my left eye. I wondered how long I had been here. Did time even move the same way here? For all I knew, hundreds of years had passed. But it felt like a few days. And I'd never felt hungry, nor had I needed a bathroom. I hadn't slept in all this time, and I wasn't at all tired.

"But you're wrong."

His statement interrupted my thoughts, making me jump. I shifted positions, trying to keep as much of myself covered as possible. I rolled myself up with my knees to my chest. I'm a little, safe egg, I told myself.

"What's your next theory, Watcher?"

I thought for a moment. Sudden anger made me what to shout at him. I didn't think, "How am I supposed to have any idea what you're doing, you sick bastard?!" would fly, so instead I said, "You're recording their memories?"

"Wrong again."

Well, sheesh. It wasn't like he let me see the finished products, anyway. He let me watch him paint the beginnings, but the final touches seemed to be for him alone.

Then, sooner than I expected, he growled. It started out like a bass, human sound, but then it must have fallen below the range of human ears. I couldn't hear anything, but I could feel it. He did this occasionally, and I wondered if maybe he was communicating with others of his kind, like echolocation. This time, though, he seemed to just be frustrated.

Always at some point, as he reached the end of a painting, he would get angry. I guess he just wasn't producing the art he wanted. Did he think that was his fault, or hers? I glanced at Abuela. Did he blame her for his failure, or was he angry with himself for making mistakes? Did he lack skill? I had no idea how to critique a corpse's art.

He seemed to hastily slap on finishing touches. This one hadn't taken him long at all. That was bad news. It meant time would be up sooner for one of us.

So, so slowly, he turned and looked down at the corpse of the old woman. There was a fury in his eyes that I had never seen before. He was much angrier than he had been over the last failure. Was he running out of time for something?

His hands were trembling. He still held the paintbrush. I wasn't ready for what he did next.

In a blur of pure menace, he swung his arm up high, then brought it down to stab the paintbrush deep into Abuela's eye. This time, I vomited. Then it was all dark.

When I came to, the floor around me was perfectly clean. No puke. I looked around. Nothing else, either. No one.

Wait, no. Curled in the corner was a small woman. A white girl with mousy brown hair. Newbie. She was staring at me.

I looked away, then cast my glance around the room. How long had I been unconscious? How many people had disappeared? There had been at least five others before...

I gagged. *Before* he mutilated that poor old woman.

Before I could turn around, I watched the white girl's face turn whiter. I froze as a shadow crept over me.

Oh God, I thought. Was it my turn?

A rasp near my ear.

Don't look at him. Don't look at him. Don't look at him.

But of course, I did. His ugly mug was right there. A grin spread across his face that didn't stop where it should have. The simper went all the way under his ears, somehow. What the fuck was this thing?

"Stand up, Palette."

What would he do if I didn't? Of course, I obeyed.

His neck stretched out and around me so his head—and *only* his head—could be level with mine. He looked me in the eye. "I expect better from you, my dear. My Palette. All of these grubs... they can't appreciate majesty when they see it. They can't begin to comprehend anything, and it shows. You, though... You are different, I think." His hands rested on my bare shoulders. They trailed down my arms, then down around my legs.

No one should ever have to feel a stranger's touch on the back of their knee. Why did that seem more invasive than the rest of my arms and legs? I wondered if anyone had ever touched me there.

How dare you, I thought. That's MY skin. My— Wait. How many hands did he have?

This wasn't a metaphor; I felt more than two hands on me. Then they were lifting me.

Here we go. Roller coaster has reached the top. Time to crest the hill and fall.

I was thrown over his shoulder, flopped like a sack of potatoes. Humiliating. Then he started towards the door. Oh, that cold, terrible door. I had watched so many people go through it before.

As he opened the door and frigid air met my naked skin, I glanced up at the girl.

She had fainted.

Then I was outside, my world was white. Snow was everywhere. It swirled through the air, and there were great banks piled on either side of the path that the monster dragged me down.

I was eerily calm.

Then I saw them.

The paintings—the portraits, I saw now—were laying in the snow on either side of me.

There were so many. So many. And they were all of... him. But they were all different.

This was how they saw him in their final moment. But why? Why did he want this?

I didn't understand. What was he looking for?

WHUMP.

He threw me into the snow. The shock of the cold made me seize up.

Oh SHIT, it's RED. The goddamn snow is RED. THERE'S RED ALL AROUND ME! NO, NO, NO! WAKE UP, WAKE UP!

WHAT IS HE DOING? WHAT IS THAT? WHY? NO, WAIT, I—

Author Bio

@ElyseRussell13 (BraveLittleTeapotThoughts)
Elyse Russell's first book, a dark, short speculative fiction collection, *My Furies and My Graces*, will be released in July 2022 (Cinnabar Moth Publications). She has several graphic novels in the works, including horror novella *The Fell Witch*, a steampunk light novel, *Sentience* (Band of Bards), and a middle-grade novel called *Curious Worlds* (Markosia).

Russell is currently pitching the graphic novel *Brunhilda and the Hex Witch*, a fantasy with hints of horror and humor.

Commissions open!

Dany Rivera is a professional artist who specializes in comics illustration, character and creature design, and book cover art. For details and rates, email her at danycomicsoriginal@gmail.com.

Follow her on Twitter: @Dany_Comics.

The Price

By Victory Witherkeigh

All she could hear was the steady thud of her heart as she adjusted her black-lace Venetian mask.

Thump. Thump. Thump. Thump.

"What do we think of this one?" The man's dismissive tone couldn't be hidden behind their own facial coverings. A small crowd walked up to her display pedestal, a sea of faces hidden behind masks with feathers, pearls, leather, and lace.

All she could see was their beady eyes staring at her offering, never looking upon her face as they hemmed and hawed with one another.

A murmur came through the crowd: "It doesn't quite do anything for me, but it's such a subjective thing, you know?"

"I see some potential. There's some interesting technique on this side and the idea is original," came another gruff commenter.

"I'm just not sure I'd be the right person for the work. It's not drawing me in the way I'd hoped a piece like this would."

"Yeah, it's not connecting with me as much either. The description was so promising as well: vulnerability."

Their voices muddled together as the first thump of a headache formed behind her eyes. The lights in the room were blurring as the dryness of her throat grew.

Should have drank more water, she thought as she tried to adjust her stance behind the display pedestal.

For the first time all evening, she was glad the Venetian mask could conceal the crease of her forehead and the pools of sweat sticking to the faux leather. It was the most awkward part of showcasing her work, trying to give off the impression of confidence and individuality as faceless crowds gathered to spew their opinions and takeaways from each piece.

"Oh..." came an unknown voice, cooing in her ear. "This one looks so raw, so strong!"

"Really? You like that one?" came a snide reply. "It's so free-form and organic. I prefer the shinier ones over there, with the gold and silver metals mixed into the pinks and reds."

"Yeah, but those artists are established. Plus, some of them look like they're just doing variations of the same thing. You can't even tell what's real or not."

"But that's what makes it cool: the mixture of organic and hard-edged metals. It's the future. It's innovative, fresh."

Innovative? Fresh? Her brow furrowed. The tingling in her lower back told her the black Louboutin heels were better suited for younger models. She shifted her weight from one foot to the other, hoping it wouldn't jostle the display too much as she tried to keep her smile as still as possible. Even with the mask, she needed an aura of disinterest, to look cool enough to talk to, but not so eager as to appear desperate or crazy.

So many rules, so many requirements...

Her eyes glanced around the hall for the first time since the industry event began. In all directions were others like her, artists trying to entice the crowd with originality. Some of them were already represented by more prominent firms, rubbing elbows with social media influencers or well-known brand ambassadors. Sure, she had sold a few pieces, accounting for the gold and silver flecks in her art, but nothing compared to her competitors' organs that glistened platinum under the spotlights.

Though she knew the futility of comparing one artist's path to another, she couldn't help but question her own piece. It was still healthy, ripe with red and pink details. From booths away, spectators could see the brilliant muscle. The small scars that built upon one another to create a cascade of tissue in budding shapes that gave her piece "depth," a look of pain and experience often sought-after at these events. Many walked by her display, commenting on the tissue's strength as if she had cultivated the rejection, heartbreak, and depression all by herself, without the aid of any naysayer. The attachments to herself were still pumping with a vibrancy that she didn't see in the better-established artists—ones with agents and publicists who interchanged various vein and muscle parts to craft the perfect presentation for the crowd.

Thump. Thump. Thump.

Yes, even though this was nowhere near her first showing, she still found herself in odd disbelief as she stood before strangers, pulling out her beating heart from the hand-scratched cavern of her breastbone. Still attached to the piece by vein and artery, she set her art—her life's work—upon the silver display dish while the crowd looked on to judge. The critiques' sting added to the growth of scar tissue if she allowed her ears to tune in too intently to the feedback.

"It's not what we're looking for right now."

"It's just not a fit for me, but it's bound to find someone else out there."

"It's gutsy, but not gutsy enough. We need more..."

She got glances from her competition as they tried to woo lookers and buyers to their organ stands, rotating the muscles at odd angles to show the most pristine pink tissue. Some were freshly grown with no marks, an image of innocence. Others had gold sewn into their blackened flesh and coronary veins, using the metals to hide the fact that the meat was rotten or stolen from other artists or cultures to make their own hearts more enticing, original.

Thump. Thump. Thump.

Could she really judge those who had clawed their way ahead into the same arena she was fighting for?

The steady beat of her heart against the metal plate was reminiscent of the knocking behind her. It reminded her of the persistence of those wanting a pedestal of their own, the opportunity to grit their teeth as she had when nails pressed into her flesh. She imagined the warmth of viscous blood as it dripped down *their* chest, as they dug further and further into their skin, until they hit breastbone.

The first time cracking the bone plate was always hardest, the first signal of exposure to the world—submitting interest in exhibiting your inner workings. She had used a chisel and hammer when she first submitted to agencies, offering chipped bone fragments, flesh, and blood to entice agents and publishers. Then came the follow-up calls.

"Can you meet these deadlines?"

"Do you understand your contractual terms if you sign with us? Your obligations?"

"Are you on social media? How big is your following?"

The crowd echoed behind her in the gallery's alleyway, hoping to be called next in case an artist collapsed from exhaustion or sheer irrelevance. What goaded her was their hunger and hustle as they surrounded her, cheering as she drove that chisel deeper and harder into the bone, cracking and splintering the protections around her heart. This was precisely what pushed her journey here, got her call-backs from agencies faster than expected. It all happened just a few weeks after her tender fingers gripped her warm, beating heart and ripped it forward to hint at what promise laid beneath.

"Last call! The last half-hour before the gallery closes this evening! Be sure to grab all your items before the doors close." The event manager's voice brought her back to the showcase and the thrum of activity bustling around her.

She looked over at her little display cards.

A handful seemed to have been taken by interested parties. More opportunities to present in the future.

"Look, Mama!" a small voice rang out. "This one is so pretty! I want to show one just like it someday!"

She smiled down to the girl with dark, curly pigtails who was dragging her mother across the gallery to point at her heart.

She looks a little like me at that age.

"Thank you." She winked beneath the leather mask.

The little girl blushed as her mother pulled her along.

Not seeing any other viewers, she began resetting her heart, cleaning along the silver platter to remove any particles that may cause harm as she zip-tied her rib cage and re-sewed her chest. It was a technique she'd only recently decided on to allow access at will.

"So," the manager whispered behind her, "what did you think of the showcase? Worth the price of admission?"

Author Bio

@witherkeigh /VictoryWitherkeigh

/Victory_Witherkeigh

Victory Witherkeigh is a Filipina author originally from Los Angeles, who currently lives in the Las Vegas area. In 2020, she was a finalist for Killer Nashville's Claymore Award and an honoree for the Cinnamon Press Literature Award. Her literary fiction and dark fantasy work have appeared in numerous online and print magazines, as well as the horror anthology, *Supernatural Drabbles of Dread.*

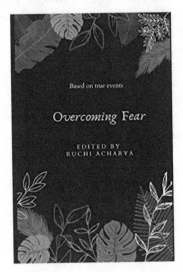

Wingless Dreamer awarded her for a short story in *Overcoming Fear,* available now on Amazon.

Thanks for reading! Find more transgressive fiction (poems, novels, anthologies) at: Outcast-Press.com

Twitter & Instagram: @OutcastPress

Facebook.com/ThePoliticiansDaughter

GoFund.Me/074605e9 (Outcast-Press: Short Story Collection)

Amazon, Kindle & IngramSpark

E-mail proof of your Amazon/Goodreads review to OutcastPressSubmissions@gmail.com & we'll mail you a free bookmark!

You can also send transgressive/dirty realism poetry, short stories, and novel query letters to the above e-mail address. Outcast Press puts out monthly poetry e-mags, bi-annual anthologies, and tri-annual novel(la)s.

CPSIA information can be obtained
at www.ICGtesting.com
Printed in the USA
BVHW070609111121
621201BV00006B/412